THE THIN GREY LINE

THE THIN GREY LINE

by

Derek Blundell

HAMISH HAMILTON LONDON

First published in Great Britain 1983
by Hamish Hamilton Ltd
Garden House 57-59 Long Acre London WC2E 9JZ

British Library Cataloguing in Publication Data

Blundell, W. D. G.
  The thin grey line.
  I. Title
  823'.914[F]   PR6052.L/

  ISBN 0-241-11046-7

Printed in Great Britain by
St Edmundsbury Press, Bury St Edmunds, Suffolk

Author's Note

Although all characters, ships, places and incidents are fictitious, a situation similar to the theme of this story could easily come about. In 1962 the U.S.S.R. attempted to set up a missile base in Cuba but, due to the strong line taken by the late President J. F. Kennedy, the threat to the 'back door' of the U.S.A. was thwarted. The People's Republic of China·already has nuclear weapons and, in the not too distant future, will have the means to deliver them. This waiting period would be cut down considerably if a foothold could be established in Africa.

Of necessity, current defence thinking, strongly influenced by a stringent economy, is mainly confined to Europe. Unfortunately, what is happening today thousand of miles away, can so easily affect us tomorrow. A strong Navy, strategically positioned, does not need costly land bases – often subject to local political whims – and is likely to prove to be the most flexible and least expensive weapon in our armoury.

On Thursday, 24th October, 1968 I was invited to attend the 46th Annual Meeting of the Royal Naval Benevolent Trust at the Mansion House. Among the distinguished speakers was the Vice Chief of Naval Staff, Admiral Sir Peter Hill-Norton, K.C.B., who delivered an excellent speech on the Royal Navy in the future. We were told of the crippling economic cuts and of the world wide commitments that were the lot of the service. In his speech Sir Peter referred to the thin grey line of British warships, their crews, small in quantity but high in quality, and the vital tasks they perform.

At that time I was writing a novel about the modern Navy, and it suddenly dawned on me that here was my title – The

Thin Grey Line. It is affectionately dedicated to the Royal Navy, present and future, from one who had the honour of serving with it.

Derek Blundell

Chapter 1

The shrill notes of the bosun's pipe echoed round the decks and compartments of the destroyer; then, as the long, last note of the call faded away, there came the message over the loudspeaker system that the crew were expecting.

'Clear lower deck. Hands fall in for entering harbour stations. Special sea duty men close up.'

In that organised bustle - peculiar to the Navy - the ratings moved quickly about the ship to take up their allocated positions on the fo'castle and quarterdeck. In the extreme end of the bows stood an officer; senior ratings - these were the special sea duty men - manned the important control positions at the helm and engine-room to carry out the entry into harbour. Two miles ahead lay the port of Toulage, capital of Zembasia, once a British colony but now an independent republic within the Commonwealth.

H.M.S. *Phoenix* was scheduled to arrive at 1000 hours, local time. In approximately ten minutes the warship would be steaming through the harbour entrance with her crew, smartly dressed in white tropical uniforms, standing rigidly to attention. If this speed of twelve knots was maintained it would be exactly 1000 hours when the traditional gun salute commenced firing at the entrance.

Towards the destroyer's stern, on top of the aft superstructure, the elderly gunnery officer glanced at his watch and nodded with satisfaction. The Captain had timed it nicely. In five minutes from now they would be gliding smoothly through the harbour entrance; four bells would be struck and he, the gunnery officer, would be responsible for the nineteen gun salute to be fired in honour of the President of the Republic.

Two young seamen gunners stood by the saluting gun,

specially installed for a flag showing voyage, awaiting the officer's order to commence firing. Long ago this same gun, a Hotchkiss Three Pounder made in 1899, had been mounted in H.M.S. *Nelson*. As a young seaman gunner himself the gunnery officer had fired it at the last pre-war fleet review. In two months time a *Seacat* guided missile launcher would be fitted there.

'Just like the entrance to Valletta harbour,' reflected the captain, Commander Clive Halton, D.S.C., R.N., gazing ahead at the opening between the two sea walls. Beyond this opening and slightly to the left lay the flagship of the Zembasian Navy, the *Alched*, once a 'COLONY' class cruiser in the Royal Navy.

She still looked the same, thought Halton, recalling his time in her as a young midshipman 22 years ago. No doubt he would be invited on board the Republic's flagship during their stay; it would certainly bring back pleasant memories.

The tall, tanned captain took one last quick glance round his ship. All was in order; they were ready to enter harbour. Pity destroyers were not entitled to Marine bands, he thought. It would just set the scene. 1000 hours, four bells of the forenoon watch, and the destroyer's bows were just coming abreast of the opening. As the ship's bell rang out clearly over the glass-still water the crew were brought to attention, and the gunnery officer gave his order:

'Fire One!'

The three pounder's deep, resonant boom echoed round the harbour. From the *Alched* came the reply. At five second intervals the destroyer would fire nineteen rounds, the flagship replying to each one. It was all part of a naval tradition that went back hundreds of years. In the days of sail and muzzle loading guns it signified that a warship came with peaceful intentions when she discharged her guns; by the same token the salute was returned by warships or fortresses in the harbour.

Moving slowly and gracefully towards her mooring buoy, the destroyer passed within a hundred yards of the cruiser. As they neared each other, the gun salutes having finished, each ship acknowledged the other by pipes from their bosun's calls, their crews still at attention. Ahead of the destroyer went one of her launches carrying the ratings who would secure her to the large buoy.

2

At 1015 hours H.M.S. *Phoenix* came to rest in the middle of the harbour. The Captain telegraphed 'Finished with engines' then made his way aft to receive his first visitor, the resident British Naval Attaché, who was approaching in a fast motor boat.

As Commander Halton walked on to his quarter deck he noted with satisfaction that all was in order to receive the senior naval officer who would shortly be coming on board. The piping party were in their correct place, at the head of the gangway. Slightly to one side of them stood the officer of the watch with a telescope under his arm. Standing by the microphone of the loudspeaker system was the duty quartermaster, ready to call to attention personnel on the upper decks when the first visitor arrived.

The ship was to spend three days here at Toulage, and Commander Halton was aware that just about everyone of any importance would be coming on board. Although not an anti-social person by nature, he reflected somewhat ruefully that the greater part of the last eleven weeks had followed a very similar pattern. Eight visits had been made during this period, each one virtually a repetition of the others. After this, all things considered, he would not be sorry to depart for Portsmouth! After a quick refit, during which *Phoenix* was to be fitted with new radar and a guided missile system, he would be taking her to the Far East for six months.

Speculations on the future were interrupted by the officer of the watch, who approached to make his report.

'Excuse me, sir,' said the young Sub-Lieutenant. 'Naval Attaché's boat is coming alongside.'

'Thank you Mr. Harding. Normal compliments. Carry on please.'

Acknowledging Halton's instructions, the officer of the watch gave his order to the quartermaster to bring the ship's company to attention. The four seamen of the piping party prepared to sound their bosun's calls, and as soon as the motor launch reached the foot of the gangway and the attaché, a Captain R.N., mounted the bottom rung of the ladder, the long pipe shrilled out over the calm waters. Halton and the officer of the watch stood at the salute as the attaché stepped on board the quarter deck. Acknowledging the salutes, the short, rather

3

thickset officer came forward and shook hands with the destroyer's captain.

'Nice to see a British warship in this harbour again,' he said genially. 'Halton, isn't it? I don't think we've met before. My name's Morrison.'

'Glad to meet you, sir. Perhaps you would care to come below to my cabin? I've heard the situation here is a bit tricky, but no doubt you will be telling me something about what's going on.'

On the way to his cabin Halton wondered what information the attaché would have for him. The press had reported that Zembasia was threatened by local communists. If the present government fell, Britain would lose a staunch ally in this part of the world. It would also mean another foothold for the communists in Africa, who were already gaining much ground. This much the British commander knew already. Indeed the whole idea behind the recent series of visits had been to give a tangible demonstration of Britain's interest in these new republics.

However, as became a professional naval officer, Halton was not very interested in politics as such, feeling that he had enough to do to keep abreast of his job in this modern navy. Showing the attaché into his cabin, Halton offered him one of the two comfortable leather armchairs and rang for the wardroom steward. While waiting for their drinks to be served Morrison steered clear of Zembasian politics, seeking instead the latest news of the service and its characters. Having served in destroyers himself several years before, he and Halton found that they had many acquaintances and experiences in common.

Later, sipping his ice cold shandy, the attaché began to tell Halton about the situation in Zembasia, and not that reported by the popular press, which only hinted at the problems. The President of Zembasia was undoubtedly a good man, with the real interests of his country and his people at heart. Unfortunatley he was old and in poor health. His potential time as leader was obviously very limited, and the immediate problem was who would succeed him?

In Moscow, and more latterly in Peking, several Zembasians had been thoroughly trained by the communists to a high pitch of efficiency. They wanted to take over the country ostensibly in the name of glorious revolution – but once in power they

4

would bleed it dry of its young men and its wealth of mineral resources. China would supply advisors and technicians, and thus achieve a long desired foothold in Africa.

Even more far reaching consequences were possible claimed Morrison. According to secret and reliable sources, there would almost certainly be an establishment of a missile base. China was rapidly developing medium range rockets with nuclear warheads, and with a base in Zembasia, these would threaten all of Africa and most of Southern Europe. The fantatical communists must be prevented at all costs from taking over the country.

In opposition to the communists was Zembasia's popular middle-aged Vice President. Educated in England, he had gained a double first with honours at Oxford. A successful lawyer by profession before entering politics, he was convinced that the democratic way of life was best. It was through his active efforts that education, working conditions, social benefits and housing were improving throughout the land, but with all the best will in the world it was slow work to bring this country up to the standards of a modern European country. Given the time, the Vice President and his supporters were certain that they could get their country well and truly on its feet. From their achievements so far it was obvious that they were sincere men who were leading the people wisely and well; indeed in a free election they would almost certainly have been given a large majority by the voters.

The real danger lay in the fact that the communists might well seize power, on the death of the president, by illegal means. It was known that they had filtered their way into many of the responsible positions, including the civil service and the armed forces. To just what extent this had been achieved the attaché was not sure; neither, unfortunately, was the present government. A nucleus of an intelligence service did exist, but it was too small and inexperienced as yet to be of much practical use. There were far too many known communists – let alone the unknown ones, who would almost certainly constitute the real danger – for it to be possible to keep them all under surveillance. In the not too distant future, probably sooner rather than later, this explosive situation would undoubtedly come to a head, with far reaching consequences.

The presence of a British warship might possibly have some

restraining influence on the more intellectual of the rebels. They would realise that Britain would help the legally constituted government to hold free elections as, of course, would the United Nations. However, by the time the latter body had decided on a course of action, it would be too late. One fact was certain. The coup, when it came, would be swift, and in a matter of a few days the country would be in the iron grip of the communists.

Halton, listening intently, was fascinated by what he had heard. The old fashioned concept of 'send a gunboat' had gone out many years ago, but even in this modern nuclear age, it was still surprising what a sobering effect could be achieved by the presence of a warship in the middle of a harbour.

At last Morrison, having discussed the political situation at some length, went on to talk about the arrangements that had been made ashore for the destroyer's visit. There was to be no real restriction on shore leave, and Halton was relieved to hear this. It had not been possible to allow his crew ashore in the last country they had visited.

Just after their arrival, an R.A.F. 'V' bomber, on one of its long range patrols, had force landed in the sea about 200 miles off the coast. The *Phoenix* had raced to the scene of the crash through foul and heavy weather, evidence of which still showed in her paintwork. Fortunately she was in time to pick up all five of the bomber's crew, who were little the worse for their adventure. Under orders from the Ministry of Defence Halton intercepted a Union Castle liner, homeward bound from South Africa, and transferred the aircrew to it four days later. So the R.A.F. men went home in style and the destroyer proceeded to Zembasia.

Having spent almost a fortnight at sea, the ship's company would be looking forward to getting ashore again. As in most sea ports, some specific areas of the town would be out of bounds. The crew would also be well advised, said the Attaché, in view of the political situation, to keep together in groups of at least four at all times. Other arrangements included the inevitable round of cocktail parties and a football match between the Zembasian Navy and the *Phoenix*. It seemed it was going to be quite a full three days.

The Royal Fleet Auxiliary, *Tide First*, was due at Toulage in the early afternoon, and would be coming alongside

6

the destroyer to re-fuel her near empty tanks. Fresh water and food supplies had been taken care of by the Attaché, and should also be brought out to the *Phoenix* in the afternoon.

Most of the routine work could be left in the hands of Halton's first lieutenant. He had a very capable second in command in Lieutenant Commander Harold Drew, and it would be good practice for Drew; he would have command of his own ship one day. As soon as the Attaché had gone, Halton decided he would let Drew and the other officers know about the local situation. Chief Petty Officer Gray, the coxswain – the destroyer's most senior rating – would know how to get the message across to the other ratings in a manner they would understand before they went ashore. He would probably tell them to stay away from the local women and drink too – for what the warning would be worth to men who had been at sea for a while.

Chapter 2

Soon after Captain Morrison had been piped ashore – it was now 1130 hours – Halton sent for the coxswain. Conversation was easy between the two men, who had a mutual respect for each other which had developed from an acquaintanceship begun fifteen years previously, when they were serving together in a destroyer during the Korean War. Gray was a leading seaman at that time, and Halton a fairly junior lieutenant.

One wild, cold night off the west coast of Korea, in the desolate Yellow Sea, the destroyer struck a floating mine, and half her bows were blown off. Nearly all the senior officers and ratings were on the bridge. The ship had been at a high state of war readiness at the time, because of reports of mines being laid in their patrol area. Hurrying to the bridge with Gray from their action station – Halton was the officer in charge of two stern 4.5 inch guns, Gray was one of the gun captains – their eyes met a sight that would remain with them for the rest of their lives.

Everyone on the bridge was either dead or seriously wounded, and the destroyer hopelessly out of control. Halton, realising that he was senior executive officer fully fit, took command, and two days later, after a nightmare voyage, brought the ship safely into the naval harbour of Sasebo, in Japan. He was the first to admit that without the staunch support of Gray he could never have done it.

Gray was awarded a well earned D.S.M. – Halton got his D.S.C. for the same incident – but something else happened to Gray. He suddenly matured. Until that terrible night his approach to life in general and the Navy in particular had been light hearted, to say the least. Now, much to everyone's surprise, he settled down and studied hard. Passing the necessary examinations, he was promoted to petty officer, and then to chief petty officer a few years later. Halton was delighted, on taking command of the *Phoenix*, to find that Gray was to be his coxswain, and between them, as was well known throughout the fleet, they ran a very happy ship.

The Captain gave Gray a brief outline of present conditions in Zembasia, and told him to warn the liberty men that there was to be no nonsense ashore. The last things he wanted were brawls or any other incidents involving his crew. Unfortunately there was little doubt that some communist agitators would try to create all types of incidents – especially at such a volatile time as this – to get the British embroiled. Even if a small group of locals were losing a fight with what appeared to be an overwhelming mob against them, the sailors were not to try any heroic type of rescues. The British sailor ashore abroad hates to see any kind of injustice, and will go plunging in to set things right, full of good intentions but without serious thought. The communists often played on this trait in sea ports in order to cast diplomatic sneers at Britain.

After lunch Halton talked to his officers, assembled in the small wardroom. There were eleven of them all told, not counting the gunnery officer, who had the afternoon watch. Once again the Captain ran over the poltical situation for their benefit, and outlined the expected happenings of the next few days. The eyes of some of the younger officers lit up at the mention of cocktail parties. They were quite keen on meeting members of the opposite sex.

Drew, the first lieutenant, had a very different reaction to this type of social occasion. 'Seen one, seen 'em all!' he was heard to murmur – and most of the older married officers agreed with him. Still, it would be nice to get ashore again, even though it meant getting all togged up in his best white uniform. However, that would have to wait. With the *Tide First* coming alongside this afternoon, he was going to be busy enough supervising the replenishments that they needed.

Sub Lieutenant John Gordon's thoughts were not about politics nor the loading operations. He was more concerned with the possiblity of agreeable female company. He had heard that the ambassador had two charming girls, and was determined to get in before the other young officers rushed along. However, first he had to work out an excuse to go to the embassy. Official mail, he decided, might be the answer.

The senior engineer, Lieutenant Commander Roger Smythe, was busy calculating the amount of oil fuel required from the *Tide First* this afternoon. As soon as he had worked out this figure his thoughts turned to a completely different subject – the ship's football team. He was its manager, and was aware that the team had to be got together and given a practice before their official match two days from now.

When the Captain had left the wardroom, the officers split into groups of twos and threes, eagerly discussing immediate future plans. Only the first lieutenant, the senior engineer, the gunnery officer and his relief at 1600 hours were required to stay on board. The rest were free to go ashore. Half the ship's company had been given shore leave, and the first liberty boat had just left. Normally the destroyer's two 25 foot motor launches would have had to make several runs, but owing to the efforts of the naval Attaché, the Zembasian Navy had loaned a large motor launch, complete with crew, to the *Phoenix* for the duration of her visit. One of the destroyer's launches could now be exclusively used by the officers. By popular vote all those officers not required for duty decided to go on a tour of the town and buy 'rabbits' for their relations and friends at home. 'Rabbit buying', or in other words getting presents, has been a popular occupation with sailors throughout history.

Standing before the mirror in his cabin, Halton brushed an almost invisible speck of dust from his uniform and ran a comb through his fast receding hair. In five minutes time the boat from the Zembasian flagship should be alongside for him. Soon after their arrival he had made a signal to her captain requesting permission to visit the flagship. This request had been readily granted, and the *Alched*'s captain had kindly offered to send one of the cruiser's boats for him. Apart from wanting to see his first ship again - it seemed only yesterday that he was a midshipman on board her - Halton was looking forward to renewing acquaintance with her Captain.

Four years ago, on a staff college course at Greenwich, he had met John Rhaman, then a lieutenant commander in the newly established Zembasian Navy, but now a full Captain in command of the cruiser. Promotion was a damned sight quicker in this little navy than his own, he mused. Still, it had to be in such a young republic. In the Zembasian army corporals of four years ago were now colonels.

John Rhaman could not really be compared with the colonels, however, as he was well used to responsibility and command. For many years, before his country had become independent and formed its own armed forces, he had been one of the few coloured officers in the British Merchant Service, and an extremely good one at that. Halton had liked what he had known of the man, though he was perhaps a shade too thrusting and ambitious. Perhaps time had changed him for the better, however, and it was a rare opportunity for Halton to inspect his old ship again.

There was a knock on the cabin door.

'Compliments of the officer of the watch, sir, and the *Alched's* launch is alongside,' reported the young duty quartermaster, a twenty year old able seaman.

'My compliments to Lieutenant Thomson. Tell him that I'll be right up,' replied Halton, and having allowed the quartermaster half a minute's start to warn the officer of the watch of the captain's impending arrival, he walked on to the quarter deck. He returned the salutes of Lieutenant Thomson then had a quick word with the officer.

'Good afternoon Mr. Thomson. You know where I am going. I shall be coming back on board about 1600 hours. Carry on, please.'

10

Halton crossed to the head of the gangway, to the sound of pipes from the quartermaster's bosun's call and the salute of the officer of the watch.

'Attention on the upper deck, face aft!' blared the ship's loudspeaker system.

The young Zembasian sub-lieutenant saluted as Halton entered the stern sheets of the 32 foot motor cutter. It was more than likely, Halton reflected, as he sat down on one of the wooden benches, that he had commanded this same boat himself when he was a midshipman. Having given the orders to get under way, the sub-lieutenant turned to Halton and began to explain that the captain's launch was having an engine change at the present time, otherwise it would have been sent for him. The young Zembasian spoke excellent English, although it was doubtful if the ratings of the cutter's crew understood a word of the conversation.

Just after they left the destroyer, Halton noticed the *Tide First* entering the harbour. The 17,000 ton fleet auxiliary looked enormous as she moved slowly towards his 2,500 ton destroyer, and he realised that his old *Phoenix* was quite small for a destroyer these days. Compared with the larger 'Daring' and the 'County' class guided missile destroyers – the latter were the size of some of the light cruisers used in the Second World War – the *Phoenix* did not amount to much. Indeed if it had not been for a tricky political situation in the Far East a few years ago – the period of Indonesian 'Confrontation' – she would probably have been scrapped along with the rest of her class.

Still, she was a first class little ship, and undoubtedly had a few more years of working life ahead of her. With her four 4.5 inch guns, anti-submarine weapons and complex radar system she could be reckoned on as an effective warship; it was a pity, though, that they had had to remove both sets of torpedo tubes to keep down the top weight on their last re-fit.

Engrossed with thoughts of his own ship, Halton did not notice how near they were getting to the *Alched* until, looking up, he got a near perfect side view of her looming ahead. She had not changed much over the years since he had last seen her. The tripod masts had been replaced with lattice ones, to carry modern radar equipment, and one of the two rear triple 6 inch gun turrets had been removed, but in most other

11

respects she seemed to be the same ship in which he had served.

Indeed she could have still been a British cruiser except for the mass of black faces, thought Halton, as he was piped on to the quarter deck of the *Alched*. Years of continued scrubbing were reflected in the almost snow white deck, the brasswork shone brilliantly and there was not a thing out of place, Rhaman certainly ran a smart ship!

The cruiser's Captain came forward to meet his old acquaintance with a smile and a warm handshake.

'It's good to see you again, Clive. Welcome aboard your old ship,' he said, in his excellent English. Introductions were made to the cruiser's senior officers, who were all keen to meet the British officer. Halton thought that Rhaman looked slightly drawn, but apart from that he had not changed at all since their last meeting.

Pleasantries were exchanged between the two officers as they went below to the Captain's cabin. Conversation flowed easily over the pot of tea one of the stewards brought in almost immediately they were seated. The cabin suite was large and comfortable, comparing more than favourably with Halton's own quarters aboard the *Phoenix*.

Both men were married and had children, and each asked after the other's family, Halton adding that he was looking forward to meeting Rhaman's wife that evening at the naval Attaché's cocktail party. When they were at the staff college together Rhaman's wife had not been with him. He had seldom mentioned her, and the British captain was curious to see what kind of a woman she was.

His thoughts dwelt briefly on his own family. There would probably be some letters from Sheila when he got back on board the *Phoenix*; indeed with any luck the fleet auxiliary should have quite a lot of mail for the destroyer. The three boys were quite a handful for her, he felt, with just a slight suspicion of guilt. Still she had married a sailor, and knew the score from the very beginning. He could not have had a better partner, he thought, with gratitude. Many a promising career had been ruined by the constant separations and the lack of understanding by the wife left at home.

Presently conversation turned to the *Alched*, and the affairs of the Zembasian Navy. Evidently the Zembasian

Admiral was away in South America to see if another warship could be acquired. Halton wondered whether Rhaman was involved at all with the political unrest in the country. He was beginning to gain the distinct impression that the Zembasian Captain was far too ambitious to be contented with the navy as a career, although he stood every chance of becoming an admiral before long. However, when Halton tried to sound him out discreetly on this subject, Rhaman became somewhat withdrawn and changed the subject, inviting his colleague to take a turn around the ship with him.

His demeanour became pleasant enough again as they strolled round the upper decks of the *Alched*. Rhaman, with almost disarming charm, tried to give the impression that he was merely a simple sailor, without the slightest interest in the politics of the Republic. Halton was not convinced, but accepted that this was obviously neither the time nor place to pursue the subject. Perhaps tonight, when Rhaman had drunk a little, his talk would be less guarded and it might be possible to extract more information. Halton had discovered years ago like many other officers, that there was often more to be learnt over a pint of beer than in the class room.

When they reached the deck the two men paused behind the rear funnel, where the 4 inch anti-aircraft guns were mounted. There were four twin turrets, two each side of the ship, and Halton explained that his action station as a midshipman had been second in command of these guns. During the Russian convoy runs they had been fired many times at the attacking German bombers, but, he added ruefully, despite the thousands of rounds fired only three enemy planes had been destroyed. Rhaman listened politely enough to Halton's little story of the past, and then remarked, quite out of the blue, that with his own Navy's potential guided missiles, a hit would always be registered on any aircraft.

This last remark was extremely interesting. Where, Halton wondered, were the missiles going to come from? He knew that they would not be provided by Britain or the U.S.A.; then he suddenly recalled the Naval Attaché's remarks about China. If Rhaman was a mere simple sailor, as he claimed earlier, he would not have known of any forthcoming communist aid. Therefore, just as Halton had suspected, the Zembasian Captain must be mixed up in the plot to take over the country.

13

It was easy enough for Halton to conceal his supicions from the other man, who had obviously not realised just how much he had let slip by this chance remark. Halton encouraged Rhaman to talk about the importance of a Navy to a small country such as Zembasia, and in the course of this it began to dawn on him that the said Navy was an extremely important factor in the country's future. This in itself was strange, for it was usually given to the Army, in these smaller countries, to impose the wishes of a government on the population. When questioned a little more closely on this, however, Rhaman shut up like a clam.

During the subsequent lull in conversation Halton glanced casually towards the *Phoenix* and saw a motor launch leaving her side. There seemed nothing remarkable in this, until he realised that the launch was heading at full speed straight for the *Alched*. Rhaman must have read his thoughts, for he remarked:

'That boat of yours is rather early, Clive. I thought you were not going back for at least another hour.'

Halton nodded.

'That was my intention. I hope to hell nothing has gone wrong on board, or with the refuelling. Drew, my number one, is a first class man, and can handle most things. I wonder what the trouble is.'

As they walked towards the quarter deck Halton noticed one of his officers seated in the launch. This was unusual – destroyer's boats seldom have an officer in charge – but he decided not to mention it to Rhaman. Soon the smartly handled launch was coming alongside the cruiser's rear gangway, and the officer prepared to come aboard.

Stepping on to the quarter deck of the *Alched*, Lieutenant Rawlings saluted the warship's ensign, then hurried towards the two watching Captains. Halton made a quick mental note to tell the young officer not to rush around so much, especially when he was visiting other warships. However, Rawlings saluted both senior officers smartly enough before addressing Halton.

'First Lieutenant's compliments, sir. He requests that you come back on board again immediately.'

Why? Halton wondered. What on earth had happened to make Drew take this serious step of recalling his Captain? Still,

14

better not let Rhaman think that he was at all concerned.

Returning the young officer's salute he said calmly:

'Very good, Rawlings. I'll join you in the launch in a moment. Carry on please.' Turning to Rhaman, he smiled, and went on, 'Sorry about this, John. I'd better go and find out what has happened. Thank you for letting me come aboard. I hope you'll pay us a return visit before we go.'

When, after a brief farewell to Rhaman, the *Phoenix*'s launch got under way, Halton spoke tersely to the lieutenant.

'Now then Rawlings - what is this all about?'

'Couldn't say much on board the *Alched*, sir. The first lieutnant received a Top Secret Operational Immediate signal which he said you ought to know about. Here it is, sir.'

Good old Drew, thought Halton gratefully. Several minutes would be saved by his being able to read the signal while they were returning to the destroyer. Taking the small buff envelope which the lieuenant had produced from his top pocket, Halton opened it and took out the paper bearing the message. Skipping the usual headings, he got down to the text at once.

'Civil war in Zembasia imminent,' he read. '*Phoenix* to leave Toulage soonest and remain in a position twenty miles off coast. Further instructions will follow. Use *Tide First* at your discretion. British population will be evacuated by R.A.F.'

Chapter 3

Stepping aboard the *Phoenix* to the shrill piping of the bosun's call, Halton saw that the first lieutenant and the senior engineer were waiting for him, together with a small, wiry man in his mid fifties whom he, Halton, had never seen before. Probably the master of the *Tide First*, he thought. Good. It would save sending for him later on.

Hastily acknowledging the first lieutenant's salute he demanded:

'How long is it going to take us to get out of here, Harry?'

'If we can get the liberty men back – half the crew and seven officers were ashore – almost immediately, sir. As soon as I received the signal I sent a patrol ashore to start rounding up anyone they could find. The plumber,' Drew jerked an irreverent thumb at the senior engineer, 'had steam for one hour's readiness, but thinks he can now make it in about twenty minutes. We've started disconnecting from *Tide First* and should be finished in five minutes. Our tanks are only a third full, though. By the way, sir, I completely forgot; this is Captain Stubbs of the *Tide First*.'

Halton, shaking hands, thought the wiry little man looked reliable enough. He was going to have to be, he thought grimly!

'Hello Captain,' he said aloud. 'Didn't think we'd meet under *these* circumstances. Are any of your men ashore?'

Much to Halton's relief, the master had not yet allowed any of his crew to go. It would have been a different matter though, in two hours time, when the refuelling had been completed. Most of his men would have departed for the shore. Just as well, Halton thought. It was going to be difficult enough to get his own men back, let alone about eighty merchant seamen as well.

'Thank you, Number One. Well done.'

Now that he gathered his wits about him Halton spoke more formally to his first lieutenant. Christian names off duty by all means, but not here. He had forgotten himself for a moment when he first came on board!

It was time to take stock of the situation, and it was going to require some hard thinking. His orders were to depart at once, but if he complied with them, half his crew would be left behind. The ship could be worked by those on board, but to leave his men there was unthinkable; or was it? God, how he wished that they were all on board. Either of the only two decisions open to him might well prove to be disastrous, and in this situation there was no chance of a compromise.

If bloody revolution broke out ashore – and it was almost certain that it would, judging by the rapidity with which the situation was developing – then the British sailors would be caught right in the middle of it. Most of them would try to make for the British embassy, but even if they made it, there could be no guarantee of their safety in the lightly constructed building.

Years ago, in the North Korean sea port, Halton had seen the damage and casualties caused by a communist led mob. It was not a pretty sight, but at least then the sailors had been armed and organised, and were able to take care of themselves. Here they would be spread out all over the town, in small groups of two and three, completely unaware that a civil war had broken out. Some, he knew only too well, would be too drunk to care. He could not, in all conscience, leave half his crew behind under these circumstances. On the other hand, if some trigger-happy fool with the shore batteries fired on the British ships, even more casualties and damage would be added to the toll.

Tide First – bloody fool for forgetting – must be got out of here at once. If she went up with her inflammable load it would be the end of the matter for all of them! Turning quickly to Stubbs he said:

'Captain, I want you to leave at once. Wait for us twenty miles west of here; I'll join you there. If I am not with you in twenty-four hours, head for Cape Town and signal to the Admiralty that you suspect I am in trouble. With any luck at all they may be able to send me some assistance.'

'Don't worry. I'll come back in and get you myself if you are not there,' replied the *Tide First*'s master.

Somewhat irritated and yet at the same time touched by this gallant but foolhardy gesture, Halton repeated his orders politely, adding with unmistakeable firmness that the *Tide First* was not to return under any circumstances whatsoever. The fleet auxiliary should be able to leave within a half hour, her Captain estimated, as he departed for his own ship.

Momentarily Halton envied Stubbs. He had had his orders and had no problems. His crew was intact. He watched the other man cross the narrow gangway between the two ships and make his way to the bridge, but before his thoughts could return to gloomy speculation, a telegraphist approached, saluted and handed over a signal that had just arrived.

The destroyer's Captain heaved a sigh of relief as he read the message. This was going to give him enough time, he reckoned, to get all his men back on board before they left. Once again he scanned the signal.

17

'R.A.F. transports arriving Toulage 1200Z, should be ready to depart within two hours of arrival. *Phoenix* to remain in Toulage and render assistance, if considered necessary, to ensure complete evacuation of all British personnel. *Phoenix* to depart immediately after this operation.'

1200Z meant 1600 local time; Zembasia was four hours ahead of Greenwich time. Halton glanced at his watch. 1530. The R.A.F. should be here in thirty minutes; meanwhile there were quite a lot of things to be done. First he had better get through to the Naval Attaché on the ship-to-shore telephone. While he was doing that the first lieutenant could organise an armed landing party from the already badly depleted crew. They would almost certainly be needed to ensure that civilians were safely embarked on the transport aircraft.

With civil war imminent, the airport was likely to be in a state of chaos. Rich people - merchants mostly, and politicians who knew what to expect if the communists took control - would be scrambling to get out of the country in anything that could fly. Desperate people might try to get on board the R.A.F. aircraft, or even to commandeer them at gun point, and if this happened the handful of aircrew would have the utmost difficulty in controlling the situation.

At the present moment, though, hardly a man could be spared from *Phoenix* until the liberty men came back. He had barely enough men aboard to steam and - should it prove necessary - to defend the destroyer. Leaving instructions with Drew to form the nucleus of an armed landing party - other men could be added to it as they came on board - Halton went to the ship-to-shore telephone which had been installed on the quarter deck.

As he expected, it took some time to get through to the embassy; he would not really have been surprised if the line had been dead altogether. However, he eventually managed to speak to Morrison. Both men had to be guarded in their conversation. If the local population got to hear that the British were pulling out so quickly and completely, it might easily prove to be the spark to the tinder. In any event, the communists were determined to take over within the next few days, and before this happened it was imperative to evacuate the British civilians. Once they were out of the way, Halton would be able to concentrate on giving what help he could to the

18

government of Zembasia. He wondered whether the ageing president or the energetic vice president were preparing counter moves to the threatened rebellion. As far as was known, the army was almost completely loyal, and could be used effectively.

Captain Halton decided that out of a total ship's company of 250, he could spare fifty men for a landing party. Thomson, the gunnery officer, would command it, and take one of the three sub lieutenants with him. Gordon would do. He had just arrived back on board, certainly not having had time to meet the ambassador's daughter! Halton made a point of knowing his officers well.

If there had been the slightest chance, the Captain would have gone with the landing party himself, but quite clearly his place was on board his ship. In the two hours that would elapse while the men were ashore anything could happen, and he had to be in close touch with the rapidly developing situation.

When the *Tide First* was almost ready to depart, Halton sent the first lieutenant across to her to give the captain the latest information. Drew was also instructed to emphasise discreetly – taking care not to annoy Stubbs at all – that she was to remain in her rendezvous position. No matter what happened, the fleet auxiliary must not enter the harbour again. Halton vividly remembered the horrifying result of a tanker blowing up on an Arctic convoy run; the effect in this harbour would be devastating. He had also read the official report of the Halifax disaster; the Canadian port had suffered damage almost equivalent to that of the dropping of a nuclear bomb when an ammunititon ship had exploded there in the First World War.

Besides an abundance of oil, the fleet auxiliary carried ammunition and a host of other explosive materials that were necessary to supply a sea-going fleet. Not unnaturally Halton was anxious to get rid of the tanker, even though it was only a one in a thousand chance that a disaster might occur. However, with that innate sixth sense of a seaman, he knew that if one took the thousandth chance into account one was covered under most other cicumstances.

Almost imperceptibly at first, the gap between the two ships widened as the *Tide First* slowly got under way. Skilfully manoeuvering the large ship – 17,000 tons was quite a handful

– Stubbs sailed her out of Toulage. Almost immediately the *Alched* started signalling to the destroyer. Her signalman was slower than his counterpart in the Royal Navy, and Halton could read the message as it was sent.

'Why is the *Tide First* leaving so soon, she had been scheduled to stay for three days?'

The reply from the *Phoenix* had to be quick and convincing. Even now the *Alched* could stop the *Tide First*: a shot across the bows and a signal to heave to would have to be complied with. It might bring down the wrath of Britain but that did not matter under these circumstances. In any event the wrath of Britain would probably be only a formal diplomatic note, Halton thought. The small destroyer was not in a position to force the cruiser to let the fleet auxiliary proceed.

At that moment the telephone from the bridge rang. As Halton expected, it was the duty signalman with the message from the cruiser; what reply did the Captain wish to make?

'Murphy, isn't it?' Halton said, recognising the tall Irishman's voice; a youngish chap, but reliable enough. Should make leading rate in about two years time.

'Yes, sir.'

'Well, listen carefully. Send "*Tide First* leaving to search for missing British aircraft. Will return when survivors are found." Now repeat that back to me, and send it right away. By the way, transmit slowly. They can't read fast Morse.'

Within seconds Halton heard the clickety click of the signal searchlight's shutters as the signal was flashed across the harbour.

'Landing party ready to leave, sir,' reported the first lieutenant, coming up to him and saluting. 'We can't spare fifty men – there are still quite a few ashore – but we have mustered thirty-five.'

'Good. That will have to be enough. I'd like a quick word with Thomson before he goes, though. Get the rest of them on board the launch.'

When the gunnery officer appeared, Halton told him briefly what was required, and what he was likely to meet ashore. He was to march his men straight to the airport – it was only half a mile away. The R.A.F. aircraft should have landed by then, or at least be in the circuit. At the airport Thomson was to report to the Naval Attaché for further instructions. If Captain

20

Morrison was not there then he, Thomson, was to supervise the quick, safe embarkation of the British passengers. Some of his men would have to guard the aircraft throughout their time on the ground. He was to leave the airport as soon as the last aircraft had taken off. One more thing, Halton added before he departed; hang on to the Zembasian launch with a small armed guard.

It was just as well that he had remembered to tell Thomson to leave some of his men in that large, fifty foot Zembasian launch. They were going to need it; the destroyer's boats, one twenty-seven foot whaler and two twenty-five foot motor boats, would have never managed all the men in this situation. How much longer would it be, Halton wondered, before the Zembasians wanted their boat back? The R.A.F. transports would be arriving very soon, and that was going to cause a stir. Rhaman would certainly want to know why.

Time was what was desperately needed; time to get the civilians away safely before the inevitable penny dropped. Obviously he could not keep this game of bluff going much longer, but there was still one thing he could do to keep the Zembasians guessing. Picking up the bridge telephone, Halton asked for the duty signalman.

'Murphy, I want you to send a signal to the *Alched* right away. Now listen carefully and take this down. "R.A.F. aircraft diverted here from air sea rescue search, should be arriving shortly." Repeat the message back to me.' He listened to the signalman repeating his message, then went on. 'Good. Now get that message off – not too fast though.'

Once again the destroyer's signal lamp blinked like a shining eye across the glassy waters of the harbour.

After a five minute delay a brief acknowledgement was flashed back from the cruiser. Rhaman certainly had something extra to think about now, decided Halton. Looking out to sea he saw that the *Tide First* was almost hull down over the horizon. Stubbs must have put on full speed once he had cleared the harbour; that was one problem less, he thought thankfully.

His thoughts were interrupted at that moment by the arrival of tea and sandwiches. The first lieutenant had sent the duty quartermaster down to the wardroom for refreshment for the Captain and himself. Halton had been far too busy to think about such things, and would probably have gone hungry for a good deal longer. Trust Drew to remember his stomach, he mused – not unkindly – as he munched the thick cheese and onion sandwiches.

It suddenly struck him as amusing that so far all the ship's business had been conducted by him on the quarter deck. Traditionally, and in practice too, most decisions he had ever made came from the bridge. Still, no point in going up there for the moment. If he did there would have to be a continual stream of messengers or telephone calls; he was much better off here on the quarter deck.

Just as he was finishing his last sandwich he heard the sound of aircraft engines, faint at first but becoming louder every second. Drew and the officer of the watch spotted them together and pointed out the four aircraft. Britannias. Halton recognised the type instantly; a year ago he had been flown back to the U.K. from the Far East in one of them. He remembered that they could carry about a hundred passengers, so that meant four hundred people could be evacuated. Suddenly, to his horror, he realised that he had not the slightest idea of the number of British people in Zembasia. Still, if the worst came to the worst he could take a fair number on board the *Phoenix* and then transfer them to the *Tide First* when they rendezvoused later in the day.

From where the destroyer was moored it was impossible to see the airport, which was a pity. Halton would have liked to keep an eye on the situation through his binoculars. The four aircraft began to orbit above the airfield; it seemed strange to the onlookers aboard the destroyer that the aircraft were kept circling for at least ten minutes before they went in to land. At one stage the startling thought occurred to Halton that perhaps they would not be given permission to land, or that the runways had been blocked, making landing impossible. If this proved to be the case, the situation would be serious indeed. Apart from the non-evacuation of the British civilians there would be another grave problem; these aircraft were short of fuel, and could not possibly divert to another airfield. Halton was still pondering this potential problem when the first aircraft went in to land, followed in quick succession by the other three. Glancing at his watch, the Captain noticed that it was 1615 hours. He had only returned to his ship just over an hour ago, but already it seemed an age. So much had happened in such a short time.

Thinking of time, Halton realised that it would be sunset in less than three hours. But here in the tropics darkness fell very suddenly, and he did not relish the prospect of taking the *Phoenix* out of a strange harbour at night. Still, with any luck at all the men ashore might be back on board before then. There was little doubt that the sooner they left for the open sea the better.

Chapter 4

The Zembasian launch which had been loaned for the destroyer's visit was approaching the *Phoenix*. No doubt the launch's crew were feeling bitter at having the British take over their boat; still, that did not matter for the moment, thought Halton. What *was* important was the fact that they could not communicate with their own navy. He saw, thankfully, that the remainder of the destroyer's liberty men were on board the boat.

As soon as the launch came alongside, the leading seaman, who had been in charge of armed guard, came running up the gangway and reported straight to the Captain. Even before the man spoke Halton knew from his expression that something had gone wrong. One of the Zembasian seamen had escaped, and with him would go the news of the loss of their launch. This man before him, thought Halton furiously, had, by a moment's inattention, put the whole operation in jeopardy.

Evidently, it transpired, one of the Zembasian sailors had indicated that he wanted to relieve himself over the side of the boat. No captor could really refuse such a request, but none of the British seamen were watching the man as he supposedly answered the call of nature. Suddenly there was a splash. The Zembasian had dived over the side and disappeared.

He must have swum over fifty yards under water, because he

was next seen surfacing alongside one of the harbour steps. He ran up the steps, and next moment was lost to view in the fast gathering crowd. It was impossible to give chase. There were only three British seamen, and they certainly could not shoot at him.

Halton's anger subsided almost as quickly as it had been aroused, for he had to admit to himself that under the circumstances he would probably have been caught out in exactly the same way. The leading seaman had been completely honest and did not try to excuse his actions, and it would clearly be most unfair to punish him. He put the man at ease at once by telling him so, at the same time conceding, albeit grudgingly, that the Zembasian sailor had outwitted them, and had also shown a lot of courage by his desperate plan of action.

Drew, the first lieutenant, brought his Captain's attention to a small motor boat that had just left the shore and was heading at high speed straight for the *Alched*. Halton realised at once that it must be the escaped Zembasian sailor on his way to report the loss of his launch to the British. This was serious; quick action must be taken. It would be impossible to intercept the motor boat; the only other alternative would be a quick signal to the *Alched* which would confuse or delay the issue; something on the lines of an apology for a dreadful misunderstanding between the launch's crew and the British. The other incident Halton would have to account for was the armed landing party. Once again it had to be another lie convincing enough to be credible. Anything to gain a little more time.

Seizing the bridge telephone, Halton asked for Murphy and then dictated the following signal:

'Report one of your men suddenly left the launch. Deeply regret misunderstanding which has arisen over this matter.'

Just as the motor boat was drawing alongside the *Alched* she sent a brief acknowledgement of the signal. Halton had decided not to make any reference to the armed party which had just landed. It was just possible that the Zembasian sailor, in a natural state of excitement, might omit to mention it to Rhaman. All Halton could do now was wait and see what move his Zembasian opposite number would make next.

As he waited he wondered how Thomson and his men were getting on at the airport. Glancing at his watch, he saw that the

24

time was 1715 hours. The first Britannia should be ready for take off in less than an hour. Ashore, apart from the crowds gathering and the police dispersing them, all seemed quiet; rather too quiet for Halton's liking. Still, give it time, he thought. Sooner or later no doubt incidents would start to happen; an explosion here, a fire there, a riot somewhere else – enough action to keep the police and the army running round in circles while the communists consolidated their grip on the town. There was little doubt that, once Toulage was in their hands, the rest of the country would soon be subdued.

Presently, predictably, the *Alched* started signalling again.

'Why have you landed army party. Request immediate reply.'

There could be no evading a signal as direct as this one. Now what the devil could he send back as an answer? Too much hesitation on his part would make Rhaman even more suspicious; he had to reply as quickly as possible. At first he thought of saying that it was normal routine for the Royal Navy to land a large shore patrol in a foreign port, but then he dismissed the idea. Rhaman would not accept that as an explanation; he had been around too many sea ports to know that this was not true.

Halton was still trying to work out a convincing reply when the bridge telephone rang. No doubt it was the duty signal rating, wanting to know what reply he must make to the cruiser.

As he slowly picked up the telephone an idea which at least had some semblance of logic occurred to Halton. Murphy, the signalman, repeated back his Captain's message before training the signal searchlight on the *Alched*'s bridge.

'Some of my crew detained by your police. Police refuse to release them unless I provide an armed escort to bring them back to *Phoenix*.'

It might do the trick, Halton thought. After all it was not a rare thing for a few sailors to get a little drunk. After he had sent the message Murphy, somewhat puzzled, was heard remarking to another sailor, 'Sure I could have sworn I overheard the first lieutenant saying all the crew were back on board!'

25

Halton neither knew nor cared about the Irishman's bewilderment. His only anxiety was whether the signal that he had just sent would suffice, and for how long. It was more than likely that Rhaman would check the signal with the police, by ship-to-shore telephone. If he did, Halton realised only too well that someone was going to look very foolish. Still he, Halton, could always try 'wearing the green coat' - the traditional Navy way of acting dim and pretending not to know anything about the subject under discussion. Nevertheless, with a man as astute as Rhaman he would have to be very careful, and could not hope to get away with it for long.

Now that he had started this cat and mouse game of lying to Rhaman, the British Captain found, much to his surprise, that he was beginning to enjoy himself. With the serious situation developing here, however, and its far reaching consequences which could certainly lead to a grave international crisis, there was no time for frivolity. Intelligent anticipation of Rhaman's moves and necessary countermoves from the *Phoenix* were of paramount importance.

Obviously Rhaman was going to be furious when he found out, all too soon, that there was no truth in the *Phoenix*'s last message. The next signal from the destroyer would have to be on similar lines, but this time there must be a semblance of authenticity. It would read, Halton decided, jotting it down on a blank message pad, on the following lines:

'Have been misinformed about detainment of crew by police. Information originated from Zembasian army officer. Have sent out recall for armed detachment.'

The crusier's Captain could pick the bones out of that one, remarked Drew, when Halton outlined his strategy. There must be at least five hundred officers in the Zembasian army, and Rhaman could hardly be expected to know which one passed on this information. Indeed it was probable that Rhaman would not have time even to begin to try and trace the originator of the message.

It was just as well that Halton had prepared an answer, for within five minutes the *Alched* was signalling again. Rhaman had not been deceived and must have been furious, as was evident by the tone of the message.

'None of your crew detained by police. Why have you landed armed detachment? Acknowledge.'

This time the *Phoenix* was ready with her reply. Any feelings of slight relief Halton may have had quickly evaporated as he read the next incoming signal from the cruiser. There would be no chance of not complying with the message, which amounted to an order:

'Return my launch and men immediately. Acknowledge.'

So Rhaman was going to be awkward, mused Halton. Well, he was about to discover that the British could play the same game. A wild idea flashed through the destroyer Captain's mind of putting the launch out of action, but he dismissed it almost immediately. It would only add insult to injury, and could serve no useful purpose. All the same, this was a bitter pill to swallow. He could have done with that launch; now the landing party would have to be brought back in the destroyer's small boats.

Just before he gave permission for the Zembasian sailors to take charge of their own launch – they were huddled together in the front of the boat with two of the *Phoenix*'s crew on guard – Halton had another plan which would further obscure the situation as far as Rhaman was concerned. It would have to be done quickly; meanwhile he ordered the duty signal rating to acknowledge the *Alched*'s signal and say that the boat was being returned shortly.

'Go below to the wardroom, please,' Halton went on abruptly to the officer of the watch, 'and bring me up a bottle of whisky and some large glasses. I am going to entertain some people.'

The officer hurried away, puzzled by the strange order he had just been given. Drinks on the quarter deck in the middle of a serious situation? It seemed oddly out of character for the Captain.

While he was waiting Halton had the Zembasians brought up from the launch to the quarter deck. While none the worse for having been tied up for the last half hour, they did look a little scared and subdued to find themselves standing before the Captain of the British destroyer.

Presently the officer of the watch returned with the bottle of whisky and glasses. Fortunately one of the sailors spoke a little English, so Halton was able to address his remarks to him. He apologised for the British taking over the Zembasian boat, explained that there had obviously been a slight misunderstanding and offered them a farewell drink before they returned to the cruiser. He was banking on the fact that most native seamen were keen on alcohol, and would usually give anything to obtain it. He also knew from long experience that the Zembasians would not be used to a lot of alcohol, and would get drunk far quicker than their British opposite numbers.

The Zembasians accepted the proffered drinks with gratitude, if with bewilderment, which was just as well because Halton fully intended, if they did not drink voluntarily, to get them drunk by force. If the sailors returned to the *Alched* drunk, that would account for the British having to take control of the launch. Rhaman could not argue against that and, more to the immediate point, would not waste time listening to the explanations of drunken sailors. Halton felt almost sorry for the men, who were tossing back whisky with joyous abandon. They were in for a very cool reception.

A little later, watching the launch make its erratic way back to the *Alched*, Halton knew that he had got over another immediate hurdle. It would be several hours before those sailors sobered up enough to tell the real truth, and a bottle of whisky was a cheap enough price to pay for time thus gained.

Suddenly, from ashore, came the sound of a deafening explosion, and a column of thick black smoke curled upwards from one of the large oil storage tanks situated just out of the town. The fun had begun in earnest and no doubt the British company which owned the refinery was going to be very upset. How many plants, Halton wondered, had been destroyed or confiscated by revolutionary governments since the end of the Second World War?

Oil refineries were attractive targets for coups. An explosion and a fire were spectacular in the first instance, and secondly, much more important, required most of the local fire services to deal with them. A large number of police would be needed to keep the roads clear for the fire services and their equipment; a large, curious crowd would gather – it never failed – and would need controlling. Meanwhile other disturbances would break out, usually in the form of demonstrations and riots, and the authorities would, in a very short time, be kept literally running around in circles.

Those Britannias should be ready to take off soon, Halton

28

thought, glancing at his watch for the umpteenth time. It was coming up to 1800 hours. In just over an hour's time it would be sunset, and he hoped desperately, that the landing party would be reporting back soon so that they could get out of Toulage before it got dark.

It was a ten minute journey to the shore in a motor launch. To save a little time, Halton decided to send one of the motor boats and the whaler to the quayside. Fortunately the whaler had been fitted with an outboard motor; a few years ago there was no provision for motors, and it would have had to be towed. Halton remembered what an awkward proposition that used to be with a fully laden boat. The two boats, he decided, would be just adequate to recover the landing party. It was essential, in case of another unforeseen emergency, to retain the destroyer's third boat.

Drew, the first lieutenant, was the first to hear the aircraft engines amongst the little group on the quarter deck. The Britannias had started up. With any luck at all the landing party should be back in twenty minutes. The two boats would be waiting for them; fifteen minutes would be required, Halton estimated, to get the men and the boats on board. H.M.S. *Phoenix* would be ready to proceed to sea shortly before sunset and, just before they departed, he would send a signal to the *Alched* saying that they were urgently required for the air sea rescue search that was in progress.

The first transport aircraft had taken off and passed over the harbour. Within three more minutes two others followed and then, quite suddenly, the noise of aircraft subsided completely, leaving a hollow silence. Where was that fourth transport? Halton wondered anxiously. There was a complete hush on the quarter deck as they all strained their ears for the slightest sound. If it had started up, or was taxi-ing, they would have heard it - but nothing happened.

Slowly it began to dawn on Halton that he might well have to take the aircraft's passengers with him, and the prospect filled him with gloom. For a start, with only three small boats it would take a long time to ferry all these extra people to the destroyer. In any case, with all the extra activity involved, the *Alched* would be certain to notice and start asking questions. Besides, it was desirable to keep the British withdrawal a secret for as long as possible. All the white faces and the women and children on the quayside and in the boats would undoubtedly be quickly spotted by the cruiser. Even if it was dark there was still a damned good chance that Rhaman would see or hear or even sense that something was going on.

If the cruiser threatened to stop *Phoenix* when she was leaving harbour Halton could not, with women and children on board, consider fighting his way out. With no room to manoeuvre, no torpedo tubes to threaten or use against their opponent, the destroyer would not stand a chance, at virtually point blank range, against the six inch guns of the *Alched*.

For a fleeting second Halton thought that he heard aircraft engines. His heart thumped – but the relief was short lived. It must have been wishful thinking, for all remained quiet. As the minutes passed slowly by, what had been an unpleasant possibility was fast becoming an awful reality. Any decisions taken would have to be his, and his alone. There did not seem to be any easy way out of it this time.

After a long time, it seemed to Halton – in reality it was only about one minute's thinking – he began to formulate his next plan of action. To hell with politeness and niceties – he would take the destroyer alongside the jetty. There he would embark the people and recover the two boats. In five minutes he could get everyone on board. Then he'd get out of the harbour, fast.

'In two minutes time I want you to fire one round from the saluting gun. Carry on please,' he said to the officer of the watch, who, somewhat startled, went off at the double to organise the firing of the gun. Grabbing the bridge telephone, Halton contacted the duty signal rating.

'Within two minutes the saluting gun will fire one round. Exactly one minute after it has fired you are to make the following signal to the *Alched*.:

"Explosion on board *Phoenix*, twelve men seriously injured. Am taking ship alongside jetty to land hospital cases. British Naval Attaché arranging ambulances".'

The signalman acknowledged and repeated the message and instructions back to his Captain. There was just time, before the firing of the saluting gun, to give the first lieutenant his orders and – over the ship's loudspeaker system – prepare the crew for what was going to happen. As Halton made his way forward he noted with satisfaction the men running to their stations for getting under way. Thank God, he thought, we have a full head of steam.

Although he was expecting it, the saluting gun's sudden, sharp report made Halton jump as he reached the ladder to the bridge. All was in order and personnel standing by as the Captain went on to the bridge platform. On the fo'castle a group of men, under the command of Drew, were ready to let go the mooring line to the buoy. The coxswain was at the helm and the senior engineer officer down in the engine room to ensure that everything went off without a hitch. The signalman was just commencing to transmit his message, which gave Halton time to pause and collect his thoughts. One more look round assured him that they were ready to move.

The *Alched* would doubtless have been taken by surprise by the explosion which had echoed across the still waters of the harbour. The signal from the *Phoenix* would follow immediately, and then her move to the jetty; it was quite logical for a Captain to want to land seriously injured men straight from ship to ambulance if at all possible. Halton knew the water was deep enough by the jetty for a deeply loaded 5,000 ton cargo ship had left there only that morning. So far so good, he thought. Once alongside the jetty he should be able to embark the refugees and landing party without the cruiser being able to see what was going on.

One more lie would not matter, after all that had happened. As the destroyer left harbour a signal would be made saying that she had been ordered to look for aircraft survivors. The civilians would have to stay below decks until the *Phoenix* was well clear of Toulage.

Halton gave one final check look round. The signal had been sent and acknowledged by the *Alched*, and he was now committed to go through with his plan.

'Let's go fo'rard,' he ordered, and then to the engine room: 'Slow ahead.'

Slowly the destroyer moved towards the jetty. With very little room to manoeuvre, the Captain had to concentrate closely on handling his ship; no time to wonder whether the landing party would be there or not, or how long he might have to wait. Small harbour craft skipped out of the destroyer's way as she made her way steadily towards the jetty. A large crowd had gathered on the quayside, but it was impossible to tell if they were black or white people. It was just as well, the British Captain thought, that he had told the first lieutenant to organise a party of armed men to spread out along the ship's side that would be nearest the jetty. He could not afford to have the *Phoenix* swamped by local, panic-stricken refugees as soon as he came alongside.

In the destroyer's bows and stern stood small groups of ratings ready to secure the ship to the shore at the Captain's command. Judging the speed to a nicety, Halton took the way off his ship at just the right time, so that she slid neatly alongside the jetty. She was swiftly secured by the bows and stern; men would now remain at these positions ready to cast off at a moment's notice.

Sunset, sudden darkness in a half an hour's time. Glancing yet again at his watch, Halton wondered how long it would be before his passengers turned up. A signal from the *Alched* was received inquiring after the 'injured' men and – perhaps more to the point – asking how long was the destroyer going to remain at the jetty. Halton dictated a reply and also mentioned what might be required. That would do at this stage; the rest could come as they departed for 'air sea rescue operations'.

Below decks, hasty preparations were being made to receive the huge influx of passengers. Destroyers are crammed full of machinery and fighting equipment, and there is precious little space for the crew to live in, let alone passengers of both sexes.

Still, better the discomfort of a night at sea in a crowded destroyer than being left behind to the uncertainties of a revolution. Although on the surface the British sailor might appear to be rough and sometimes crude, he is basically of a kind and generous nature. The civilians, especially the women and children, would be made as comfortable as possible. Halton's main concern now was to get them on board and depart quickly.

Once again he noted the time. Ten minutes had passed, and still no sign of them. Suddenly there was a stirring among the mass of people gathered on the jetty, and above their heads Halton caught a fleeting glimpse of a naval white cap. More and still more began to appear. The landing party were returning, and trying for force their way through the crowd. To help clear a passage for them Halton sent an officer and thirty armed men on to the jetty. Even more effective was the sight, a

32

few moments later, of the 4.5 inch gun on the quarterdeck moving slowly round to cover the crowd, its gun crew at the ready. Sheer bluff. Halton could never have used the gun there, but the crowd did not know this, and the move paid off handsomely.

The sailors began to usher the British civilians on board, quickly, firmly but gently, especially with regard to the women and children. Halton did not attempt to count them, but it was obvious that there were more than the hundred or so he had anticipated. Spotting some men in khaki drill uniforms among the motley mass coming on board, he realised that these must be the aircrew from the fourth Britannia. Some of his own men were wounded, with blood-stained uniforms, and many were hatless.

He hoped that nobody had been seriously hurt, but there was not time to inquire after them now. He had to get his ship out of here; time enough in the morning to get a full report from Thomson. Within five minutes Drew was reporting the ship ready for sea. Now at long last they could get under way.

Leaving the jetty, the destroyer headed quickly towards the harbour entrance and the open sea. Already Halton was beginning to feel less anxious, and able to appreciate the cool evening breeze blowing over the upper deck. As they swept passed the *Alched* he made his last fictitious signal to her. His game of bluff worked; he wondered if any other naval officer had told so many lies in so short a time and got away with it. Tomorrow they would rendezvous with the *Tide First*. There would be time then to sort things out – and Captain Stubbs was in for a surprise.

Chapter 5

The tropical sun shone brilliantly on the two ships lying alongside each other, and anyone unwise enough to walk the steel decks unshod would suffer burns to the soles of his feet.

Land, twenty miles away, was out of sight, and apart from the two ships moving slowly ahead together, the calm wastes of the sea were tranquil and undisturbed. A closer look at the ships, however, would have revealed a considerable amount of activity.

Soon after leaving Toulage the *Phoenix* had made radar contact with the *Tide First*, and joined up with her during the night. By means of the signal lamp - Halton did not want to reveal by radio signals that the two ships were just over the horizon from Zembasia - the fleet auxiliary had been informed of the situation. As soon as dawn had broken Halton had taken the destroyer up alongside the other big ship.

In a calm sea such as this, there was no problem in trasferring the destroyer's passengers. Halton had been prepared to use the two motor launches, but this proved unnecessary. The two ships were able to keep moving slowly about ten feet apart, and it was a simple matter to rig a breeches buoy transfer by which the passengers and their few belongings were transferred. Captain Stubbs had boarded the destroyer by the same means to be put completely in the picture. He was not enthusiastic about taking so many passengers - the final count was just over two hundred - but obviously there could be no alternative now.

At the same time Halton took advantage of the opportunity to replenish the destroyer's fuel tanks, and felt vastly relieved when the senior engineer officer reported that the operation was complete. Now he could be completely indpendent of the auxiliary and the land. The *Tide First* would go to Cape Town and disembark her passengers, and from there it would be a simple enough matter to arrange air passages back to the United Kingdom for the refugees. So, with the exception of the *Phoenix*'s crew everyone knew exactly what his or her immediate future was.

The previous night Halton had sent an urgent coded signal to the Ministry of Defence, reporting what had happened and asking for further instructions. The reply to this had been:

'Transfer passengers to *Tide First*. *Phoenix* to remain in position, further instructions to follow. Well done'.

He was pleased with the commendation, and hoped that due credit would be given to Thomson, who had done so well with his landing party.

There had been no time yesterday to hear the elderly officer's report – everyone else had been far too busy – but this morning Halton had him up on the bridge after he had read his report. The report was brief enough, but, reading between the lines, it was clear that Thomson had done a damned good job. Halton listened carefully as the officer verbally filled in the details as to what had happened ashore.

After they had left the Zembasian launch in the charge of a small armed guard, Thomson had formed up the detachment and marched the men through the narrow streets to the airport. On the way they met with only a little trouble. One mob seemed determined to stop them, so Thomson halted the party and made a deliberate show of fixing bayonets. When the sailors advanced again the mob dispersed, and they were able to get through to the airport without any more incidents. In all it had taken fifteen minutes.

When they got there the Britannias were not in sight, but Thomson knew that they would be arriving in a few minutes. There were only a few air liners on the tarmac, and he noticed to his dismay that the airport officials were having difficulties with the crowd of potential passengers. Meanwhile the first British passengers had begun to arrive, and he made sure that the detachment was alert and ready.

Soon the Britannias appeared overhead and began to circle the airfield. After what seemed a long time, Thomson began to puzzle why the aircraft were not attempting to land, for there seemed to be no other planes in the vicinity. Here Halton remarked that he had wondered the same thing. It seemed to Thomson that, at the rate things were going, the Zembasian air traffic control were not going to give the Britannias the necessary permission to land, and he also realised that the aircraft would be getting short of fuel. Something would have to be done quickly to get them down.

Leaving young Gordon in command of the main body, he took six men and hurried over to the control tower. There he found five air traffic control officers. Two were dead, lying in pools of blood on the floor; the other three were being menaced by pistol carrying young communists. One of the latter fired at the sailors as they entered – fortunately he missed – and a burst from Thomson's sub machine gun almost cut him in half. The remaining communists surrendered instantly, and were quickly secured with the rope the sailors had brought along. Then an air traffic control officer, on Thomson's orders, switched on the R/T and gave permission for the transports to land, after which Thomson and his men were able to rejoin the main body on the tarmac.

Most of the British civilians had arrived by this time, and Gordon had very sensibly placed his men around them in a protective cordon. More trouble quickly followed. The Zembasian ground crew refused to refuel the aircraft and once again Thomson had to intervene. He commandeered the fuel bowsers, and the Zembasians were forced to refuel the aircraft at gunpoint under the supervision of the flight engineers from the British planes.

While this was going on the Naval Attaché, Captain Morrison, arrived, and said that the ambassador was being held as a hostage in the embassy. Thomson sent Gordon and ten men - all he could safely spare - with the Attaché, and the ambassador was extricated from a nasty situation. After that they managed to get most of the passengers on board the transports without too much trouble.

Just as Thomson was watching the aircraft taxi-ing along to the runway, relieved to see them go, a fanatical communist ran out from the crowd and threw three hand grenades at the last Britannia. Two of them caused only superficial damage, but unfortunately the third went straight up the jet pipe of the starboard outer engine. The engine blew up and started a serious fire. The passengers and aircrew escaped unhurt, but it was obvious that the aircraft would never fly again.

Gathering his charges together - Thomson remarked ruefully that he now knew how the Pied Piper of Hamelin felt - they set out for the harbour, Thomson and ten men in front with fixed bayonets and guns loaded, Gordon bringing up the rear. It had only been necessary to fire one volley over the heads of the crowd to demonstrate that no one was going to stop them, and only minor incidents had occurred on the way back to the jetty where, much to their surprise and relief, they had found the *Phoenix* right alongside.

Sub Lieutenant Gordon had been a very able second in command, Thomson stated officially. Privately he had been agreeably surprised by the efficient way the young officer calmly carried out his orders. Before this episode Thomson had been convinced, along with most other members of the wardroom, that all Gordon ever really thought about was women.

Thanking Thomson for carrying out his most unenviable task so well, Halton told him that he would be mentioning his good work in his official report.

By noon, having completed the transfer of passengers and oil, the *Tide First* made her departure for Cape Town. Halton decided to give his crew as much rest as possible, for it was doubtful if many of them had got much sleep the previous night, having given up their bunks and hammocks to the passengers. This afternoon would be 'Make and Mend' routine; the Royal Navy's quaint phrase – its origins lay in the days of sail – for having an afternoon off. Halton wondered when and what he would be hearing from the Ministry of Defence. As the Naval Attaché had remarked earlier in the day, he was bound to get a signal soon. British destroyers were far too few, for the many commitments they had to carry out, to be allowed to lie idly off the coast of Africa.

Morrison had requested to stay on board the *Phoenix*, and Halton was more than pleased to have him there. If the destroyer was to become involved in any way with the Zembasian situation, then the Attaché's local knowledge was going to be invaluable. In addition he could also speak the local language and knew many of the African dialects and was furthermore much better trained in the art of diplomacy than the Captain of a destroyer was ever likely to be.

On the other hand, if they were not required to return to Zembasia, Captain Morrison was a pleasant enough person to have on board for a while, and would certainly appreciate a few days at sea. There was a possiblity that the *Phoenix* might be getting orders to return to the U.K. direct, but then again, the legal government of Zembasia might well request British aid quickly in this crucial situation. In this case the destroyer was right on the spot – although just exactly how the *Phoenix* could help Halton was not sure at the moment. His orders and instructions would be coming from the Ministry of Defence. All he could do at present was make sure that his ship was prepared and ready for anything.

Thick smoke could be seen billowing on the horizon from the direction of Toulage; a useful aid to navigation if they had to return there. Meanwhile Halton was determined to have an early lunch and catch up on some badly needed sleep. Apart from the odd cat nap on the bridge it was nearly forty-eight hours since he had slept properly. That morning he had insisted that Drew spent a few extra hours in his bunk so that in the afternoon he could take over while Halton himself caught up. Until they received definite instructions from the Ministry of Defence about their immediate future, either the Captain or the first lieutenant must remain on the bridge ready to take instant action.

Halfway through his lunch, Halton was wanted on the bridge telephone. Drew reported that a British tanker was heading their way from Toulage, and suggested that it might be a good idea to seize the opportunity of questioning the skipper about the latest situation in the harbour. Halton agreed, adding that he would be up on the bridge shortly. As soon as lunch was over he and the Naval Attaché made their way up to join Drew.

In brief, the first lieutenant reported, it seemed as if the government was beating the communist revolution with the aid of the majority of the Zembasian Army. It was becoming apparent though, according to the Captain of the tanker, that the real and as yet unknown leaders of the rebels had still to be caught.

This was the most likely pattern, the Attaché said, when Halton invited him to comment. Nobody wanted to be on the losing side. In most revolutions there were many – usually minor politicians and men well advanced in their professional careers – who kept very quiet until they knew which side was winning before joining in. All the same, it was not like the communits to go off at half cock. To attempt a half hearted coup like this and fail would put their cause back many years.

Then there was China to consider. If she did not back the efforts of the communists in Zembasia – with action and not mere propaganda – then her relationship with other pro-communist countries in Africa would be set back many years. Still, even if the Zembasian communists did send off a frantic plea for military aid, it was difficult to see how China could help, as she did not possess many long range strategic transport aircraft in which to rush troops to the trouble spot. In any event, the Attaché was reasonably certain that the government was now in full control of the airport, thanks, in the first instance, to the landing party of the *Phoenix*. As the landing party left the airport, the Attaché went on, two companies of armed soldiers loyal to the government marched in. Both officers agreed that there was obviously a lot more to the situation than was apparent at the present time.

While they were talking, Halton asked Morrison for more information about Rhaman, who must by now be one of the most senior officers in the Zembasian Navy. The Attaché replied that he did not know the man very well, but it was common knowledge that he was extremely ambitious and wielded a great deal of influence in the Navy. There was no doubt he had once wanted to become the Commander in Chief of the Zembasian Navy but, under the present régime, stood no chance of further promotion. In consequence he had become sullen and obviously embittered. However, it was not certain whether or not this bitterness had steered him towards the communist cause.

Halton was suprised to learn that Rhaman had been passed over for promotion, for he believed him to be one of Zembasia's best and most experienced seamen. There was no disputing that fact, replied the Attaché. Unfortunately when Rhaman was on the staff college course in England he had been indiscreet enough to seduce the Zembasian ambassador's wife – and the ambassador was the President's youngest brother. Now he understood, Halton remarked with a wry smile, why Rhaman had never completed the course, and was rushed back to his own country in such a hurry!

While most of the *Phoenix*'s crew slumbered – only the first lieutenant and the few ratings on essential duties remained awake – the destroyer steamed in a wide, lazy circle at a very slow and economical five knots. All was quiet on board. Even the ship's bell, normally rung every half hour, failed to mark the passage of time, for the Captain had given orders that it was not to be used until 1600 hours, eight bells marking the end of the afternoon watch. The men would begin to stir as tea time approached. The average British sailor will never willingly miss his afternoon cup of char!

Up on the bridge, Drew altered the destroyer's course to take her near a Union Castle liner, homeward bound from Cape Town, which he had spotted a few minutes before. With her

39

graceful bows cleaving through the calm sea, the 20,000 ton, lavender hulled liner looked magnificent as she approached the *Phoenix*. Passengers were beginning to crowd her port side to get a better view of the destroyer, and – much to the delight of the ratings on watch – pretty girls in bikinis left the liner's swimming pools to wave vigorously to the warship's crew. To the professional sailor and land lubber alike, the sea is always lonely, especially when out of sight of land, and another ship is a welcome sight.

Signals were exchanged between the two ships as they passed each other. The liner's Red Ensign was slowly dipped in salute, in the centuries old tradition of the sea, just as she came abeam. Returning this salute with the destroyer's white ensign, the first lieutenant wished the liner 'bon voyage'.

His eyes on the fast disappearing liner, Drew had to admit to himself that he would not mind being on board. In a mere fourteen days she would be steaming up the English Channel. Still, if they were lucky, he thought, the *Phoenix* would be returning home shortly. However, he realised only too well that the situation in Zembasia could cause a considerable delay. No signals had come through from the Ministry of Defence yet, and Drew had given orders to the duty telegraphist to contact the bridge immediately contact was made.

At ten minutes before 1600 hours, the first lieutenant sent Sub Lieutenant Gordon, who had the watch, to organise some tea for the bridge. Seagulls screeched and circled the ship; it almost seemed as if they knew that food was approaching, Drew felt at peace with the world as his thoughts dwelt on family and future.

Although he had had only three hours sleep, Halton felt greatly refreshed when he awoke to the sound of eight bells being rung at 1600 hours. Years at sea had taught him to make the most of any time that was available for resting. Picking up the telephone to the bridge, he asked Drew if anything much had happened during the afternoon, and having listened to the first lieutenant's reply, said that he would be coming up shortly. Ringing the wardroom steward, Halton told him to take tea and sandwiches to the bridge, and five minutes later he was there himself, immaculate in clean white shirt and shorts.

Halton had almost finished his tea when the lookout reported sighting a fast moving ship coming from the direction of

Toulage. Training his powerful binoculars on it, Halton studied the approaching ship for a full minute. Suddenly he gave a muttered exclamation. It was a Zembasian destroyer heading towards them at high speed; there was no mistaking her, for she was one of the old British 'K' class. During the Second World War probably the most famous ship of this class had been Lord Louis Mountbatten's immortal *Kelly*; most officers of the Royal Navy were familiar with her outline. Zembasia's three destroyers had been away on an exercise while the *Phoenix* was in Toulage. They must have been recalled when the revolution broke out.

'Action stations, Number One!' rapped out the destroyer's Captain, and alarm bells clanging throughout the ship destroyed any ideas of peace and quiet for the slowly waking crew. A rapidly increasing bow wave was ample evidence that the engine room had responded to the orders from the bridge telegraph to bring the ship up to half speed as quickly as possible. Halton was not taking any chances with the strange warship that was approaching at such speed. Although the *Phoenix* was so far a neutral observer in the Zembasian dispute, there was no knowing what mission this destroyer had been sent to carry out.

The chances were that her intentions were peaceful, and that Halton's precautions were quite unnecessary. Still, whatever happened, it was useful practice for the ship's crew in preparing her for action. On the other hand it was quite possible that the Zembasian vessel was in the hands of communists who would not hesitate to blow the interfering British ship right out of the water. No doubt if this did happen it would later be ascribed to a dreadful misunderstanding – the communists thought the destroyer was on the other side, and so on – but that would not bring back the *Phoenix* or her crew. Once again, thought Halton, if one was thoroughly insured for the thousandth chance one could take the rest in one's stride.

As the Zembasian destroyer drew nearer she began to slow down. Halton noticed that her guns were trained fore and aft; clearly she intended no hostile action. A few seconds later her signal lamp began flashing, and Halton and the others on the bridge read the message at first hand:

'Have on board the Vice President of Zembasia'. The Naval Attaché, standing beside Halton, gave an exclamation of genuine surprise. 'He wishes to speak to you urgently. Am sending a boat over'.

Halton gave instructions for the quarter deck gangway to be lowered and then, just before going aft with the Naval Attaché to meet their visitor, gave orders for the crew to stand down from Action Stations. As the two officers made their way to the stern of the destroyer, the Attaché suggested that one reason for the Vice President's arrival could well be that he was seeking refuge. However, he added, this seemed unlikely for a man of such strong calibre. Tanjong was a brave and intelligent man, and not the sort of politician to desert his country in its hour of peril.

To the sound of pipes from the bosun's call – Halton thought that this was the least ceremonial he could lay on – the tall, well built politician came on board. Halton liked the look of him from the start, and knew instinctively that here was a man who would not leave his people to their fate while he saved his own skin. He escorted his visitor and Morrison below to the wardroom, and as soon as they were alone the Vice President began to speak urgently, in excellent English.

Several people on both sides had been killed, he said, and many wounded. Public buildings had been damaged or destroyed by the communists in wanton acts of sabotage. However, the revolution was almost over, and government troops now had control of Toulage, except for a few isolated pockets of resistance.

The Zembasian Army had remained almost completely loyal; it would of course have been a different story altogether if the soldiers had gone over to the communists. At first the position of the Navy, and in particular Rhaman, seemed to be very uncertain. Rhaman almost certainly had communist sympathies, but was far too clever to furnish any proof of this. With the timely arrival of the Zembasian Navy's three destroyers, the issue of the Navy's loyalty never arose. Two of their captains – one of whom commanded the destroyer which had brought Tanjong out to the *Phoenix* – were known to be genuinely loyal to the government, and the third was thought to be so.

The old President – Tanjong spoke of him in almost reverent tones – was still very much alive, and had handled the extremely delicate situation perfectly, although recent events

42

must have put a severe strain on his already poor health. It had been his, the President's, wish for Tanjong to find the *Phoenix* and request her to return to Toulage, his reasons for this being simple and twofold.

Firstly the presence of a British warship in Toulage harbour would clearly demonstrate Britain's continued interest in and solidarity with Zembasia. Secondly, he wanted the officers of the *Phoenix* – they would be in effect Britain's representatives – to be present at the trials of the arrested rebels and see that justice was meted out fairly. The Zembasian government intended to get as many countries as possible to witness these forthcoming trials; meanwhile Halton was requested to return with his ship. *Phoenix* would, by her mere presence, help the pro-British government to quell any doubts that remained in the minds of those members of the town's population as to where their loyalties lay.

Halton was no politician, but he could see quite clearly now the importance of Tanjong's mission. The Naval Attaché might be able to give him advice, but in the final analysis any decision would have to be made by Halton. Unfortunately whatever he decided to do could quite easily turn out to be a grave error of judgement. If he assented to the request of the Vice President, then he might later be accused of high handedness in plunging headlong into Zembasian domestic affairs without first seeking his own country's advice and political guidance. On the other hand, if he refused he might well be equally criticised for losing Britain a valuable ally in this part of the world. The Zembasian government, if they won the day – and there was every indication now that they would – would not be interested in future relations with Britain if she refused to help them in their hour of need. There was little doubt too that other Commonwealth countries would lose a great deal of respect for Britain if she did not help. Paradoxically enough, some Commonwealth republics, especially the emergent African ones, would be angry if a British warship interfered with the domestic affairs of another country.

The British Captain, though well aware that either of the only two decisions open to him could be equally wrong, realised also that he would have to make one very quickly. The T.C.I.C. (Thank Christ I'm Covered) type of officer might have done nothing and waited for someone far senior to make a decision, but Halton had never subscribed to that theory. He knew that under the present circumstances he had to make a decision on the spot, and follow it up with quick action.

In a little less than three hours it would be sunset. If both ships left now they could be back at Toulage in one hour. A speed of twenty knots – the ex-British destroyer looked as though she was still capable of a fair turn of speed – would be required. Having made up his mind on this course of action, Halton decided to send an immediate signal to the Ministry of Defence informing them of the situation, and at the same time stating his intentions. He might even, with a bit of luck and quick action from the Ministry, get an answer to this signal before reaching Toulage.

The British Captain suggested to Tanjong that in order to give a practical demonstration of Britain's solidarity with Zembasia, it might be a good idea if he remained on board the *Phoenix*. The Vice President agreed that it would indeed impress the Zembasians to know that he had entered harbour in the British warship. A few minutes later, when the Zembasian destroyer had recovered her motor launch, the two ships set course for Toulage in line ahead formation.

As Halton watched the old 'K' class destroyer, positioned about three hundred yards ahead of the *Phoenix*, he thought back to her days in the Royal Navy. Her record had been an honourable one, first in the Mediterranean and then on the wicked Arctic convoy runs. Two Italian and three German submarines had been sent to the bottom by her, besides numerous enemy aircraft. During the withdrawals from Greece and Crete she managed, in spite of heavy damage and casualties, to get back to Alexandria, and lived to fight again. When the Second World War ended many fine ships of all classes were ruthlessly scrapped by successive governments. Even now the Navy was still feeling the long term effects of this, with the huge number of worldwide commitments that had to be carried out. Halton was pleased that the grand old ship steaming on ahead had managed to escape the fate of the ship-breaker's yard.

Some of this he managed to convey to the Vice President, whom he had invited to stay on the bridge for the short voyage. Tanjong listened with obvious interest. Although not a sailor himself, he clearly took a great interest in ships and sailors, as much of the potential growth of Zembasia lay with the export and import trade.

Seeing Zembasia's coastline in sight ahead, with Toulage's taller buildings already beginning to stand out, Halton wondered fleetingly what sort of reception the two destroyers would receive. They would be entering harbour in about twenty minutes. Would the Ministry of Defence send an answer to his signal before then?

When the entrance to the harbour lay only a mile ahead, Halton peered through his binoculars, exclaimed, and peered again. No – he was not mistaken. What he had seen was the superstructure of one of the Zembasian destroyers, sunk just inside the harbour. What the devil had happened there? It looked mighty suspicious, and could well be a trap.

Instantly he ordered the ship to go hard about, at the same time flashing a warning to the other destroyer which had put on speed and was nearly at the harbour entrance. He had no time just then to look at the signal which the duty telegraphist was trying to hand him.

Too late the Zembasian destroyer spotted the *Alched*'s three triple six inch gun turrets training round on to her. The cruiser opened fire. At that range it was impossible to miss, and within a half minute the destroyer was reduced to a blazing wreck, completely out of control. Chain reaction from a flash must have ignited her magazine, for in one tremendous explosion the mortally wounded destroyer disappeared completely.

At thirty-five knots the *Phoenix* headed out to sea; the firing from the *Alched* ceased as suddenly as it had begun. The Vice President wept unashamedly, at having witnessed the death of so many of his unsuspecting countrymen, and who could blame him? The disintegration of the old British destroyer was a sight that would remain with the horror-stricken crew of the *Phoenix* for the rest of their lives.

If there had been the slightest chance of survivors Halton might have been tempted to return – but he knew in his own heart that he could never have so compromised his crew and ship. Once again he stared at the signal. If it had only arrived five – even two minutes earlier, this disaster could have been avoided.

'Phoenix must not, repeat not enter Toulage. Reliable

report indicates Zembasian Navy have rebelled against government. *Alched* dominates harbour and town'.

Chapter 6

The *Phoenix* spent another night at sea off the Zembasian coast, but this time, in contrast to all the activity and overcrowding of the previous night, her crew managed to get a reasonable amount of sleep. Only a third of the men were required on duty at any one time, to keep the destroyer at partial action stations. This comparatively high state of readiness was necessary, Halton had decided, in order to avoid being caught out by any treachery Rhaman might be planning. Radar was in use, its probing, invisible fingers on search throughout the night, helping to guard against surprise.

An almost continuous stream of signals passed between the destroyer and the Ministry of Defence; signals which had to go through the secret coding and de-coding processes in order to avoid allowing other listening ears to know what was happening. In reply to Halton's message describing the sinking of the Zembasian destroyer, the Ministry of Defence had replied that the *Phoenix* was to render all possible aid to the pro-British government.

Easy enough to say, difficult to put into practise. One destroyer pitted against a cruiser and another destroyer stood little chance of achieving anything worthwhile – except to get itself sunk, observed Morrison drily. If only the *Phoenix* had been able to retain her torpedo tubes ... Still, no use crying over spilt milk, thought Halton.

The two renegade Zembasian warships certainly had their country in their grasp for the moment – but how long would Rhaman be able to maintain this high pressure? Gathered round the wardroom table, the three men upon who so much depended racked their brains to find an answer.

Suddenly the conference was interrupted by the arrival of a

messenger from the bridge. Reading the latest signal from the Ministry of Defence, Halton smiled with grim satisfaction. Here at last was some good news. A 'Tiger' class cruiser was being despatched from Gibraltar, and should be arriving in about four days. This would certainly even things up for the pro-government forces.

Both the attaché and Halton agreed that had Britain not scrapped so many cruisers – there were only three left now – one could have been on the spot much sooner. However, provided the communists did not gain too much of a stranglehold on the country in the next four days, the British cruiser and destroyer would be more than a match for Rhaman's ships. Armed with automatic six inch guns, the 'Tiger' class cruiser had a high rate of firing which would take Rhaman completely by surprise. If the *Alched* chose to try and fight it out she would very quickly be reduced to a battered wreck.

Halton had taken the *Phoenix* to a distance of five miles from the harbour entrance at which, although within the range of the *Alched*'s six inch guns, he reckoned they were safe enough for the moment. By steaming at a fairly high economical cruising speed, almost twenty knots, and zigzagging at irregular intervals to alter the range, it would be impossible for the cruiser to zero in her guns on the destroyer. Even if she opened fire unexpectedly the chances of getting a direct hit were fairly slim. Toulage, and the two warships anchored in the harbour, were being kept under observation by the officer of the watch and other lookouts with powerful binoculars.

So far this morning – three bells of the forenoon watch had just sounded 0930 hours – there had been no movement of shipping. Motor launches had exchanged visits between the Zembasian cruiser and destroyer, and in addition visits to and from the shore had been made. The *Alched*'s three triple six inch gun turrets, trained on random targets in the city, altered their aim every few minutes to indicate that they were manned. It looked convincing enough to Halton; to the citizens of Toulage it must have been even more terrifying. It seemed most unlikely however that the cruiser would open fire on the *Phoenix*. She appeared to have enough problems to contend with, and it would be sheer stupidity to stir up a hornet's nest at sea by provoking the British destroyer into action.

Coffee was brought to the three men as they sat in the

wardroom discussing the situation, to which it seemed impossible to find a practical answer. For a start Tanjong, not unnaturally, wanted very much to get ashore to join his President and other members of the government. Halton could understand and respect the Vice President's motives only too well, but at the same time, as he pointed out, it was just possible that Rhaman might suspect that Tanjong was on board the *Phoenix*. If Tanjong left in one of the destroyer's launches Rhaman might open fire on it or, perhaps worse still, intercept it when it was beyond the destroyer's reach. With the Vice President in his hands Rhaman would have a powerful hostage for bargaining purposes. Fortunately Tanjong could see the wisdom in this and did not insist, much to the relief of Halton and Morrison. Had he done so, Halton realised, there would have arisen an extremely delicate situation. The Captain of a British warship could not hold such a prominent person prisoner in time of peace. If it was at all possible, Halton said, he would try to land the Vice President secretly after dark.

Another signal then arrived from the Ministry of Defence, instructing Halton to use the utmost discretion in this delicate situation. It was all very well for a staff officer sitting in London to dictate this sort of message, Halton remarked angrily to the others. What the hell did he think the destroyer's Captain *would* be doing? However, he was mollified, on reading the rest of the message, to learn that the British cruiser would probably be arriving to join *Phoenix* half a day sooner than estimated.

There was no doubt, the Naval Attaché said, that everything depended on the prompt arrival of the British cruiser. Then, in theory, all that needed to be done was to invite Rhaman to surrender in view of the odds against him. A guarantee of his personal safe conduct by the British might possibly be added as a further inducement if he appeared reluctant. Should neither of these courses of action appeal to him, then the *Alched* would be smashed into submission by the British cruiser.

Meanwhile the *Phoenix* would continue to patrol, just off the harbour entrance, keeping a general eye on the situation until help arrived. Halton was just about to remark that, although this sounded relatively simple, a lot could happen in the next few days, when a message from the first lieutenant broke up the conference. Halton made his way quickly to the bridge, closely followed by the other two men.

A motor launch had left the *Alched* and was heading straight for the *Phoenix*, a white flag of truce flying conspicuously at her stern. This was indeed a surprise development; the communists must have something important to discuss. Halton wondered, as he watched, why the *Alched* did not make a signal instead of going to the trouble of sending out a boat. It was unlikely that Rhaman himself would be on board this launch.

Suddenly a thought occurred to Halton. Rhaman would not know whether the Vice President was on board the British ship or not at this stage. After all, it was most likely that Tnjong would have been returning to Toulage yesterday evening in the sunk Zembasian destroyer. It would be a good thing to let the rebels keep on wondering if the Vice President had been killed, decided Halton; even better still if they were convinced that Tanjong was dead. Come to think of it, yesterday's bloody trap had probably been laid on with the Vice President in mind. If the government lost its strong second in command, there was little doubt that this would cause even some of its staunchest to falter and lose heart.

Explaining quickly to Tanjong what was in his mind, Halton requested the Vice President to go below and remain out of sight. Meanwhile preparations were made to receive the launch which was coming up alongside.

By slowing down to five knots – Halton was not going to risk his ship by bringing it completely to a standstill while still in range of the cruiser's guns – the Zembasian launch was able to approach the destroyer's stern. There would be no formal reception on the quarter deck this time, the destroyer's Captain had decided. Orders had been given to throw a scrambling net, normally used for picking up survivors, over the side for the officer from the *Alched*. This officer was to be brought to the bridge, under armed escort, and the launch would be told to keep her distance.

A Zembasian lieutenant commander came up on the destroyer's bridge. He had an arrogant manner, and was quite young for such a rank. Personnel on duty looked at him with suspicion and anger. Here was a man who had been partly responsible for the mass killing of his own countrymen in yesterday's treacherous episode. Halton felt the same as his men, but was well aware that it was no use engaging in dramatics if he was to get any sense out of this officer. Accordingly he demanded in a frigid manner the purpose of the Zembasian's visit.

'Admiral Rhaman wishes to meet you on board the *Alched*, Captain Halton.'

If Halton was surprised by this bald statement – it almost sounded like a royal command, he remarked later – he did not show it, and let the Zembasian continue.

'He personally guarantees your safety. As the future President of Zembasia, he desires very much to have friendly relations with Great Britain. If you will accept his invitation, sir, my boat is completely at your disposal.'

For several moments there was complete and utter silence on the bridge. It seemed as though all had been struck dumb by the officer's cheeky demand; then an excited babble of conversation broke out. Who the hell did this officer think he was to invite their Captain to walk into a deliberate trap? Rapping out a command for silence Halton made his frosty reply:

'After yesterday's destruction of innocent, unsuspecting sailors – your own countrymen – I do not trust your leader. I have no intention of returning with you – but if *Admiral* Rhaman would care to come on board the *Phoenix* I will give the same guarantee. You can tell him also that a British officer's word is to be trusted.'

The Zembasian officer replied that the counter invitation by Halton was unacceptable, and it seemed for a moment that impasse had been reached, neither leader being willing to put his head into the lion's mouth. Then the Attaché, Morrison, came up with a compromise that might be acceptable to both sides.

Suppose, he said, that the two Captains – he, too, was not yet used to the idea of Rhaman's self promotion to the rank of Admiral – met exactly halfway between the two warships; a sort of no man's land? All that was required to effect their meeting was a launch from each ship to take the respective Captains to the rendezvous point. This way neither would endanger his ship or himself.

As far as he was concerned, Halton said, this was acceptable;

did the officer from the *Alched* agree? The Zembasian said that he did, in principle, but only his leader could make the final decision. He would pass on the message to Rhaman and an answering signal would be made from the *Alched*.

Halton and Morrison watched the cruiser's launch as it sped across the smooth sea between the two warships. The distance was approximately five miles, and would take the small boat about twenty minutes. Allowing a further ten minutes for the officer to report to Rhaman and the latter to make a decision, within a half an hour from now – it was 1000 hours – an answering signal should be coming from the cruiser. Leaving Drew on the bridge, Halton and the attaché retired to discuss the latest development, calling in at the Captain's cabin on the way to invite Tanjong to join the conference in the wardroom.

When the Zembasian Vice President was told of the proposed meeting, his reaction was one of alarm and concern. It could be a trap, he declared vehemently. They had already seen an example of Rhaman's ruthlessness – what was to stop him overpowering the British launch and taking Halton prisoner? The two other men had to agree that Tanjong had a valid point, but Halton felt that the meeting must take place, otherwise they would never get to know just what Rhaman was planning. In that case, remarked the Attaché, it would be best if he, Morrison, went along. After all, he was a trained diplomat, and might be able to handle the meeting better than Halton, whose place was surely on board his own ship. For a moment Halton considered this proposition. Then he dismissed it, saying that he must keep to his side of the agreement. The chances were that if Morrison went, Rhaman would be annoyed at Halton not turning up and the meeting would not take place at all.

To offset any treachery – Rhaman was certainly not to be trusted – the destroyer's Captain proposed a counter move that was simple but drastic. On the stern of the *Phoenix*'s launch a depth charge would be fitted set to go off at thirty feet. This would be pointed out to Rhaman, and in the unlikely event of trouble, the depth charge would be released, which would result in the destruction of both boats. Horrified, the other two men tried to talk Halton out of this drastic idea, but the destroyer's Captain was adamant. He pointed out that while he was no fanatical idiot, and certainly had no wish to die in that or any other way just yet, he did not give much for his chances of survival if he was to become Rhaman's prisoner.

Anyway, he felt quite certain that the depth charge would act as an effective deterrent. Whatever opinion Rhaman may have formed about Halton during their time as fellow students on the Naval Staff College course, recent events had proved the British Captain to be a man of action. Therefore it was extremely unlikely that Rhaman would dismiss the depth charge ruse as sheer bluff.

When it really came down to it, Halton went on, all the British stood to lose was a naval commander. The communists, on the other hand, stood to lose their leader and the future President of Zembasia, so, he continued jocularly to his two companions, stop looking so glum, and stop trying to talk me out of it! In any case, he added, he was a natural coward from way back, or else he would not be here today! All the same, Halton's light hearted approach did not fool the other two men completely. They knew only too well that this was the decision of a brave but very modest man, and they respected him accordingly.

Two seamen and an officer would be required to accompany Halton in the launch. The latter would have preferred to go alone, but there was no alternative for he knew he could not manage the launch and handle the depth charge single handed. Picking up the telephone to the bridge, he told Drew of his intentions. Apart from the boat's crew, who were to be true volunteers who knew the nature of the mission, the first lieutenant was to arrange the preparation of the depth charge.

There remained little to do now until the signal came from the *Alched*. It would not be wise to start making preparations for lowering one of the launches, for the *Phoenix* would be under close observation, and Halton did not want the communists to think that he was over-anticipating the proposed meeting.

Presently the wardroom telephone rang. *Alched* had made her signal, and Rhaman was agreeable to meeting Halton in half an hour's time – 1100 hours – midway between the two ships, as had been suggested.

Having ordered the launch to be lowered, the destroyer's Captain had it brought round to the seaward facing side of the ship; he did not want an astute observer on board the

Alched to spot the depth charge being lowered into the boat. The lethal object was lowered with the utmost care and then secured to the stern of the boat. The greater part of the depth charge was out of the water; had there been a rough sea running Halton would never have attempted such a hazardous operation, but it looked quite safe. When the two motor boats were approaching each other he intended fitting one further refinement – a 'dead man's handle'. If this was released the depth charge would drop into the sea, so that if the holder was badly wounded, or even killed, he still carried out his duty to its ultimate end. All this would be made plain to Rhaman although, with the sensible precautions that he had taken, Halton did not expect any serious trouble from the meeting.

A spontaneous burst of cheering broke out from the ship's company of the *Phoenix*, nearly all of whom had gathered along the upper decks of the destroyer, as the launch made her departure. In most ships of the Royal Navy, particularly in the smaller ones, the latest 'buzz', or news, did not take long to filter round. Every member of the crew knew what the Captain was setting out to do, and that somewhat ragged cheer was their way of showing their respect and admiration. Halton, touched but embarrassed, acknowledged this completely un-official salute with a gesture that was half wave, half salute. Five miles away another Captain was leaving his ship, but his departure was unmarked by such informal nonsense.

Thank God the water was so calm, thought Halton, as they made their way towards the *Alched's* launch. If there had been any waves at all that depth charge would certainly not have been fitted behind them. This was one of his trump cards and, in addition to the depth charge, he had another two which he intended to use when the opportunity presented itself at the forthcoming meeting.

Firstly, the Vice President was safe in British hands. It would be interesting to see Rhaman's reaction to this news, for Halton was almost certain that the general belief ashore was that Tanjong must have been killed in the Zembasian dest-royer. However, it would not do to give away this titbit of information too soon. His second string was the pending arrival of the British cruiser; if necessary he might even bluff a little, and state that it would be arriving much sooner than the three or four days he knew must elapse.

It was just possible that he might be able to persuade Rhaman that the game was up and then, if he were to accept this, offer him a guarantee of personal safety on board the *Phoenix*. How simple things would all turn out to be if Rhaman chose to follow this course! The political situation would stabilise, and peace be restored to Zembasia without any more bloodshed. The bitter fact was, however, that Rhaman was not likely to give in so easily. The die was cast as far as he was concerned, in which case Halton would, sooner or later, have to take much stronger action than mere talking.

As the two launches neared each other Halton noticed, without surprise, that the Zembasian launch was crowded with well armed sailors. It was obvious that Rhaman meant to overpower the British boat and take its occupants prisoner. Very well, thought Halton to himself, I'll wipe that smug expression off his face! He could see Rhaman clearly now, sitting in the stern of the Zembasian boat, smiling because he thought that the British boat contained only Halton and three unarmed sailors.

There was a perceptible stir amongst the Zembasians as Halton turned the launch to show to advantage the deadly weapon it carried. Ominously he pointed to it – no words were necessary – and to the sailor holding the 'dead man's handle'. Rhaman was no fool. He got the message at once, and the Zembasian sailors put down their guns. Halton's ruse had ensured that this was going to be a peaceful meeting.

When the boats were within speaking distance Rhaman began, without preamble, to state his case. He said that he intended taking over Zembasia for the communists, and then becoming the President. For years the pro-British government had governed the country badly and oppressed the people. Now things were going to change for the better. Every person would be given full employment with good pay, there would be no social divisions and all would have an equal chance. Gone were the days of Zembasian subservience to the imperialists and the capitalists – and so on. It was the usual communist line, full of half-truths, which Halton had heard before in various parts of the world. Still, he thought, if he let Rhaman rave on for a while something useful might slip out which he could use when he got the chance to reply.

One fact which was going to be useful was that Rhaman

54

thought the Vice President had been killed in the destroyer which had been sunk the previous day. With this popular politician out of the way, and the guns of the *Alched* trained on the shore, Rhaman effectively controlled the country.

Here was a golden opportunity for Halton, the Zembasian Captain declared, as Britain's official representative on the spot, to be one of the first to recognise the new régime. After all he, Rhaman, respected the British up to a point. It was silly for Britain to continue to support a tottering governemnt. Rhaman would cut off all trade with her if she did not take a more sensible attitude. Why not, he enquired, signal London and suggest that, under the prevailing circumstances, it might be the best thing to acknowledge Rhaman's powerful régime?

It was Halton's turn to reply, and he began by declaring he had never heard such a load of bloody nonsense in all his life. For a start, he went on, the Vice President was very much alive on board the *Phoenix* – he noted with pleasure Rhaman's startled reaction to this revelation. Also, he continued, very soon now a British cruiser would be arriving. If Rhaman still wanted to continue this role in power politics, then it was inevitable that the *Alched* would be blown out of the water. Britain would only recognise a freely elected government.

Rhaman might be able to terrorise the Zembasians ashore in Toulage with his six inch guns for a little while longer, but his time was limited. What on earth was the use of being the President elect for three days at the most? He could only expect a death sentence, after his outrageous attack on the Zembasian destroyer. However, if he gave himself up to Halton, here and now, the British would guarantee his personal safety. If he wished, Halton added, they would give him a safe passage to anywhere in the world.

In spite of this generous offer, which under present circumstances seemed more than reasonable, Rhaman remained adamant and hostile. It was obvious that an impasse had been reached; neither man was going to give way to the other.

Halton wondered why Rhaman had entered into the political game with such deadly intent. Not so very long ago really, this man would have been more than content to be the master of his own merchant ship. Still, it would serve no useful purpose to reflect on the past, nor to appeal to any sense of decency that

Rhaman must once have had. Obviously the Zembasian was too obsessed with his dreams of power to pay any heed.

The one thing that did puzzle Halton, though, was that Rhaman, who was no fool, should even begin to imagine that he was going to get away with his deadly game. Before the meeting finally broke up he made one more effort to get the Zembasian officer round to his way of thinking. With all the odds stacked against him, he asked, how on earth did Rhaman think he could possibly win? The answer that Halton received shook him to the core. There was nothing foolish and nothing had been left to chance in the communist plan of action.

All Rhaman had to do, in effect, was to control the port for two days; then four Communist Chinese supply ships would be arriving, crammed with arms and military equipment. The last two ships would also carry three battalions of infantry to act as 'military advisors' to the new Zembasian Army that would be formed. Once in Toulage, the Chinese would link up with the local communists, many of whom were now lying low. The country would quickly be taken over, and Rhaman had been promised the Presidency.

As the Zembasian launch pulled away, Rhaman shouted a final warning to Halton to stay out of Zembasian affairs. Everything had been settled now, he said, and the British could do nothing at all about the matter.

It was a very grim looking Captain who arrived on to his quarter deck twenty mintues later. Halton had much on his mind, and so very little time left to form and carry out any plan of action.

Chapter 7

Shortly after Halton's return to the *Phoenix*, every officer, with the exception of two on essential duties, assembled in the wardroom. They all knew that the situation in Zembasia was becoming serious, and it was obvious from the Captain's expression when he came on board that the meeting with Rhaman had not been a successful one. Animated conversations with wild speculation were interrupted by the arrival of Halton, accompanied by the Vice President and the naval Attaché. The Captain had decided to call together his officers so that he could tell them what had happened. After this meeting he intended to clear the lower deck and put the rest of the ship's company in the picture. Like most naval Captains he firmly believed that his crew ought to know what was going on, maintaining that men who knew why they were doing a job performed it far more willingly and efficiently.

First Halton briefed the officers about the situation ashore. Very simply, he began, Rhaman had everything in his favour for the moment. The guns of the *Alched* were being used to blackmail the government into submission. Even if the government held out against a threatened bombardment, there was a good chance that Rhaman would not revert to this measure, as he would need the harbour later. The fact remained however that the communists controlled the harbour. No ship could enter or leave without Rhaman's permission; trade agreements with other countries would be ruined. Once the Chinese ships arrived and unloaded their deadly cargo there would be nothing to stop the communists.

In addition to the active intervention of the Chinese there were also many – how many was unknown at present – local supporters, fully armed and prepared to participate in the revolution when called upon. An even greater menace were the 'strap hangers' as Halton put it, men from all walks of life who would join the winning side en masse when they saw which side was most likely to come out on top. When all these groups combined, the government would stand little chance of survival. However, there were still some factors in the government's favour.

For a start, if things had gone according to plan the communists would not have started this revolution until the Chinese supply ships were about to enter harbour. It would also have been better for them if the *Phoenix* had departed after her official visit was over. In normal cicumstances both these events would have taken place; however, thanks to the premature actions of a few young hotheads, the revolution had begun three days earlier than had been intended by Rhaman

57

and the other leaders.

All the same it was difficult to see at the moment exactly how to stop the increasing momentum of communist control. Obviously the real fly in the ointment was the presence of the *Alched* in the harbour – had the British cruiser been there it might easily have been a vastly different story. If the *Alched* could be destroyed, or persuaded to leave the harbour, then the government stood a good chance of restoring order. With the government in control the Chinese ships would not be allowed to enter harbour; the revolution would be finished and China would lose her chance.

As things were at present, Halton went on, it would be ludicrous for the *Phoenix* to try to get into the harbour and attempt to sink the *Alched*, or put her out of action. Long before the destroyer reached a position where her own guns could be used she would be sunk by the heavier armament of the cruiser. Simple blockade seemed to be the answer. If they could stop the Chinese ships from entering Toulage, then the full armed rebellion could not take place as the communists had planned it. If any officer present had any ideas at all, now was the time to come out with them, Halton concluded, looking around at the attentive faces of his listeners. He would be grateful for any practical suggestions, having discovered long ago, the hard way, that good ideas were not the monopoly of high rank.

One of the first suggestions put forward extended the destroyer's Captain's own idea. Blockade the harbour and stop the Chinese ships by all means – but why not let Rhaman know that this was going to be done? Make a signal and state the intentions of the *Phoenix* loud and clear. The communists could not afford to ignore such a threat at this critical time; Rhaman would have to take the *Alched* out of harbour to remove the menace. With her superior speed the destroyer could evade the cruiser's guns and, under these circumstances, there should not be too much risk involved. Meanwhile, in the absence of the *Alched*, the government could regain effective control of the harbour.

This was not a bad idea, Halton agreed, but the real problem was that Rhaman could not afford to stay away from Toulage for long. If he did submit to the temptation of a long, stern chase to catch the *Phoenix*, which was most unlikely, then he would lose control of the harbour. There was a good chance too that he would get very annoyed at not being able to get to grips with the destroyer, and in this case, he might return to the harbour and start an indiscriminate bombardment to demonstrate that he really was in command of the situation.

If only they knew the present position of the Chinese supply ships, the ship's Captain went on, it might be possible to intercept them and prevent them from going into Toulage. Unfortunately, though, there was no real indication of their position and the course that they were steering, and it would be impossible to find them in the vast wastes of the sea; even if they managed to locate one, they might easily miss the others. Then again there was the diplomatic angle to consider. No warship could, in peacetime, intercept merchant ships on the high seas and order them to turn back to their home ports. However, if the worse came to the worst, it was possible to act first and ask questions about the niceties afterwards.

Sub Lieutenant Gordon was the first officer to speak. Basically his idea was to lay depth charges at the *Alched*'s stern, at night, by means of the launch. With a time fuse on each charge to give the launch a reasonable chance of getting away, the cruiser's stern, together with its propellors and rudder, would be damaged, and she would not be able to steer or move. As Drew, the first lieutenant remarked, this was not a bad idea; it was a pity they did not carry limpet mines, which would do the job even better.

Halton agreed in principle with Gordon, and said that although they would not carry out the scheme just yet, he would keep it in mind should the chance come about. Thomson, the gunnery officer, had an entirely different idea. He was in favour of a good old fashioned boarding party which, carried out in the middle of the night, would take the *Alched* completely by surprise. The Captain replied that if all else failed he might be prepared to carry this out, but it could prove very costly in British lives. Then, just as he was about to call the conference to an end, having more or less made up his mind to carry out a blockade, another young officer came up with an idea which was going to have a great influence on the situation in the next few hours.

Sub Lieutenant Rawlings who, Halton knew, wanted a transfer to the Fleet Air Arm as soon as he could get one, asked if there was any chance of getting an aircraft carrier to come to their aid within the next few days. It could fly off its striking force of aircraft four or five hundred miles from the harbour, the young officer pointed out enthusiastically, and therefore would be in action a full day earlier than any other type of warship.

Unfortunately, replied Halton, none of the few remaining carriers were available. According to the latest information from the Ministry of Defence, *Eagle* was in the Far East, *Hermes* was having a re-fit and the *Ark Royal* was on a N.A.T.O. exercise north of the Arctic Circle. However, there was no reason why they should not send a signal off to request help from the R.A.F. A 'V' bomber or a 'Canberra' light bomber might possibly be available.

Rawlings' suggestion, aerial bombing of the *Alched,* was undoubtedly a sound one. In the Second World War it would have been a more difficult task. The German battle cruisers *Scharnhorst* and *Gneisenau* had, in the French harbour of Brest, survived numerous bombing attacks. On the other hand there was Pearl Harbor, where the U.S. Fleet had been taken completely by surprise. That vital element of surprise would be present in this situation if the R.A.F. could send a bomber, and a jet aircraft coming in at high speed would spend very little time over the target.

A low level attack would be necessary, with conventional 1,000 pound bombs. Two or three bombs on the decks of the *Alched* should prove sufficient to put her right out of action. As soon as possible after the bombing had been carried out the *Phoenix,* taking advantage of the resultant confusion, would enter the harbour and take control of the situation. The *Alched* would be in no position to offer much resistance, and would almost certainly surrender. If she did not, then the British destroyer would open fire, and if necessary – although Halton sincerely hoped that it would not be – sink her.

A signal was at once sent off to the Ministry of Defence, giving full details of the situation and requesting the urgent assistance of the R.A.F. Halton mentioned that the airfield was in government hands, for if a Canberra was used there might be a fuel requirement immediately after the attack had been carried out.

Meanwhile the officers' conference broke up for lunch, during which there was only one main topic of conversation.

While he was sipping his coffee after lunch, Halton received, to his astonishment, a signal from the Ministry of Defence stating that the requested air support was available in the form of a Canberra bomber. Evidently, by some lucky coincidence, the aircraft was carrying out a re-deployment exercise from the R.A.F. base of Akrotiri, in Cyprus. It was already airborne and had set course for a neighbouring republic only one hundred miles north of Toulage.

When the signal from the *Phoenix* arrived at the Ministry of Defence requesting air support, the duty staff officer had acted very quickly. He had got in touch with the R.A.F. at Akrotiri who, after being told the nature of the mission, had in turn contacted their bomber. For the redeployment exercise the Canberra was carrying a war load of conventional bombs which under normal circumstances would have been dropped on a bombing range at the end of the flight. This was fortunate, Halton thought. Had the aircraft been carrying a tactical nuclear weapon it would have been no use in this situation. The bomber's captain had been given his orders and would be coming in to attack at 1330 hours, local time – which, Halton realised, glancing at his watch, was precisely twenty minutes from now.

Since a number of the crew of the *Alched* were probably not communists at all, but merely carrying out the orders of their officers as naval discipline demanded, Halton determined to make one last attempt to avoid more bloodshed. Rhaman had had time to think things over since the meeting that morning, and it was just possible he might be of a more reasonable mind, and be prepared to accept the British offer of asylum. A carefully worded signal – it was vital to avoid giving Rhaman any hint of the forthcoming attack – was sent from the *Phoenix*, repeating the offer of asylum for Rhaman, and this time Halton extended the offer to include any of the *Alched*'s crew.

While he was still waiting anxiously for an answer to his latest signal, the Canberra checked in with the *Phoenix* on R/T. It was twenty miles away, out of sight and hearing of the ships, losing height before coming in for a low level attack. Halton gave instructions for the aircraft to orbit and delay for a few minutes, and the pilot was told that there might be a last minute cancellation of his mission.

When the reply came from the *Alched*, it was on the lines that Halton expected. Rhaman had no intention of giving himself up, and it would be best for the British to stay out of Zembasian affairs before there was real trouble. Reluctantly, Halton ordered the Canberra to carry out the attack, and gave the pilot his final instructions regarding the target and its relative position in the harbour.

Most of the *Phoenix*'s crew had assembled on the upper decks of the destroyer to watch the attack, and just in case anything went wrong, Halton had ordered 'Action Stations'. Suddenly out of nowhere the Canberra came in, sweeping low and fast over the harbour heading straight for the *Alched*. The cruiser, taken completely by surprise, did not have time to open fire. One 1,000 pound bomb scored a beautiful hit on the quarter deck by the rear six inch gun turret, but the other one dropped on this run was a near miss.

The crew of the *Phoenix* cheered as wildly as any cup final crowd while the bomber climbed away to position itself for the next bombing run. This time the *Alched* was prepared, and her four inch anti-aircraft guns commenced firing, followed by the rapid fire of the many 400mm 'Bofors'. The Canberra pressed on gamely to the attack through the heavy barrage, but then, disastrously, it received a direct hit on one of the engines. Breaking off the attack it clawed desperately for height, dense black smoke pouring from the shattered engine.

While the crew of the *Phoenix* looked on in dismay, Halton told the pilot, over the R/T, to head for the destroyer if he intended to abandon the aircraft, which seemed almost certain now. A brief acknowledgement came from the pilot; he obviously had all his work cut out in trying to control his badly damaged aircraft. These were his intentions, he said, and the navigator was just about to use his ejection seat.

Two parachutes blossomed seconds before the Canberra exploded. The crew had only just left in time. Halton gave orders for the *Phoenix* to head for the gently descending parachutes, at the same time telling the surgeon lieutenant to be prepared in case the airmen had been injured.

Suddenly the wind freshened, and began blowing the parachutes in the direction of the harbour. Almost simultaneously a launch set out from the *Alched* and began racing to intercept the airmen.

Ordering full speed ahead, Halton steered the *Phoenix* towards the area where he estimated the parachutes would land. It did not take much imagination to realise what sort of a reception the airmen would get from the Zembasians, and although the *Phoenix* would be placed well within the range of the *Alched*'s main armament, the risk had to be taken in order to attempt a rescue. A signal was flashed from the cruiser to her own launch. Halton did not have time to read it, but he could guess it was instructing the launch to get right out of the way.

Bringing her two fore six inch gun turrets to bear – thank God the Canberra had knocked out one third of the main armament, thought Halton – the *Alched* opened fire. At first her shooting was wild, the recent air attack had probably shaken the crew, but then accurate salvoes commenced. Desperately zig-zagging to a position inshore of the airmen, who were now in their rubber dinghies, the *Phoenix* laid a thick smoke screen. Under the cover of this smoke it was a fairly straight forward matter to stop and pick up the airmen, neither of whom was seriously hurt, and then head out to sea.

It was astonishing, Halton thought, how quickly time slipped by in situations of crisis. From the initial sighting of the bomber to the rescue of its crew had taken only twenty minutes. Having made the two R.A.F. officers welcome on board – at the moment they were being royally entertained in the wardroom, none the worse for their adventure – the destroyer's Captain sent a signal to the Ministry of Defence informing them of the situation.

He had to face the fact that they could now rule out any further ideas of air support. Removal of the *Alched* and restoration of peace to Zembasia was a problem to be solved by *Phoenix* alone.

Chapter 8

Through his binoculars Halton studied the damage suffered by the *Alched*. The bomber's gallant attack had not been entirely in vain, for the rear six inch gun turret was completely out of action. One of the three guns had disappeared completely, the other two were bent and twisted, pointing grotesquely towards the sky. If it came to a pitched battle between the *Alched* and the *Phoenix*, Halton estimated, the destroyer would have more of a chance now with three out of the cruiser's nine six inch guns missing.

It would be vital to keep the destroyer close behind the cruiser's stern – her blind spot – and keep up a rapid and accurate fire with the *Phoenix*'s 4.5 inch guns. With concentration of fire there was a reasonable chance of damaging the *Alched*'s rudders and propellers, after which the destroyer would have the cruiser at her mercy. During this kind of action the destroyer's Captain would have to be sure that the *Alched* got no opportunity at all to bring her two forward turrets to bear on his ship. To stay in the arc of safety, about 45 degrees each side of the dead astern position of the cruiser, would mean being in at short range; one slight miscalculation on the part of Halton would result in severe damage or destruction for the *Phoenix*.

Six inch shells weighed 100 pounds, and against the thin plating of a destroyer the results were deadly. One of Halton's friends had been in the *Glasgow* when she and another cruiser, the *Enterprise*, had engaged German destroyers in the Bay of Biscay during the Second World War. Both cruisers had been armed with six inch guns, and the destroyers were virtually wiped out, only one or two returning to France, badly damaged, to tell the ghastly tale. The moral was obvious; destroyers did not take on cruisers under normal circumstances. However, the situation in Zembasia could hardly be described as normal.

As he pondered thus, the ghost of an idea flashed through

Halton's mind. One of his officers had mentioned the subject during the conference, and it was just possible that he might be able to bluff the cruiser after all. Rhaman would not be in a position to know whether or not limpet mines were carried by the destroyer. If he, Halton, could convince the Zembasian Captain that this type of mine had been placed on the *Alched*'s bottom and, perhaps more important, that they would explode at a certain time, then the cruiser might be abandoned by her crew. No matter how hard Rhaman ruled his ship, Halton thought that it was extremely unlikely that the Zembasian sailors, and Rhaman himself for that matter, would just wait on board for their ship to be blown up, and certain death. When, as Halton hoped, the cruiser started abandon ship routine, then the *Phoenix* would seize the opportunity of dashing into the harbour and taking over the *Alched*.

Having sent for the first lieutenant and the Attaché, Halton told them of his proposed plan and asked if they had any comments to make about it. Both officers agreed that it was worth a try.

'It might even work,' added the Attaché. 'The reactions of these people were hard to predict.'

'Right,' Halton said. 'Let's get down to some practical planning. In the first place, it seems to me, the sooner we carry out this operation the better; secondly, it will have to be done in a convincing fashion.'

He went on to explain briefly just what he had in mind. Taking into account that the *Phoenix* was being kept under constant observation – this could be safely assumed, all agreed – one of the destroyer's launches would depart from the ship and head towards the harbour. This departure of the launch would be an elaborate affair, with diving and associated equipment lowered into it slowly and deliberately, so that the lookouts from the *Alched* could not miss seeing what was going on. Then the launch would leave the destroyer and take up a position about three miles from the *Alched*. When the launch had stopped divers would be seen to leave the boat and disappear; in fact they would merely swim under the boat and be picked up on the opposite side to the cruiser.

All this would take place within the range of the cruiser's guns. Admittedly the *Alched* might commence firing, but a small launch was a difficult target, and there should not be too much danger of a direct hit from a random shot. If the cruiser did not open fire, or send out a boat to investigate, the launch would stay in position for about two hours. At the end of this time she would burst into activity, and having apparently recovered the divers, would head back to the *Phoenix* with all possible speed.

If the *Alched* opened fire as soon as the boat from the *Phoenix* got into position, of course, the launch would have to return quickly, but even so, a pretence of launching the divers would be made. Two hours later the launch would go back again and simulate recovery action of the divers or, to be technically correct, frogmen. On the whole Halton rather thought that he would have to put his second plan into operation, but the prospect did not dismay him unduly. At least it would confirm that Rhaman was taking note of what the British were doing.

When the operation had taken place – Halton estimated this would be at about 1700 hours – he would send a signal to the *Alched* stating that limpet mines had been planted on her bottom and were due to explode in half an hour. Many Zembasians besides Rhaman would read that signal, and with any luck the crew might panic and even abandon ship. Once this was accomplished the *Phoenix* would make a high speed dash into the harbour and board the cruiser – all of which was going to call for perfect timing, because if the *Alched's* crew were not sufficiently far from their ship when the destroyer made her dash, they would have time to get back on board and repel the boarding party from the *Phoenix*.

For a time the destroyer's Captain considered going with the launch himself. Apart from wanting to ensure the success of the mission, he was deeply concerned about sending men out on these dangerous tasks while remaining himself in the comparative safety of his ship. However, his companions pointed out, his place was really here on board. After all, if any orders or instructions came from the Ministry of Defence, especially if the signal was of a particularly urgent nature, valuable time would be lost with the Captain away in a small boat taking charge of a comparatively minor operation. Reluctantly, Halton had to admit that the officers were right. Drew would take command of the launch, and was quite capable of ensuring that the operation was carried out according to plan.

Like most ships of the Royal Navy, the destroyer carried a set of skin diving equipment. Being practical and quick to put on, it was most useful when it came to inspections of the hull or propellers. Quite a show was made of loading the underwater gear into the launch, and ordinary cans of paint, representing limpet mines to the distant observer, were lowered with much care. To create an effect of testing their equipment Halton had a practice submarine grenade exploded in the sea near the destroyer. These made an effective looking explosion, but in reality were quite harmless; they were generally used against friendly submarines, during exercises, to show that the submarine had been located and was under depth charge attack. At this stage of the operation the significance of this explosion might well escape Rhaman, but later, when he saw the frogmen leave the launch, he would realise what it had meant, and might be convinced that limpet mines had been planted underneath his ship.

After all this carefully rehearsed demonstration the launch left the *Phoenix* and headed at high speed towards the harbour. At first it seemed that the *Alched* either had not noticed, or was not interested in the activities of the launch. Drew had got his men into the water and was recovering them, out of sight of the cruiser, when the first shell arrived, taking them all by surprise. It was a damned sight too accurate for anyone's liking, remarked Halton, grudgingly forced to admit that the standard of Zembasian naval gunnery was good. The launch got the men on board with all speed and wove her way out of range back to the *Phoenix*.

Rhaman, on board the *Alched*, had been watching the British destroyer and launch with interest. He was in his cabin with the Chinese consul, discussing the pending arrival of the supply ships, when the officer of the watch reported that the *Phoenix* was lowering a motor launch. The two men had just reached the cruiser's bridge when the submarine grenade exploded near the destroyer. Neither Rhaman nor the consul thought much about it, however, except perhaps to hope some of the British sailors had been killed or wounded.

There was no doubt that the attack by the Canberra had made Rhaman feel extremely suspicious and bitter towards the British. He would never have believed they could commit such an unsportsmanlike act. Fortunately the only real damage caused was the loss of the *Alched's* after turret. A few of his crew had been killed or wounded, but this was of no consequence to Rhaman. All that really counted, as far as he was concerned, was complete domination of the harbour with the cruiser's forward gun turrets. In two days time the Chinese supply ships would be in Toulage and, within hours of their arrival, he would be the new President of Zembasia. He had merely to keep his ship intact for this period and, as the Americans would say, he had it made.

At one stage Rhaman had been sorely tempted to take the *Alched* out to sea, especially after the sneak air attack, and sink the impertinent small British destroyer. However, common sense prevailed after his rage had subsided a little, and he realised that the harbour might be taken over by the government forces during his absence. The Zembasian destroyer which would be left behind if he carried out this plan might well be overpowered, and besides, like most dictators, he did not like relying too much on subordinates. So, he decided to remain where he was. He knew that he held all the trumps.

His main worry at the moment was whether or not the British would launch another air attack. The first bomber had taken him completely by surprise, and had almost succeeded in wrecking his plans. However, another attack, though possible, seemed unlikely at present, for two reasons. For one thing, the communists had shot down one aircraft, which – and he would have liked to capture the crew for interrogation – Rhaman was almost sure was on a random patrol. Secondly, thanks to his British staff college course he knew that the R.A.F. had far more commitments than their small force of operational aircraft could cope with.

Still keeping the launch from the *Phoenix* under observation through his binoculars, Rhaman began to wonder why it was heading in the direction of his own ship. When it stopped he became interested and suspicious, and stared intently at what was happening. Then when it became apparent that the British were launching frogmen, he gave swift orders for the *Alched'* six inch gun turrets to be manned. As soon as they were trained on the launch, firing was to commence. It was just possible that a lucky shot might hit the small boat, although Rhaman was experienced enough to know that this was extremely unlikely. However, the real object of the barrage was to act as an effective deterrent. If men were swimming under water, the exploding shells would create shock waves that might cause concussion or death to the frogmen; thus there was a reasonable chance that none of them would be able to press home with the attack. To ensure that no frogman who might have survived the barrage could get through, four motor boats were detailed to patrol the sides of the cruiser. With the almost certain prospect of becoming President in the next two days, Rhaman was not going to take any chances.

Halton could not read his opponent's mind, but the actions of the *Alched* subsequent to the supposed dropping of the frogmen were enough to convince him that the first part of the operation had been a success. Rhaman's reactions were identical to what his own would have been in the same situation. Although he detested all that Rhaman was fighting for, Halton could not help feeling a sneaking admiration for the sheer audacity of the man who, like Julius Caesar, had burnt his boats behind him.

It was not often that a mere naval Captain could cause such a political upheaval; Rhaman must have been planning all this down to the last detail months, possibly even years before. If the hotheads of the Zembasian communist party had not been so impatient at the last moment, Rhaman would have been able to take control very much more easily and quickly than was now likely to be the case. There was certainly no saying that he would not be able to even now, but at least the government and the British knew about the plot, and were going to try and stop him.

All feelings of admiration vanished, however, when Halton suddenly remembered the dreadful slaughter of unsuspecting Zembasian sailors as their destroyer tried to enter harbour the day before. A man like Rhaman did not deserve to live at their expense, he resolved, although he had pledged his word to take the potential dictator to safety if he surrendered soon. Not that the latter event was very likely, and even if it did happen, no doubt the Zembasian government would demand that the prisoner be handed over. Still, it was no use speculating, for the moment anyway. That bridge could be crossed if and when they came to it.

As the afternoon dragged on, Rhaman's feelings of acute anxiety began to fade, but he still kept his crew on the alert.

At frequent but deliberately irregular intervals, the motor boats from the *Alched* dropped explosives in the water around the cruiser. If any of the frogmen had managed to get this far, after the effects of the shelling, there was a good chance that they would be killed or spotted by these local counter-measures. All the same the fact still remained, which any captain would be a fool to ignore, that one or two determined men could with luck get through and sink the cruiser.

(When the British battleships *Valiant* and *Queen Elizabeth* had been 'sunk' in the Second World War by the intrepid Italian frogmen in Alexandria harbour, the Royal Navy was quick to realise that a new naval weapon had arrived, and not slow to exploit it. Fortunately for the British, their two battleships had been moored in shallow water, and sank only a few feet before coming to rest on the sea bed. By putting it out that these ships were still in active commission, until they could be patched up enough to make voyages to repair yards, the British government concealed the affair from the rest of the world until long after the end of the war.)

Just before 1700 hours, Rhaman decided that the attack must have been thwarted by one of the counter-measures he had used. If anything was going to happen it should have taken place by now. He invited the Chinese consul below to the wardroom for some tea, and as the two men left the bridge, there was a noticeable relaxation by all on board the *Alched*.

at the same time the feeling on board the *Phoenix* was, if anything, completely opposite. Halton had organised an early tea for all the ship's company, since it was not at all certain when the next decent meal could be served. Once again the launch set out, at exactly 1700 hours, from the destroyer's side to go through its routine. Another good performance was put on by the first lieutenant and his party for the benefit of Rhaman. Any onlooker must have been convinced that the launch was undertaking the recovery of frogmen.

This time, surprisingly, the *Alched* did not open fire, and the launch was able to make a much more leisurely return. Resisting the urge to make a signal to the cruiser immediately after the launch's return, Halton deliberately waited another five minutes. During this enforced interval he spoke to all the

70

crew over the ship's loudspeaker system, explaining what his intentions were if the limpet mine ruse came off. Extreme caution would have to be used during the approach to, and the actual boarding of the *Alched*, he warned. All four 4.5 inch guns would be manned, plus the four sets of Vickers twin machine guns. He himself would be leading the boarding party, consisting of the whole of the starboard watch – approximately fifty percent of the total crew.

He finished speaking, then gave orders for the signal to be sent which stated, simply and concisely, that limpet mines were secured to the *Alched* and were due to go off at 1800 hours.

All feelings of complacency that Rhaman may have had quickly vanished as he read and re-read the signal from the *Phoenix*. So they had penetrated his defences after all! Or ... had they? This could well be another piece of British bluff; he had experienced more than enough of that during the past few days. Nevertheless he could not afford to ignore the warning. Word had spread fast around the *Alched* about the latest British signal, and the crew were getting restless. While it was one thing to die in battle it was, even to the fanatical communists among them, an entirely different matter just to stay on board the ship and wait to be blown up.

1800 hours. Rhaman had nearly half an hour to make up his mind what to do. He must arrive at a decision soon, for he could sense the restlessness mounting in his crew. If only he had some divers available he could have them inspect the cruiser's hull, but unfortunately that was now impossible. All the Zembasian Navy's divers and their equipment were on board the fleet's salvage ship, which was several hundred miles away in another country. Rhaman's careful planning of the rebellion had taken into account, intentionally, that most units of the fleet would be absent carrying out manoeuvres and courtesy visits.

Suddenly the incident involving the two British battleships in Alexandria flashed through his mind. They were sunk in shallow water, or else they would have been lost completely. Two could play at that game! He decided that he would take his ship into shallow waters, which were only a quarter of a mile away; then, if the British were not bluffing, the *Alched* would only sink four feet before coming to rest on the sea bed. She would become, in effect, a fixed steel fortress in the middle of the harbour, and still be able to dominate the situation. His destroyer would be fully mobile, if he had need of a warship that could move, and in two days time the Chinese ships would be arriving. All he had to do was to hold out until they came.

Having made up his mind, Rhaman acted fast, signalling his destroyer to come and take the *Alched* in tow. Instructions were passed to the senior engineer officer – Rhaman did not intend to take any unnecessary risks now – to reduce all steam pressure in the boilers just in case of an explosion. Nobody was left below decks as the destroyer towed the cruiser towards the shallow water. They made it with five minutes to spare.

From the *Phoenix* Halton had watched the manoeuvre in a state of suppressed fury. Another plan had to be written off! Was there *any* way out of this increasingly serious situation?

Chapter 9

Sunset in the tropics never failed to impress Halton. Each one was slightly different in beauty and magnificence from any he had seen before. Over the many years at sea – it must be nearly twenty now, he realised – he had witnessed many tropical sunsets, mainly in the Far East, and had never regretted not becoming a specialist which would have involved long spells ashore. The vivid colouring of the sky, with red tipped clouds near the horizon, gave him a feeling of deep satisfaction; there was something so vast, so awesome about the whole scene which made a man realise that perhaps religion was not all just an old fashioned fable.

Long ago he had reconciled himself with God, although of course many smart and clever men professed to be atheists, or at least agnostics in this modern age. It was strange though, he recalled; he had never really met an atheist in any action or tight spot in which he found himself! As the sun dipped finally below the horizon he wished, for the umpteenth time, that he had the talent to capture the scene in paint.

Glancing round the ship, he noticed that many other sailors were just as fascinated by the sunset as he was. Looking towards the stern, he was pleased to see, on the small quarter deck, the two R.A.F. officers from the ill-fated Canberra taking exercise and looking well. According to the surgeon lieutenant there was nothing to worry about. However, there would be little chance of disembarking them for a while.

It had been pleasant to relax for a few minutes, thought Halton, turning his mind to the more pressing problem of the Zembasian situation. Tonight they would be sending ashore the Vice President, who was going to need an escort. Tanjong had been quite willing to go alone, but an officer and a dozen men were to accompany him. Most of the communist activity was confined around the *Alched* and the rebel destroyer, but all the same, Halton declared that he was not prepared to risk the life of the Vice President by letting him go by himself.

There was another reason, though, why Halton wanted to send a party ashore. He needed an officer – one who must be selected with the utmost care – to find out about the real situation in Toulage at the moment. Several questions needed to be answered. Was the morale of the pro-government army high? Were the men dependable? Could they be relied upon to hold out until the British cruiser arrived? Was there any chance of diversionary activity against the two communist warships? Did the government know about the pending arrival of the Chinese supply ships? If so, had any plans been made to resist their unloading?

Once again Halton would have liked to go ashore himself, but he knew this time that it really was out of the question. Eventually he decided that Morrison, the Naval Attaché, would be just the man to lead the expedition. He was the obvious choice, for he knew the Zembasians and their ways well – far better than any of the *Phoenix*'s officers could be expected to do.

'Captain Morrison?' Halton was 'phoning the wardroom from the bridge. 'Sir, this is Captain Halton speaking. I would like you to go ashore with the Vice President this evening.'

Although as Captain of his own ship, his word was law to all on board in the strict technical sense, Halton knew that it was best to put the matter in the nature of a request to the more senior officer.

73

'The boat will leave in one hour's time, so there is time for dinner first,' he went on. 'I'll be down for dinner myself in twenty minutes. I'd like to talk to you about it then, sir.'

Morrison assured him that he was more than willing to go along with the Vice President. Meanwhile there was one more thing for Halton to do before going below for dinner.

Gray, the destroyer's coxswain, was sent for; the reliable chief petty officer was just the man to act as second in command of the landing party. Briefly Halton explained to him just what was going on. To give the boat a good chance of not being seen from the shore, he intended to take the *Phoenix* further along the coast before dropping the landing party. It would mean that they were in for a long walk, but would be in far less danger of being intercepted. At all costs the Vice President had to be got safely to government headquarters. When Gray had left the bridge to get the men of the landing party organised and armed, Halton felt completely satisfied that his old Korean shipmate would be able to handle the situation.

Dinner in the wardroom that night was a very pleasant affair. Most of the destroyer's officers were able to attend the informal little gathering, and animated conversations took place about the situation in the Zembasia in general and the prospects of the landing party in particular; a venture in which the majority of those present would have liked to participate. During the meal Halton spent most of the time talking to Morrison and Tanjong about the forthcoming operation.

It was more than likely, the destroyer's Captain said, that the government did not know about the pending arrival of the Chinese; he was almost sure Rhaman had let slip this vital piece of information in an unguarded moment during their last meeting. Tanjong, who appreciated fully the implications of this intervention, assured Halton that he would inform the government and make certain that measures were taken to stop them unloading.

Both the Attaché and the Vice President were advised to stress the arrival of the British cruiser in three days time. Halton reminded the two men upon whom so much depended that the government must hang on till then, whatever happened. Admittedly the Chinese were due to arrive twenty-four hours before British reinforcements, but unless the government wanted to see an end to democracy in Zembasia, the Chinese would have to be repelled most strongly. It was just possible, Halton added cautiously, that he might be able to provide effective help over this matter. With a little luck the *Phoenix* would be intercepting these ships, and it was hoped it would be possible to delay them until help arrived. Meanwhile, the destroyer would wait off shore – they were nearing the secluded spot Halton had selected – for the Attaché and landing party. If there was any trouble during the landing and recovery parts of the operation, Morrison was told to fire three red Very cartridges and the *Phoenix* would send reinforcements.

The landing having been successfully accomplished, the party of men made their way through thick jungle to the government headquarters. It took them three hours to cover the distance of five miles from the beach, but it was worth taking this route as they had the advantage of not being spotted by anyone. The route could have been a damned sight harder, Gray remarked to a cursing young sailor, if it had been through virgin jungle. They would have had to hack their way through – in some parts of Borneo, where Gray had served during the period of Indonesian 'Confrontation', they were lucky to cover two miles in a day. On these old logging paths, along which elephants had pulled timber at one time, the going was comparatively easy.

In the dark the Naval Attaché smiled to himself. The coxswain certainly knew how to get the best out of his men without being officious, and Morrison felt instinctively that here was a good man to have around if an emergency arose. Tanjong, who had known these forests as a child, was a great help to his escort giving them practical tips about jungle navigation, including the marking of trees, which would be a useful guide on the return journey to the *Phoenix*.

Eventually they emerged from the lush greenery, and made their way to the government headquarters situated in the outskirts of Toulage. This was not the normal place of government, but an army camp where the troops were known to be loyal. Also – of equal importance – it was out of range of the *Alched*'s six inch guns.

It was a tremendous surprise to the assembled ministers and senior army officers to see Tanjong again. Rhaman had

75

informed the government that he had been killed in the Zembasian destroyer, and the old President was overjoyed to learn of his survival. Morrison, after he had been introduced to the President, was invited to speak to the assembly about the plans that the British had and how the Zembasian Army could help them.

Briefly, Morrison outlined the situation. His revelation of Chinese intervention caused much alarm and dismay. No one had really considered this as a possibility, although it had been rumoured that something of the sort was in the wind. To reassure them the attaché emphasised the fact that a British cruiser would be arriving, and that, with the odds stacked up against him, Rhaman would be forced to surrender. However, he went on, there was going to be at least a day between the arrival of the Chinese and the British. The *Phoenix* would do her best to stop these supply ships, but could not guarantee being able to intercept all four of them. So, in the event of one or more getting through, the army would have to take action to prevent the Chinese ships from docking. It would mean occupying the quaysides and, should it prove necessary as a last resort, opening fire on these ships.

This was easier said than done, pointed out one of the army officers. If the army interfered with the unloading of the Chinese ships, then Rhaman would almost certainly carry out his threat and open fire on the town. No matter how brave the soldiers were, the town and the civilian population would take a heavy battering, and it could only be a matter of time before the morale of the people cracked under a sustained bombardment. Then all the efforts of the army would have to be concentrated on trying to control an enraged population, leaving the Chinese ships to carry out unloading uninterrupted. So, concluded the officer, the situation would deteriorate, and become far worse than if they, the army, had done nothing.

Morrison had to concede that the army officer had made some valid points but, he argued, the Zembasian Army could not just sit back and let the communists overrun their country. After all, he reminded them sharply, the price of freedom was high, and almost invariably sacrifices had to be made. The Zembasians were stung by his remarks, as he had fully intended them to be, and began to stir from their apathetic approach to what was going on around them. Tanjong came to the Attaché's aid, and between them they injected new hope into the government and its supporters. Basically there was nothing very much wrong with the army officers. No one doubted their honour or physical bravery, but they were fast losing their sense of purpose, which had to be restored. Morrison suspected that there might be communists among them who had sapped their minds with subtle propaganda, and he was determined to give them some fresh hope.

Cautiously, for he did not want to commit Halton to an irrevocable decision, he sounded them out on other lines. If the *Alched* was not in the harbour when the Chinese came, would the army take positive action then to stop the supply ships from unloading? A very definite assurance was given under these circumstances, but how, he was asked, could the British guarantee this, and how did they propose to achieve it?

The Naval Attaché replied that there was no need at this time to go into specific details, but broadly speaking, the *Phoenix* would make it necessary for the *Alched* to leave harbour. To achieve this Halton would be stating quite openly to Rhaman that he intended to intercept the Chinese ships well out at sea. Rhaman would then have the choice of remaining in harbour – in which case the Chinese support, upon which so much depended for the communists, might never arrive – or putting to sea to stop the *Phoenix* from interfering. Somehow, concluded Morrison, he was convinced that Rhaman would choose the latter course.

One of the four Zembasian naval officers, who had up till now remained silent, said bluntly that a mere destroyer would stand little chance against a cruiser. That might be the case under normal circumstances, replied the Attaché quickly – he did not want more cold water poured on his plans – but with her superior speed the *Phoenix* would be able to keep out of harm's way. Besides, he added, they had in Halton one of the most skilled and experienced destroyer Captains in the Royal Navy. The conference ended with an agreement that, if the British could get the *Alched* to leave Toulage, then the Zembasians would do their utmost to prevent the Chinese ships from entering harbour.

Just before Morrison took his leave he raised a query which had been bothering him all evening. Where, he asked, was the

Vice Admiral who commanded the Zembasian Navy? The reply he received startled him. No harm could be done in telling him now, said the naval officer, with a glance at the others. The Admiral had gone to South America ten days ago to collect the latest addition to the Zembasian Navy – a 10,000 ton eight inch gun cruiser.

Why had all this been kept such a secret? asked Morrison. Surely there could have been no harm in the rest of the world knowing about it; the next edition of 'Jane's Fighting Ships' would reveal it anyway. True, the naval officer admitted, but at this stage it was considered best to keep the deal a secret. Several of the African republics were interested in acquiring warships, and if they had known that Zembasia was after this particular ship, they might have stepped in and forced the purchase price up considerably. Zembasia was not as rich as some of her neighbours, but nevertheless she was determined to be an effective naval power in this part of the world. The new cruiser would help to ensure that.

Over the years Morrison had become a pretty good judge of character, and now, looking at the earnest faces of these Zembasian naval officers, he could see that they were not power crazed men. They were proud of their country and their service, and had made no bones about the fact that they wanted to have the best navy on the African continent; which, in these troubled times, the Attaché reflected, was not such a bad idea. When, he enquired, was this cruiser due to arrive at Toulage, and was the Admiral loyal to the present government?

There was no doubt about the loyalty of the Admiral, Morrison was earnestly assured. He had a wonderful record of service to Zembasia, and before that to Britain. Financial rewards would mean nothing to him as he was, in his own right, one of the richest men in the country. Politically he was sound, having turned down many high ministerial posts to remain in the Navy. Furthermore, he and the old President were close friends.

As to the exact position of the *Umled*, as the new cruiser was called; of this the officers could not be at all certain. After the Admiral left the South American port his intentions were to exercise the new ship and her crew in the South Atlantic before returning to Zembasia.

When the revolution broke out the Admiral had been

contacted immediately and informed of the situation in Zembasia. Wireless contact with the cruiser was very bad, and had finally been lost completely. However, as far as could be established the Admiral had received the message and was returning as soon as possible. It was difficult to work out his estimated time of arrival, but it was unlikely to be before the arrival of the British cruiser. At this point an army lieutenant colonel interjected that as neither of the cruisers were going to arrive in time to help, the *Phoenix* had better come up with a good plan before it was too late. Morrison was angered by this sneering remark, but knowing that there was nothing to be gained by indulging in a slanging match, he held his peace. The Zembasian naval officers were deeply offended, however, and only the diplomatic intervention of the British Naval Attaché averted a heated exchange of words. Subsequently, to Morrison's surprise, the lieutenant colonel became quite cordial, and offered to provide the naval party with an escort of soldiers back to their ship.

Glancing at his watch, Morrison realised it was high time they departed. Halton expected them to return to the *Phoenix* at about 0200 hours, and three hours of hard walking lay between them and the spot where the launch was beached. He gratefully accepted the lieutenant colonel's offer, and was delighted to learn that the officer who was to accompany them would be able to save them valuable time with short cuts. After a final word with his naval counterparts, Morrison was ready to move off.

Chapter 10

About an hour after they had left the headquarters, Chief Petty Officer Gray stumbled and fell. Morrison felt sorry for the elderly coxswain as he bent down to give him a helping hand. He ought not to have been trekking through the jungle at his age. Putting an arm round the Attaché's shoulder, the coxswain started to hobble along with him. The Zembasian officer came back to see the cause of the slight delay, but after Gray and Morrison had assured him that they would be able to keep going, he went on ahead to continue leading the party. After he had gone Gray murmured in a low tone, so that only Morrison could hear:

'Keep a straight face, sir, don't look surprised and let me hang on to you for a while. I'm not hurt at all. I fell over deliberately so that I could have a quick word with you.'

Morrison, although naturally startled, concealed his reaction and the coxswain continued:

'These soldiers are taking us the wrong way. I don't like it at all, sir.'

'But Chief, they know the jungle better than we do,' replied Morrison, also in an undertone. 'Besides, their colonel said that there would be some short cuts back to ...'

'Short cuts be damned, sir!' interrupted Gray. 'They're taking us miles out of the way. Look – our main heading for the beach should be south west. For the last twenty minutes at least we've been heading south east, right into the thicker part of the jungle and away from the sea. That officer – a nasty piece of work, sir, if you ask me ... has been whispering to his men, one at a time, ever since we started out. It could be a trap of some sort. After all, we don't know for certain whose side anybody is really on out here, do we? I thought you'd better know about it, sir.'

As the coxswain was speaking Morrison was unobtrusively taking random compass headings. Gray was perfectly correct. There was something bloody suspicious going on here!

* * *

Making quite certain that no one else was within hearing distance – after all, a staff officer using a telephone was not an unusual sight in the headquarters – Lieutenant Colonel Kualur indolently dialled a number, blessing the day when automatic exchanges had been installed throughout Zembasia. Now conversations were almost secure, and callers very hard to trace.

The person he was calling did not keep him waiting long.

'Rhaman here,' said a well known voice.

'Sir, this Kualur. I must be quick, but I have some important news for you.'

Briefly the army officer realted how the British had visited government headquarters that evening. He outlined the plans made by the British and the Zembasian Army, laying special emphasis on the fact that the *Phoenix* would try to intercept the Chinese ships. Then, having informed Rhaman of the naval news, he went on to reveal the most important part, as far as he was concerned; a plan that he had worked out personally, on which would depend his future career.

When the landing party left the headquarters to return to their ship, he had obligingly provided them with an army escort. This escort consisted of soldiers loyal to the communist cause and an officer who could be trusted; Kualur had given the officer orders to lead the party into thick jungle and then take the British prisoners. Rhaman could, if he thought it worthwhile, use these sailors as hostages for bargaining purposes with the *Phoenix*'s captain. After all, one of the captives was Morrison, the Naval Attaché, and this senior officer must be worth something to the British. What did Rhaman want done with the sailors, he enquired? They could either be killed, or held prisoner for a while. He, the colonel, had arranged to get in touch with the officer by radio.

Kualur could almost imagine those two stars, the insignia of a major general, on his shoulders; this was to be his reward, so Rhaman said, for his part in the revolution. The British sailors were to be kept alive until they had outlived their usefulness as hostages. Once the communists had taken over control properly in Zembasia it did not matter what became of them. They could be disposed of and their bodies never found in the thick jungle far from the sea.

Kualar, extremely pleased with himself, decided that he had done a good night's work for the communists. It had been a difficult personal decision to make, whether to join the communists or remain loyal to the government. When Zembasia had been a British colony it had taken him twelve years to rise to the rank of sergeant. Then came independence, and in the last four years he had been commissioned and risen to his present rank. Although he would never admit it, this rapid rise had aroused a latent streak in his nature; ambition now overruled all else. It was another progressive step in his career to join with the communists. Rhaman had spotted his ambitious streak from the first, and knew how to exploit a weakness to further his own ends.

The British destroyer, Kualur realised, could do very little now to stop Rhaman from becoming President.

* * *

After he had landed Morrison's party successfully – the beach was deserted, and no one had seen the landing – Halton quickly removed the *Phoenix* from that part of the coast. A stationary destroyer which was expected to be patrolling would undoubtedly attract attention and suspicion. He had estimated that the landing party would be returning to the beach between 0200 and 0300 hours, and intended returning then.

He positioned the *Phoenix* five miles off the harbour entrance, a familiar area from which he could observe all that was going on in Toulage and, quite intentionally, let Rhaman know that he was being watched. Visibility was good tonight, with a full tropical moon shining brightly on the calm sea. Speed was reduced when the destroyer reached her patrol position, and a wide circle pattern commenced. Two extra lookouts kept their powerful night glasses trained on the Zembasian warships while the other duty personnel – the officer of the watch, quartermaster and normal lookouts – went about their usual duties.

* * *

In his cabin on board the *Alched*, Rhaman was sitting pondering the implications of the telephone call he had just received. He was well aware that Kualur, who had triggered off an entirely new chain of action with his call, was a greedy opportunist, who only wanted to ensure his own future by siding with the communists. Therefore, in the long run, he could not be trusted. It would be necessary to get rid of a man like that as soon as he, Rhaman, came to power. (By some strange quirk Rhaman did not see many of his own characteristics reflected in the army officer.)

The capture of the British Naval Attaché had been an excellent move though, and he resolved to make the most of this unexpected piece of good luck. He wondered what Halton's reactions would be when he learnt that Morrison and a dozen other members of his crew were hostages. He knew, from years of experience, that the British placed high value on human life, and would himself utilise this in endeavouring to strike a bargain with them.

First, he decided, he would send a signal to the British destroyer as soon as possible, stating that the lives of the hostages were entirely dependent upon the *Phoenix*'s non-interference with communist plans. The destroyer was not to attempt to intercept the Chinese supply ships; if any of these ships failed to arrive within the next few days, the hostages would be killed. When Halton saw the reference to the Chinese he would begin to wonder - Rhaman was rather pleased about this aspect - just how much of his plans had been revealed to the communists.

Yes, all in all the army officer had done a good night's work in furthering the communist cause. In the not too distant future he would get a fitting reward, thought Rhaman with grim amusement. Another important gain for Rhaman was the fact that the captured Attaché would not be able to pass on the information he had obtained about the new cruiser. Not that it mattered really, because Rhaman was the only person in Zembasia at that time who knew the real story behind their navy's latest acquisition. When those fools in the government found out - and Rhaman would let them know when the time was right - that the *Umled* was already in communist hands and heading for Toulage, it would be too late for them to do a thing about it.

The Zembasian self-styled Admiral estimated that ten percent at most of the Zembasian Navy knew of the existence of the new cruiser. In the strictest sense of the word this cruiser was quite old, having been completed twenty years ago, as part of the U.S. Fleet. Subsequently, being surplus to the requirements of the U.S. Navy, she had been sold to one of the South American republics where, due to a severe economic crisis, she had hardly been used at all. Therefore she was in very good condition for her age. Armed with nine eight inch guns, this heavy cruiser - a rare type these days, the Royal Navy had none - would be a powerful addition to the Zembasian Navy.

No one disputed the integrity of the Commander in Chief of the Zembasian Navy, nor his loyalty to the government. Not even Rhaman doubted it, which was precisely why he had ensured that thirty officers - the *Umled* was to carry forty altogether - were dedicated communists. These officers, who had been very carefully briefed, were to take the ship over somewhere between South America and Zembasia and bring it in to Toulage at about the same time as the Chinese ships were due to arrive.

Normally it would be impossible, in the twentieth century, for a mere 30 men to overpower 700 - the total complement of the new cruiser - but Rhaman had planned well, and knew his men. Firstly, possibly the most important factor in the take over would be the element of surprise. Secondly, the average Zembasian sailor - most of them were short term conscripts - was a fairly simple man who would obey any orders given to him by an officer without question. Once the loyal officers had been got rid of (with only ten of them this should be comparatively easy), the sailors would work for the communist officers without too much trouble. Should it prove necessary, two or three of them would be picked out at random and shot. The others would quickly accept the new régime.

Once again Rhaman inwardly cursed those idiot hotheads who had sparked off the revolution prematurely. His original schedule had included, amongst other things, transferring himself to the *Umled* for a ceremonial entry into Toulage to demonstrate to all that he held the tangible power. Still, no great harm had been done. The new cruiser would still arrive before the British cruiser, and the balance of naval power would still be in his favour if it came to an actual battle between the warships.

Rhaman's briefing to the communist officers had included one very important point; if the take-over was successful, they were to maintain a strict radio silence and keep a listening watch for the situation in Zembasia. Thus the government would be ignorant of the *Umled*'s position, and would also have no idea of the situation on board. When the cruiser came to within twenty miles of Toulage - whilst on passage she was to keep out of sight of land and avoid other shipping if possible - she was to send a motor launch to the *Alched*. No one but Rhaman would know of the new arrival. This would all be done under the cover of darkness, almost certainly tomorrow night.

At one stage Rhaman might have stayed in the *Alched*,

lying in the harbour, to keep a watchful eye on the situation ashore. Now he had decided, especially after the bombing attack by the British and the unwelcome attentions of the *Phoenix*, that he would return with the *Umled*'s launch and bring the cruiser into the harbour. In the early hours of the morning, just after dawn, she would make an imposing sight, and undermine the morale of the government so much that resistance would crumble. And heaven help the British destroyer, thought Rhaman gleefully, if it tried to stop him!

Thinking of the *Phoenix*, Rhaman glanced at his watch. It was time to send off his signal regarding the hostages. Kualur had received his instructions, and should have contacted his officer by now. The British sailors were now his captives. As he made his way to the *Alched*'s bridge Rhaman wondered how his opposite number in the *Phoenix* would react to the news. The officer of the watch on the bridge pointed out the British destroyer to him, about five miles away from the harbour, gliding slowly across the moonlit sea like a sinister ghost ship.

For hundreds of years Britain had relied on those ships of the Royal Navy, in every ocean and sea, to maintain her once powerful position in the world. Even today, Britain had the third largest navy, and was still a power to be reckoned with, as Rhaman realised only too well. Over the past two decades aircraft had replaced those ships to a large extent. However, with diminishing land bases overseas and the ever increasing Soviet Navy, Britain's defence policy was beginning to turn full circle, back to her traditional sea power. Rhaman had more than a sneaking respect for the British. 'Never underestimate your enemy' was one of the cardinal principles of war. Ironically enough, Rhaman's teachers on this subject had been the British themselves.

* * *

Halton, on the bridge of the *Phoenix*, was on the point of giving orders for an altering heading to rendezvous with the landing party when the *Alched* started to signal.

'Captain Morrison and twelve of your men are my prisoners. I will negotiate with you in the morning for their return. Acknowledge.'

Three times the message was sent. Rhaman was making

sure, thought Halton bitterly, that the *Phoenix* received it. Most of the destroyer's personnel on duty had read the message, and many faces turned towards their Captain. He was now in a very difficult position, as they realised only too well.

Although the message had at first filled Halton with dismay, a combination of thorough training and a calm personality helped him to overcome the initial shock, and he began to think coolly. This could easily be a huge bluff on Rhaman's part. At the same time, almost as if he had read his Captain's mind, the first lieutenant remarked that the message appeared genuine enough, and reluctantly Halton had to agree. At this stage he did not have much choice – certainly not with thirteen British lives at stake. He had no illusions about their fate if he did not comply with Rhaman's request for a meeting.

Turning to the duty signalman Halton told him to acknowledge receipt of the signal, and while the rating was doing this, the Captain began to write on a message pad his reply to the *Alched*, briefly stating that he was willing to meet Rhaman in the morning, at the latter's earliest convenience. Once again the clickety-clack of the searchlight broke the stillness of the tropical evening. The Zembasians were prompt in sending their acknowledgement, and Halton could imagine the smile of triumph on Rhaman's face.

Discussing the situation with Drew, the destroyer's Captain remarked that Morrison and the landing party must have been caught on their way back to the beach; otherwise Rhaman would have mentioned the Vice President in his list of prisoners. Drew agreed, pointing out that in addition to this, had the landing party been captured on the way to government headquarters the *Alched* would have signalled as much to the *Phoenix* at least two hours earlier.

It was decided that, just in case Rhaman was lying, which was unlikely, the *Phoenix* would go back to the area of the beach rendezvous and cruise just off the shore for the remainder of the hours of darkness, in the hopes of being able to recover the men. In so doing, also, the crew would spend a more peaceful night out of sight of the *Alched*, and make the cruiser wonder where they had gone. In the morning the two Captains would meet – and needless to say Halton was not looking forward to what would be a very one sided affair.

Chapter 11

Surrounded by the unfamiliar darkness of the jungle, far from the *Phoenix* and the sea he knew so well, Chief Petty Officer Gray stumbled along with Captain Morrison. Theirs was a great responsibility, for unless they acted sensibly and quickly, a dozen British lives would almost certainly be lost. Between them they had worked out a plan, and now, with time fast running out, they began to put it into action.

Gray, keeping up a convincing pretext of having sprained his ankle badly, began to inform the landing party of his supicions and what they were going to do about it. The Zembasian soldiers paid little attention as pairs of sailors came along in turn to give the coxswain a helping hand. Secretly the young Zembasian army officer in charge of the so-called escort party was pleased that the British N.C.O. had been injured. It would make it much easier, from this officer's point of view, to take the British prisoners when the time came. There was no doubt that an experienced N.C.O. - and Gray was clearly that - would stiffen the resistance of the other sailors if he was fit, so the injury was more than welcome.

Gray remarked to Morrison that it would look very suspicious if he had to be helped along by all the British sailors, so the Attaché played his part by discreetly letting the remainder of the landing party know just what he and Gray had in mind.

In numbers, the Zembasians and the British were evenly matched; a dozen on each side, and all of them armed. There the comparison ended, however, in favour of the soldiers. Gray and a leading seaman carried Sten machine carbines, whilst all the other sailors - with the exception of the Attaché, who had a revolver - were armed with rifles. Each of the Zembasians carried a sub-machine gun, of a compact looking new pattern, which would certainly give them the edge when it came to effective fire power.

Both Morrison and Gray realised only too well that in the narrow spaces of the heavily wooded jungle, the sailors' rifles were not going to be of much use. Complete and utter surprise tactics were vital; otherwise, as Gray remarked to Morrison 'As sure as God made little apples' they did not stand the slightest chance of getting away with their audacious plan. These Zembasians were trained soldiers, and used to operating in the jungle. Perhaps even more to the point was the fact that they had little regard for human life, their own included.

Gray was to be the one to start off the combined plan of action – the sailors had been warned to watch his movements carefully – by asking two of the Zembasians to help him. When they did the coxswain, who was extremely tough and strong for his slight build, would grab hold of them and yell out. Morrison, who would by this time have made his way up front with the Zembasian officer, would disable the leader. The leading seaman and one other sailor – Gray had already passed him his Sten gun earlier – would train their machine carbines on the rest of the soldiers. Should it prove necessary these two sailors had orders to open fire without hesitation on the Zembasians. All the remaining sailors had been told that when Morrison started to approach the officer, they were to get as far away from the soldiers as they could without arousing early suspicion.

In view of the situation and the type of men with whom they were dealing, Morrison realised grimly that there were no easier alternatives. If they managed to get out of this, he determined, Gray would get full credit for his initial observation, and for his help in formulating the plan which they hoped would work. If it failed, they were unlikely to get out of the jungle alive.

Quite casually Morrison began to work his way towards the front of the column of men loosely strung out along the jungle path. The Zembasians allowed him through unmolested, and when he came up alongside the army officer he started a conversation with him by asking how far they had to go. While they were talking, Morrison managed to sneak the odd quick glance behind, unobserved. Everything seemed to be going according to plan. Gray was slowly dropping back, and would soon be in a position to ask the two soldiers bringing up the rear to help him along for a while.

Once the coxswain had his arms firmly around the shoulders of these two men he would yell out at the top of his voice, and

88

at this pre-arranged signal the sailors would spring into action. With luck – which Morrison realised, they certainly needed – the Zembasian officer would turn round and see what all the noise was about, which would give Morrison the opportunity to draw out his own revolver and club him down. If necessary he would shoot him dead with no compunction. There would not be time for any indecision or half-measures. Once the Zembasian leader had been dealt with there was a good chance that further resistance might collapse altogether. In any event, with the officer out of action the movements of the soldiers would be completely unco-ordinated, and this was certainly going to help the British.

Suddenly, with a wild yell, Gray grabbed the two soldiers. Almost simultaneously Morrison knocked out the officer with the barrel of his revolver. Four of the soldiers started to unsling their sub-machine guns, but long before they could bring them into use, the two sailors with Sten guns opened fire upon this group. All four of the soldiers fell; two were killed instantly and the other two badly wounded. With their officer and four of their comrades on the ground, further resistance was obviously futile and the remaining soldiers dropped their guns and put up their hands to surrender. None of Morrison's men had been injured in that wild, short scuffle. Gray came up looking none the worse for the key role he had just carried out so well, and the two men began to take stock of the position.

Rudimentary first aid was given to the two wounded soldiers to make them as comfortable as possible. The wounds sustained by one of them would obviously prove fatal, but mercifully he was unconscious, and did not suffer. The officer must have had a thick skull, Morrison remarked to Gray, for he recovered his senses within a very short time. He was given a quick choice; guide the British out of the jungle to the beach rendezvous, or die on the spot. The officer did not hesitate to offer his services. It was abundantly clear to him that the sailors meant what they said.

Both Morrison and Gray agreed with the Zembasian's estimate that they were about five miles from the coast. While they had been walking along with the soldiers Gray had been keeping a mental plot of their position, which he thought might come in useful if anything went wrong. Almost from the start he had felt something *was* wrong, and as they progressed further it became more and more obvious to him.

Using the recognised jungle travel method of measuring distance – three paces were equivalent to approximately two yards – Gray had counted out the steps they had taken and noted them down at intervals when the party were making their way to the government headquarters. On that journey there had, of course, been no question of treachery, and the coxswain had checked the distance primarily for something to do. Now his mental exercise was about to pay off dividends. Combining distance travelled with the odd heading checks on his compass – the coxswain and Attaché carried pocket compasses as part of their equipment for the landing party – Gray had a very good idea of their position relative to the sea. There was little chance for the army officer to try and mis-direct them again, and he was made well aware of this fact.

The Zembasian soldiers, thoroughly cowed and docile after the British convincing demonstration of force, were detailed to carry their two wounded comrades. Half the landing party acted as armed escorts and watched their charges like hawks, with orders to shoot at the slightest sign of any suspicious behaviour. All the sailors now knew of the trap that the Zembasians had been planning for them, and would not hesitate to cary out those orders. Just in case there was any misunderstanding by the soldiers, their officer was ordered to tell them what was happening, and as Morrison knew the language, no mistakes were made.

Slowly the party began to move through the jungle, Gray in the lead keeping a careful watch on the Zembasian officer, Morrison bringing up the rear, and all of the sailors on the alert.

Five miles would take them about three hours at the rate they were moving, thought the Attaché. The two wounded soldiers would impede their already slow progress, but he dismissed the idea of leaving them behind, with some of their comrades to look after them. It was more than likely that the fit soldiers would run off to tell the rebels what had happened. No, decided Morrison, he would not risk the lives of his own men in a potential ambush.

Originally their estimated time of arrival at the beach was about 0200 hours, but they would be much later now. The fight, and the misdirections from their escort had cost them precious time. 0400 hours would be nearer the mark; the destroyer's crew would be wondering what had happened. It was a beautifully clear moonlit night, so when they arrived at the beach they should be able to see the *Phoenix* if she was within a five mile radius of the rendezvous.

Fortunately for the landing party, Halton had deliberately decided not to darken the ship. He wanted all ashore – especially the rebels – to know that he was cruising up and down the coast. A warship at night, without any form of lights showing, was almost invisible; its low contours blending into the background of the dark sea. There might well come a time later, the destroyer's Captain considered, when there would be a need to make his ship inconspicuous, but for the time being he wanted to be seen. Sighting reports from all along the coast would be continually passed to the *Alched*, and they should cause Rhaman concern and irritation. Most of the landing party carried torches, so it would be quite easy for them to flash a signal to the destroyer to show where they were.

If the destroyer was nowhere in sight, Morrison decided, he and his party would remain at the rendezvous point on the beach till dawn. This would enable the men to get some well deserved rest while he, Gray and the leading seaman took turns to keep a good look out for their ship. Their position would be about eight miles south of Toulage, and when dawn came they would proceed along the beach towards the town. Walking along the sea shore would be fairly easy going, and they should either spot the *Phoenix* on the way, or eventually, when they got nearer the town, see her patrolling off the harbour entrance. In either case it would be a simple matter of attracting her attention and waiting for the launch to pick them up. They could even commandeer a local fisherman's boat if necessary, and sail out to her...

The slow moving procession stopped, and the Attaché hurried forward to find out the reason. The badly wounded soldier was writhing in his final death throes, and as Gray rummaged in his small first aid kit for morphine to ease his last agonies, there was a yell from another of the sailors, followed by a burst of machine gun fire. The Zembasian officer had seized the chance of making a bid to escape – but he did not get far. He and his wounded comrade must have died at almost the same time.

Two shallow graves were quickly dug by the other Zembasian soldiers, who showed little emotion at the deaths of their comrades, and the two men were buried. Unprompted by their senior the British sailors removed their caps, and Gray, stepping forward, said a quick and simple prayer. It seemed wrong to leave them without a word.

Progress was much faster without the badly wounded man, and Morrison and Gray now estimated that they would probably get to the beach at about 0300 hours. Soon the party came across an old logging path which obviously ran in the direction of the sea, and after that it was fairly easy going for the rest of the way.

Whatever any of them had thought and said about their ship in the past – not all of it complimentary – there was not a sailor present who would not be pleased to see the *Phoenix* again. One lad cheekily asked the coxswain if tonight's efforts would be worth an extra tot of rum, and was good humouredly told just what he was worth. Secretly, though, Gray was pleased with his men, and proud of the way they had responded to a pretty rough old night. Most of them were quite young, and for many the destroyer was their first ship. He was almost sure Captain Halton would grant a request for a little extra rum for them all.

As they came at last within sight of the beach, and beyond it the sea, every one of them breathed a sigh of relief. They had made it! The beautiful silver sand, the glittering sea, the gently swaying palm trees were not noticed. All the men wanted to see was their ship – and she was not there! They stared, disbelieving. Surely Captain Halton had not left without them? There was an anxious muttering, which changed to a loud burst of cheering when quite suddenly the *Phoenix* came into view, sailing round a jutting headland less than two miles away.

Chapter 12

Commander Halton had tried to snatch a few hours sleep before dawn, but after tossing and turning for a while, decided that he was not going to get any rest in his cabin, and went up to the bridge. A quick inspection, carried out automatically by him whenever he went on the bridge, showed that all was in order. Lookouts – there was one positioned on each wing of the bridge – scanned the spaceless sea and the Zembasian coast for any sign of activity. He lowered himself into his Captain's chair and sat there in brooding silence.

Apart from brightly lit merchant ships passing by on their peaceful routes, mainly from the Far East to the U.K., nothing out of the ordinary happened. Now and again the radar rating on duty would call up the bridge and report contacts on his screen to the officer of the watch. These the officer plotted, noting the relative bearing and distance from the destroyer. With some of the nearer ones heading towards them, avoiding action might prove necessary, or investigation in case one of the Chinese supply ships was trying to slip into Toulage ahead of schedule. When investigation *was* considered necessary the officer of the watch gave orders to the duty quartermaster in the wheel house on the deck below to steer an interception course. Binoculars would be trained in the direction of the contact until the blip on the radar screen was in a position to be visually identified.

These activities helped to pass more quickly the long hours of the middle watch; 2359 to 0400 hours, least popular with most watch-keepers. More important though, apart from keeping the men on duty alert, these alterations of speed and heading kept the crew in constant practice; the watch rotas were designed in such a way as to ensure all had to be on the middle watch some time over a period of a few days. An identified blip today would almost invariably turn out to be an innocent merchant ship, but tomorrow that blip could turn out to be an enemy warship. In peace or war, the general routine in the Royal Navy was almost the same, and it was due to this constant training, Halton reflected, that the transition from peace to war was easier for the sailor than for the other branches of the Armed Forces.

In another three hours it would be dawn, and an hour or so after that – sooner, if possible – Halton had to face another meeting with Rhaman. This time almost entirely on the latter's terms. With thirteen of his men in Rhaman's hands Halton would have to tread very carefully. He was not prepared to throw away their lives, and of course Rhaman, knowing this only too well, would play on it for all he was worth. The Ministry of Defence had been informed of the situation, but under the circumstances there was little they could do to help. Halton knew that it was all up to him now and, like many another captain before him, he would have to use his own judgement to try and reach the correct decision.

Other captains of British warships had sailed in these waters for nearly four hundred years, and had faced demanding problems all over the world. Command was lonely enough in modern times, but in those days the captain of a small wooden sailing ship had no radio to keep him up to date on the current situation. Sailing out of Portsmouth or Plymouth, it would almost certainly be three or four months before he even reached his destination, perhaps longer, and by then the whole situation could have changed completely.

As well as being a good seaman and navigator, mused Halton, a captain of the past few centuries had to have many other remarkable qualities. He needed to be a politician, an astute diplomat, a tactician, had to be well versed in the art of strategy, and, although this was not mentioned in any text-book, needed a good deal of luck. Halton wondered how one of those men would have dealt with the situation he was facing at the moment, with Zembasian politics as they were, and the threat of overpowering odds at sea. Perhaps the legendary Captain Horatio Hornblower could have worked something out; in any event, he had to admit to himself, Commander Clive Halton didn't have the the answer to it!

Halton almost welcomed the intrusion on his gloomy thoughts when a messenger reported that the duty radio rating was on the telephone and wanted to speak to the Captain urgently. Picking up the bridge telephone, he listened as the

94

incoming message was read to him. He was rather surprised to learn that it had originated from the fleet tanker *Tide First*: the only signals he was really expecting would be coming from the Ministry of Defence.

'Passed a heavy cruiser, nationality unknown, ten minutes ago on a reciprocal heading. From a porthole someone flashed – "S.O.S. Inform Zembasian government that the...." flashing stopped at this point. My position follows.... Estimated speed of cruiser to be twenty-five knots. Thought must pass on this information.'

Good old Stubbs, thought Halton gratefully. The message was certainly of interest at the present time. Having given instructions to acknowledge the signal, he settled down to ponder the significance of the incident.

Could China be sending a cruiser to Zembasia to help the communists? Unlikely; he was almost certain that China had no cruisers except for the old *Pei Ching*, an ex-Royal Navy vessel, then known proudly as the *Aurora*, but now reduced to a mere hulk. A glance at the latest copy of 'Jane's Fighting Ships' confirmed these facts, and showed that China had no cruisers.

A browse through the standard naval reference book carried by most warships – Halton was already fairly familiar with it – offered no answer to the nationality of the cruiser that was heading fast towards the Zembasian area. For a start the only Navies which had heavy cruisers were Russia and the U.S.A., plus a few South American republics which had, since the end of the Second World War, acquired some from the United States. The large cruiser that had passed the *Tide First* simply had to be in this book. No country in the world could build a ship of this type and size without someone knowing about it.

There was also the interrupted message from the cruiser to be considered. Who had started to signal, and why? These additional complications were most unwelcome; the situation in Zembasia was volatile enough. In another two days the Chinese supply ships would be arriving, and unless *Phoenix* could intercept them there was going to be bloody war and revolution on a much larger scale.

If this heavy cruiser coming up fast from the south was on the side of the rebels, then the position of the British and government forces would be almost hopeless, and the revolution was bound to succeed. Even with the arrival of the eagerly awaited British cruiser the situation would still not improve very much, and the *Phoenix* alone would not stand a chance against two cruisers and a destroyer. In any case it was ridiculous, whilst his own men were being held to ransom for his non-interference, even to contemplate any action against the warships and supply ships. One manual he had studied on 'Operations' recommended that an officer did not treat with the enemy for hostages – this was not to the advantage of the men held prisoner – but pressed on with more vigorous operations if possible. While this was all very well in theory, Halton wondered if in fact it would work in practice. With the odds already against him, plus the possibility of a new threat to contend with, he could hardly follow the second recommendation – the carrying out of more vigorous operations.

Glancing at his watch yet again – he had unconsciously been looking at the time every five minutes or so – Halton saw that it was almost 0330 hours. A change of scenery might be welcome, he decided. All was quiet in the brightly lit harbour of Toulage, and looked like remaining so, so he quietly gave orders to the officer of the watch for a distinct alteration of heading to steer instead of the large circling pattern they had been following for some time. The *Phoenix* was returning for a time to the rendezvous, on the admittedly slim chance that some of the landing party might have escaped. While cruising up and down this quiet stretch of coast Halton would also have time to try and work out a plan of campaign for his meeting with Rhaman.

Just after they had rounded the thickly wooded point near the landing beach – the water was quite deep, and the destroyer was about a mile from the coast – a sudden shout brought everyone on the bridge to the alert. It was the lookout on the port wing of the bridge, reporting that he had seen a torch flashing from the shore. Instantly many pairs of binoculars were trained on the spot, while Halton ordered the duty signal rating to acknowledge the flashing with the port signal searchlight. This action would let the person who was signalling ashore – Halton hoped desperately that it might be one of the landing party – that the destroyer had seen the torch flashing and was ready to receive any message.

96

While the duty signal rating wrote down the Morse being flashed from the shore, Halton was able to read the message as it was being sent. The landing party were all safe, and they had some prisoners with them! Immediately excited chatter broke out amongst hitherto silent personnel on duty. Halton himself breathed a heartfelt sigh of relief. It seemed almost too good to be true!

Suddenly, as the first lieutenant was giving orders to lower one of the launches, it struck Halton that this could in fact be leading up to a well planned ambush. What a fool he was! They might lose many more men if he did not take adequate precautions. Orders were given for the second launch to be prepared for lowering, and at the same time a crew was detailed for it. This launch was to carry several more men than normal, each armed with automatic weapons to give support to the first launch, which would carry out the actual recovery of the landing party if it proved to be genuinely them.

Telling the two officers in charge of lowering the boats – Sub-lieutenant Gordon had taken charge of the second launch – to await his orders, Halton hurried back to the bridge. Confirming first with the navigating officer, the depth of water from their position to the shore, he decided that it was safe enough to take the *Phoenix* up to within two hundred yards of the beach. This would considerably reduce the time needed for the whole operation.

As the destroyer slowly headed in towards the beach she was thoroughly prepared for any emergency. All guns' crews were at their loaded guns, and the powerful 44" searchlight, situated amidships, was ready to be switched on. When they got nearer this strong beam would be trained on the beach, lighting it up completely to reveal any funny business that might be taking place. It would be prudent, the destroyer's Captain decided, to make one more check before lowering his boats. On orders from his Captain the duty signal rating sent one more message to the shore, asking the name of the Captain under whom Gray and Halton had served during the Korean war. Only Gray would be able to answer this question correctly.

From the shore came the answering signal that confirmed all was in order. Halton was vastly relieved. They were by no means out of the wood yet, he realised, but at least he had now all of his crew intact. If Rhaman had held these men as hostages he, Halton, would have been helpless at their next meeting. It would almost certainly have meant the end of effective British support for the Zembasian government.

As the destroyer neared the beach Halton gave orders to stop engines. The searchlight shone its powerful beam towards the beach, illuminating the landing party waving wildly at the ship. Both the launches were lowered as the *Phoenix* lost her speed, and headed quickly towards the beach. While they were away Halton gave orders for the reception of the landing party. The surgeon lieutenant was to be at hand – he might be needed, though it was hoped not – and a messenger was sent to the galley to request the laying on of hot cocoa and plenty of sandwiches.

Although it seemed a long time to those waiting aboard the destroyer, in fact it only took about twelve minutes to effect the recovery operation including the hoisting in of the launches. Halton felt quite sorry for the terrified looking Zembasian soldiers as they came on board. There was a good chance that they had never been on a ship before, and they must be wondering what the British were going to do with them. He would deal with them later, but for the moment they must not be allowed to interfere with the operations of the *Phoenix*. Halton had them handcuffed to some stanchions on the quarterdeck – after the doctor had confirmed that they had no injuries – and an armed guard was detailed off to look after them.

The landing party was formed up just aft of the fo'castle break, and as their Captain came up to them Gray called them smartly to attention. The coxswain saluted, and reported all present and correct. Morrison had already given Halton a quick run down on what had happened. A much more detailed report would be made later, but it was quite evident that Gray and the others had come through the ordeal well.

Halton felt genuinely proud of his men's showing that night, and very briefly – for they were obviously extremely tired and needed rest – he thanked them all for the good work that they had just carrried out. Like any good officer he realised the value of praising where it was deserved, and these men had certainly earned a pat on the back.

When the weary sailors had been dismissed, Halton asked Morrison to come to his cabin for a short talk before retiring.

Fresh plans for the morning would have to be made, in the light of that night's events, and Morrison's information was going to be invaluable.

Chapter 13

Captain Morrison drank his cocoa and gratefully munched the sandwiches while, between mouthfuls, he gave Halton a much more detailed account of what he and his men had been through. Both officers agreed that the landing party had been exceptionally lucky, and that this was due mainly to Chief Petty Officer Gray's innate sixth sense. Had it not been for the coxswain, they would certainly not have been there talking about it. Halton commented that he would be making a very full written report about the incident, and would emphasise that Gray had shown plenty of initiative, adding that in his opinion these experienced chief and petty officers who formed the strong backbone of the service, were given far too little recognition or reward for their vital role.

Morrison agreed whole-heartedly. He and the other members of the landing party owed their lives to the chief petty officer, he went on, and anything that Halton decided to write would be fully endorsed by him.

When Halton mentioned the signal he had received a few hours earlier from the *Tide First*, there suddenly dawned on the Attaché the importance of what he had heard at government headquarters. He had quite forgotten, in the excitement of the later events of the night, the information he had gained about the new Zembasian cruiser. Indeed had it not been for Halton mentioning that signal, he might not have remembered the matter until what might, in view of the fast changing situation, have been too late.

Having listened to the Attaché, it became only too apparent to Halton that this new cruiser must be assumed to be hostile until proved otherwise – although there was precious little chance of the latter, he had to admit. With this heavy cruiser as well as the *Alched* and the destroyer against them, the odds were far too great. If the promised British cruiser had arrived, or could get there in time to counter the new threat, it was just possible that the two British warships could engage and defeat the three rebel warships, but going into battle alone, the *Phoenix* did not stand a chance. She would be blasted out of the sea, with the superior range of the enemy's heavy guns, long before she could ever open fire herself. An eight inch shell weighed 250 pounds; it would not take many of them to rip the thin armour plating of the destroyer wide open, with devastating results.

There was little point in making a gallant gesture if in the end it was all going to be completely futile. Zembasia would still be taken over by the communists, and he doubted if any action taken by the *Phoenix* alone would delay such an event by more than half an hour. No doubt the sensible thing to do was to take his ship out of harm's way, and against these impossible odds he knew that he would not be censured for doing this.

Halton knew in his own heart, however, that this course was quite unacceptable to him. It was not the risk of jeopardising his own career – strangely enough he had never been an ambitious man; something much stronger than any personal considerations told him that he could not withdraw from this dangerous situation. Some cynics might have suggested that Halton felt this way because he was too steeped in the traditions of the Royal Navy. They may even have been right, up to a point; after all, there were precious few cases of British warships giving up a fight easily, if at all. But it was not anything like that that really affected his thinking, reflected Halton to himself. He was sure that he was far too realistic ever to become a hero.

Perhaps it was the political consequences of failure, both here and throughout the world; then again, this obstinate streak of his might simply be that he could not bring himself to tell the Zembasian government that he was going to leave them in their hour of need. There was no doubt, though, that if he did go now it could easily damage the reputation of the entire British Commonwealth. Whatever the motivation, anyway, Halton decided, the *Phoenix* was going to remain, and do her

100

best to restore peace to this country. So far they had had luck on their side, but....

His thoughts were interrupted by Morrison's voice.

'I say, Halton – what about a good old fashioned boarding of the *Alched*?'

Calmly returning his colleague's startled gaze, the Naval Attaché went on:

'We've still got two hours of darkness left, and we could take them completely by surprise. It would be the last thing they'd expect.'

For a moment the idea seemed too ludicrous. Then it slowly began to dawn on Halton thhat this might be the answer to all their problems. It was a crazy scheme, but if they could pull it off – and they just might at that – then the current Zembasian situation would be solved. The plan of attack would have to be as foolproof as possible, of course. The destroyer's Captain was not going to sacrifice his men and his ship needlessly.

As the two officers quickly got down to details, Halton was thankful that Morrison knew Toulage and the Zembasians so well.

Even at a speed of twenty knots the *Phoenix* could make the entrance to the harbour in half an hour. They still had enough time to plan and prepare for the attack and – more important – would be able to carry out the whole operation in darkness. Halton sent for the first lieutenant and the gunnery officer. Both men would be key figures in the forthcoming venture, and it was best that they should be in on the planning of the assault.

'Well, Harry, how would you like to command a cruiser?' Halton enquired genially of Drew, who, completely taken aback, stammered:

'I.... I can't see that happening for a while, sir – there are only four left, and by the time I get promoted there probably won't be any at all.'

Halton smiled grimly, thinking how often they had discussed the alarming shrinkage of the Navy over the past few years. However, there were other more immediate problems to consider just now. He began to outline his plans to the assembled officers. To save repetition, all officers not on watch had been requested to gather in the wardroom.

For a start, he pointed out, they would not be able to use the destroyer's boats. He estimated that about half the crew were going to be needed to board the *Alched*, and the three boats could not carry that number of armed men. Then again, in the doubtful event of the boats managing to get alongside undetected, there would be the difficulty of climbing the high sides of the cruiser with arms and equipment. There was only one way to do it, and that was to take the *Phoenix* right into the harbour and put her alongside the *Alched*.

An animated babble of conversation broke out among the officers at this bold suggestion. Normally Halton would not have tolerated such interruptions, but on this occasion he allowed them to think about and discuss the initial idea for a few moments before continuing. After all, while this sort of action might have been common enough in Nelson's day, there were very few, if any, recorded instances of a destroyer boarding a cruiser. Of course there was the bold episode in the Second World War of the *Cossack* boarding the *Altmark*, but the latter was an armed supply ship with a crew less in number than the destroyer.

Presently the talking died away. It was obvious from the look on Halton's face that he was waiting to go on.

This was not going to be a suicidal mission, he continued. He had considered things very carefully, and taken into account the fact that the cruiser completely outgunned the *Phoenix* with her deadly six inch guns. What he had in mind was straightforward enough, and was on the following lines:

About half a mile from the harbour entrance, and well out of sight of the *Alched*, the destroyer would launch one of her motor boats. This boat, which would be loaded with rockets and other colourful aids to pyrotechnics, should be able to get into the harbour completely undetected under cover of darkness. Once inside the harbour it would make for the far side, well away from the entrance, and commence a firework display. This unexpected action would attract the attention of everyone in Toulage, and in particular the lookouts and duty personnel on board the cruiser. Two minutes after this show had begun the *Phoenix* would make a high speed dash through the harbour entrance and go straight alongside the

Alched. If all went well, the cruiser would be taken completely by surprise.

Even so, Halton continued, he was not going to rely completely on the elements of surprise and good fortune. Once through the harbour entrance he intended bringing the destroyer hard round and making a fast approach to the *Alched* from her stern. Even if they were spotted at this stage it would not matter very much; thanks to the Canberra attack (with a nod at the two R.A.F. officers, who were also present), the cruiser's rear six inch gun turret was out of action, and they would be safe from heavy gunfire. Equally important from a boarding point of view was the fact that the destroyer's fo'castle was just slightly higher than the cruiser's quarterdeck. They would be able to board the *Alched* without any involved gymnastics.

Continuous small arms fire from the destroyer's fo'castle during the final approach would, it was hoped, dispose of any potential reception committee on the cruiser's quarterdeck, and the boarding party should be able to get across without too much trouble. The first lieutenant would lead the boarding party, while the gunnery officer was to be responsible for directing the small arms fire from Vickers and Bren machine guns during the run in. With the *Phoenix* right alongside, re-inforcements could be supplied as required. Prisoners taken by the boarding party, once they were established on the *Alched*, could be easily transferred back to the destroyer, and would not impede the operation.

Once the majority of the rebel officers had been captured or killed, resistance would almost certainly quickly collapse, and in view of this one third of the boarding party would head straight for the wardroom and arrest the officers. The remainder would be deployed between the bridge, the crew's quarters and the engine room. It was fortunate, Halton added grimly, that he himself had served in the *Alched*, and knew her layout well. An officer was detailed off for each of the main sections of the cruiser, and all were thoroughly briefed as to the quickest way to get to their objectives. Nothing was left to chance.

Halton glanced at his watch; fifteen minutes had gone by since the meeting had started. This, then, he concluded, was the plan. They had one hour and forty-five minutes to put it into action.

* * *

Rhaman, though tired, simply could not get to sleep. After tossing and turning for an hour or two he gave it up as a bad job, dressed and went up on to the bridge.

Looking out over the harbour, all seemed quiet. He was glad that he had imposed a dusk to dawn curfew the day before. Anything that moved in or around the harbour at night without his personal permission would be fired on at sight, and three launches patrolled the harbour to enforce this. The only exception, he reflected bitterly, was the *Phoenix*, which was constantly prowling round the coastline. Where was the British destroyer just now, he wondered? Nothing would have given him greater pleasure than to put paid to her once and for all, and he was convinced that but for that sneak air attack he would have achieved this.

Those arrogant British needed a lesson, he thought. By what right did they interfere with Zembasian internal affairs? Or for that matter in any other country's, ex-colony or not? For centuries they had ruled nearly half the world, but now their golden era was over, and the sooner they realised it the better. As far as Zembasia was concerned the British were going to learn this lesson the hard way, very soon.

In another twenty-four hours the *Umled* would be arriving, and very shortly afterwards the Chinese supply ships, to consolidate his position. For the moment it was a good idea, he decided, to let the British go on thinking that this was just another crackpot revolution with no real planning behind it. As the future President of the new republic, however, he intended making many changes. Zembasia was going to be the leading African power; perhaps one day a major power, if he could get nuclear weapons from China.

Meanwhile the *Phoenix* could go on patrolling off the coast just as long as she liked, for there was very little she could know that would alter the situation. There was no doubt that he, Rhaman, held the trump hand with the hostages that were being brought to him. If Halton did not do as he was told those hostages would die, and the British Commander must realise this. Life was cheaper in Africa than in the more sentimental western countries.

For a moment Rhaman was tempted to telephone Lieutenant Colonel Kualar. Then he decided against it, realising that it might betray the army officer if anyone recognised the voice of the caller. No, he decided; he would wait a while before taking this action – and in any case it was going to take time for that army patrol to send word back to Kualar regarding the whereabouts of their prisoners. Then again, the army officer would have to pick his time carefully to telephone Rhaman. At present the government headquarters must be a very busy place, and there would be far more officers than usual on duty and standing by.

Nevertheless, Rhaman was anxious to have those hostages on board the *Alched* as soon as possible, in case Halton wanted visible evidence. If the British thought that their own men had been killed, especially in cold blood, there was little doubt that they would re-double their efforts to bring down Rhaman's régime – and although in public he might pour scorn on the efforts of one British destroyer to finish the revolution, he was only too well aware in his own mind just how formidable an opponent Halton was. Behind that little ship and her highly trained crew lay something else which had been forged over the centuries. Their revenge would be terrible.

Like all experienced seamen, Rhaman glanced constantly and instinctively around his ship and the harbour. All remained still and quiet. It would be dawn in just over half an hour. He wondered where the *Phoenix* was; there had been no sighting or reports of the British destroyer for several hours. Still Halton could not be far away. He knew he must attend the meeting in the morning concerning the fate of the hostages.

At this meeting Rhaman intended to make it quite clear to the destroyer's Captain that he was not to interfere with the approaching Chinese supply ships in any way. If Halton agreed he would be told that, subject to his carrying out his part of the bargain, the hostages would eventually be returned unharmed. No alternative course of action would be considered. There would be no bargaining, nor would there be any of that strategy so beloved by the British; compromise.

Rhaman was grimly looking forward to meeting Halton

again, with everything now in his favour. As soon as the *Phoenix* was sighted he would send a signal giving details of the meeting. In the unlikely event of the destroyer's not showing up he could always send out an R/T message on the international distress, telling Halton to get in touch with him immediately.

Chapter 14

The silence that lay over the harbour was suddenly shattered by the metallic chatter of machine gun fire. It came from the direction of the entrance, and Rhaman instantly ordered a searchlight to be trained in that direction. One of his patrol boats must have run into trouble, he thought. He wondered if the British were up to something, and then, as he trained his powerful night glasses on the spot, he realised what all the commotion was about. It was his own patrol boat out there, and the other craft seemed to be a local fishing vessel.

Rhaman muttered a curse between clenched teeth. If some fools of fishermen had broken his curfew, then by the living God they were going to pay for it with their lives! His orders were made to be obeyed, and the sooner the population learned this the better. Any survivors would be publicly executed without delay, as an example to anyone else who might think of taking the law into his own hands!

When the patrol boat returned alongside the ALCHED the Zembasian Captain was not surprised to see that it had some fishermen on board. There were five altogether, and one of them had been wounded. As he had suspected, they had tried to sneak out on the tide just before dawn, to get the best haul. Their disobedience would be rewarded, Rhaman told the cowering men on the quarterdeck, by the death penalty. He sent them below to the cruiser's cells, under armed escort, and warmly congratulated the coxswain for his vigilance in the affair.

106

Time passed. Soon – in half-an-hour or so, the first pale fires of the tropical dawn would be kindled in the east. One of the cruiser's lookouts reported sighting the *Phoenix* just off the harbour entrance. 'It cannot do any harm to let them know that we are wide awake,' thought Rhaman, as he gave orders for a searchlight to be trained on the British destroyer. Looking closely at her through his night glasses, he was quite surprised by what he saw.

* * *

On board the *Phoenix*, during the hour or so before dawn, Halton had not had time to give even a passing thought to long term strategy. He had been far too busy briefing the men detailed off for the party who, thanks to their Captain's detailed knowledge of the *Alched*'s layout, were going to be in a good position once they got on board the cruiser. Sten guns and revolvers had been issued to all the men – rifles would not be of much use in the narrow spaces on board a ship – all the guns had been checked and there was plenty of ammunition available. Everything was in readiness for the final assault, and the majority of the boarding party were gathered together in their allocated groups on the fo'castle.

The destroyer steamed slowly towards Toulage, almost invisible to anyone who might be looking out to sea from the shore. Smoking was forbidden; not a light showed.

In the waist of the *Phoenix*, just aft of the fo'castle and level with the funnel, preparations were under way to make ready the motor boat on the starboard side for her role in the operation. Having got Drew to take command of the bridge for a while, Halton made his way aft to have a few final words with Sub Lieutenant Gordon.

This young officer was going to be in charge of the motor boat for the vital mission. Halton had been agreeably surprised, since the troubles had started in Zembasia, by Gordon's reactions during times of stress. For an officer of his limited experience he had kept a cool head, and on this coming trip he was certainly going to need it. That boat had to get into the harbour without being spotted, before starting its spectacular firework display. Gordon was going to be completely on his own for at least twenty minutes before the *Phoenix* came dashing in.

107

Also to be considered was the possibility that the assault might fail. If the destroyer was spotted by the *Alched* before she could get into a position astern of her – the final approach had to be made up this safety lane – Halton would have to get out of the harbour just as fast as he could. Obviously he could not risk his ship and the entire crew by stopping to recover the motor boat, and Gordon fully appreciated this. Like most naval officers, he knew that the Captain could never risk his ship in such a way.

Plans had been made, however, for such a situation. If the attack did fail, the launch was to get out of the way fast and head for a deserted part of the coast a few miles south. All being well, the destroyer, or its other motor boat, would return later to pick up the launch and its crew. If the worst happened – if the *Phoenix* was sunk or captured by the Zembasians – the launch would be on its own, and must head out to sea. There, in a shipping lane with vessels frequently passing, they were sure to be picked up.

Having made sure that the young officer thoroughly understood his instructions Halton, after a quick cheerful word with the other members of the motor boat's crew, went back up on to the bridge. There the first lieutenant had just given the order to 'Stop Engines'. The destroyer was a mile south of the harbour entrance – the pre-arranged starting point – and completely out of sight of anyone in Toulage. In another half-an-hour it would be dawn; the time had come for Halton to put his plans into operation.

First came the launching of the motor boat, which was quickly and carefully lowered into the calm sea. The top speed of the boat was ten knots, and Halton had estimated it would take approximately fifteen minutes to get into position and commence firing the pyrotechnics. Meanwhile the *Phoenix* would have to remain stationary, but even though the engines were stopped, instant power was available. They would need it soon for their high speed dash into the harbour.

Shortly after the motor boat had vanished into the darkness – the estimated visibility without the aid of lights was about a quarter of a mile – there was a sudden burst of heavy machine gun fire. As no tracer ammunition was being used it was difficult to tell exactly where the firing was coming from; it seemed to be from the direction of the entrance to the harbour.

Anxious faces turned towards the Captain to see what his reactions would be. It seemed fairly certain that the motor boat had run into serious trouble.

Knowing that hasty action might only make things worse, Halton calmly gave orders for the ship to get under way and head for the entrance at a fairly slow speed. Inwardly he was more than a little apprehensive; worried about the crew of the launch, and concerned that the chances of pulling off a surprise attack was getting less every minute. First priority, though, was the safety of his men. Afterwards another plan might have to be devised for putting the *Alched* out of action.

A searchlight's beam flashed around the harbour, then settled on a spot just inside the entrance. The motor boat could not have covered this distance in the time that had elapsed since it had left the *Phoenix*, but Halton, despite his relief, cursed himself inwardly for being so stupid as not to have taken into account the possibility of patrol boats.

Five minutes later the motor launch was spotted heading at full speed towards the *Phoenix*. Thank God, thought Halton fervently, young Gordon had had the sense to realise that the game was up when the firing started. Once the searchlight had come into play he must have decided correctly that the surprise attack could not be put into operation.

Hasty preparations were made on board the destroyer to recover the motor boat and then, just as it was coming alongside, the blinding beam of the *Alched*'s searchlight came to rest directly on the *Phoenix*.

* * *

At first Rhaman could not think why the British destroyer should be lowering one of its boats so early in the morning. Closer observation, however, showed that the boat was not being lowered at all. It was being recovered – but why?

He gave orders for the searchlight to be traversed slowly along the length of the now stationary destroyer. It was almost dawn, and the rapidly increasing light helped him to see the large number of men on her decks. Unusual, at this time in the morning; her fo'castle was absolutely packed. He puzzled over this for several moments, and then the truth dawned. The *Phoenix* had been about to enter the harbour and mount a surprise attack on his own ship! But *was* it the truth? After all, he had the hostages in his power. Would the British be prepared to risk their lives in an all out attack? It seemed out of character, especially for Captain Halton.

As it was almost daylight Rhaman gave orders for the searchlight to be switched off. He could see the *Phoenix* quite clearly now. Her motor boat had been hoisted on board and she was heading out to sea. If she had been within range Rhaman would have opened fire, without a moment's hesitation. As it was he could only stand and watch, and admit a grudging admiration for the sheer audacity of a scheme whereby a little ship was prepared to attack a much bigger one, against great odds.

Quite apart from wanting to gain control of the *Alched* in view of the overall situation, he decided, there must have been another reason for such suicidal methods. This could only be that Captain Halton thought his own men were on board the cruiser. A boarding party might have released them with a minimum of casualties, while the *Alched*'s crew were occupied with the defence of their ship. It would not be a bad idea, decided Rhaman, to allow the British Captain to continue under his misapprehension for the time being. Meanwhile, the sooner he, Rhaman, got those hostages on board the *Alched* the better, for a variety of reasons.

Gazing out to sea, he saw that the *Phoenix* had taken up her patrol position outside the harbour, just out of range. Before going to his cabin for breakfast Rhaman told the officer of the watch to signal the *Phoenix* shortly and say that he would meet her Captain at 0800 hours on board the *Alched*.

Ten minutes later a messenger from the bridge brought *Phoenix*'s reply. It read:

'Good morning. No hostages, no meeting.'

Chapter 15

Several thousand miles from Zembasia, on a cold and foggy

morning in London, a group of the Royal Navy's most senior officers were assembling in the Admiralty building. They had been called away from other duties at very short notice to try and work out a solution for the rapidly deteriorating situation in the African republic of Zembasia. The atmosphere, in this room where so many historic decisions had been made over the years, was tense. On the walls hung pictures of famous sailors of the past who had, in their time, also discussed or been discussed here. As the First Sea Lord entered the room all those present rose to their feet. He seated himself, motioning them to do the same, and an attentive hush fell over the room as he began to speak.

The Prime Minister, he said, wanted daily reports on the Zembasian situation, with immediate details of any fresh developments. It was up to the present company, he went on, to try and find a solution from the naval point of view. As usual in peacetime, it was a matter of doing things on the cheap as far as defence needs were concerned, and paying dearly later, when the chips were really down. Not that any one political party could be blamed for, he added hastily, the trend had always been there throughout the recorded history of Britain. If the Navy had had anywhere near the number of warships it required for its far-flung commitments he was certain that this sort of situation need never arise. Originally he had requested permission to send a cruiser and four destroyers on this round of courtesy visits, but had only been allowed, grudgingly, to send one destroyer.

However, in all fairness it must be said that when the *Phoenix* set out to visit the various African republics, no one had envisaged her involvement in such a delicate situation. In any case, concluded the First Sea Lord, it was no use trying to be wise after the event. The most important thing was, of course, to sort out this mess, and give the unfortunate destroyer's Captain as much practical advice and aid as they could.

He had barely finished speaking when the telphone rang. It was the Prime Minister, and in the ensuing conversation the latter made it clear that, much as he disliked saying so, the fate of one British destroyer was really of minor importance when compared with the bigger issues at stake. First, there was the potential loss of a republic hitherto on friendly terms with, and

111

from the point of view of future exports, extremely important to Britain.

Further, and perhaps even more serious, was the threat of a dangerous Chinese foothold in Africa, the possible implications of which could not be overstressed. Then again – the politician was obviously warming to his theme – there was world opinion to consider. This affair was going to have to be handled with extreme care, otherwise it could quite easily escalate to the risk of a major war.

In reply the First Sea Lord did his best to persuade the Prime Minister that there was little chance of the British being labelled as the aggressor when all the facts were revealed. After all, in this case there was only one destroyer on the spot, and the odds were obviously too great for one comparatively small ship to start behaving rashly. Even if the British cruiser arrived at the same time as the expected Zembasian heavy cruiser – which was extremely doubtful – it would not go into action except as a last desperate resort.

Political considerations apart, the British cruiser only mounted, as main armament, two semi-automatic six inch guns, as opposed to the *Umled*'s nine eight inch guns. These latter could, as well as firing a shell more than twice the weight of a six inch shell, out-range the British cruiser by at least two miles. The heavy cruiser also carried thick armour plating and could absorb a great deal of punishment from the available British guns. In fact, the only advantage that the British cruiser had over her counterpart was speed – about five knots more – which should be enough of a margin to keep her out of trouble if things became serious.

While this lengthy telephone conversation was going on the assembled officers remained silent, listening intently and drawing their own conclusions as to what the Prime Minister was saying. They did not envy their leader's position. It was quite obvious that the Prime Minister, worthy and respected gentleman that he was, had very little knowledge of purely naval affairs.

The First Sea Lord, normally a somewhat irascible and impatient man, was excelling himself this morning in the field of diplomacy, thought the elderly Vice Admiral who was sitting near him. Vice Admiral Sir Walter Halton, K.B.E., D.S.O., D.S.C. had good reasons to be present today. Apart from his outstanding professional qualifications, he was very fond of and concerned about his nephew, Commander Clive Halton, the Captain of H.M.S. *Phoenix*.

As far back as he could remember Walter Halton had had only one hero, and that was his elder brother, Clive's father. He had followed him into the Navy, and in his early career had served under him in two ships. Terence, senior by ten years and vastly superior in rank, had never allowed this gulf to breach their genuine friendship. Many times he had given his brother a helping hand, and on some occasions before the Second World War, had got him out of some awkward scrapes. Walter had been a somewhat irresponsible young officer at times.

On the 3rd September, 1939, they were both serving in the same destroyer flotilla; Terence was a Commander and had his own ship, Walter was the young First Lieutenant in another destroyer. Only a few months later the latter saw his brother's ship dive-bombed and sunk off the beaches of Dunkirk. There were no survivors. It had been his sad duty to convey the news to Terence's wife, who had unfortunately never really recovered from this tragedy. Almost deliberately, it seemed, she went out of her way to risk her life as an ambulance driver in the London blitz, and was killed on duty, not long after the death of her husband, during a heavy air raid.

Walter and his wife, a childless couple, took Terence's only son Clive, then a boy of fifteen, and a cadet at the Royal Naval College, Dartmouth, into their home and treated him as their own. As soon as he was old enough he, too, went to sea; it was the year before the Second World War ended. Clive, like his father and uncle before him, was a natural destroyer officer, with a very promising career ahead of him.

If things went badly in Zembasia, thought the elder Halton sadly, it would be a grim quirk of fate that obliterated his brother's family so completely. It must not be allowed to happen; there *must* be something that could be done. An idea had just started to formulate in his mind when he realised that the First Sea Lord was speaking to him.

'Halton,' the Admiral was saying sympathetically. 'I know that you have more than a passing interest in this affair. Are there any suggestions you would care to make?'

'Well, sir...' Halton paused, considering. Then he went on.

'As a matter of fact I *was* thinking along the lines of bluffing this man Rhaman into believing that we have several ships, including an aircraft carrier, close at hand and hurrying to the aid of the *Phoenix*. If we can convince him that this is the case, or at least put grave doubt in his mind, it might deter him from taking any drastic action against us at this stage.'

The others present looked puzzled when they had heard the Vice Admiral's opening remarks. Surely they had covered all this before? Quite simply, there was no carrier available at all; they were all fully employed on commitments far away from the Zembasian area. Halton, knowing what must be in their minds, went on quickly to point out that during the Second World War the old battleship *Centurion* had successfully masqueraded as the modern battleship *Anson*. The *Centurion* was a battleship which had been laid down before the First World War, and after that war she had been converted into a target ship. In the Second World War she had found more honourable employment by impersonating the newly constructed *Anson* for some time, ending up finally as part of the break-water in the Mulberry Harbour which had been constructed as the invasion port for Europe on 'D' Day. That, concluded Halton, was a case of visual deception and – most important – it had worked. If they could persuade Rhaman that the cruiser heading towards Zembasia was an aircraft carrier – this time it would be more of a case for radio deception – then they might have a chance to retrieve the situation and turn it in their favour.

Probably the most charitable thought in the room at that moment was that Halton had either become suddenly senile or gone completely off his rocker. The First Sea Lord, nonplussed, remained silent, but audible protests began to come from the other officers against the absurdity of the proposal and the necessity to stop wasting time.

Halton had deliberately paused at this stage to observe the reaction to his suggestion; it also gave him a brief respite to work out some quick practical details for the implementation of his plan. As patiently as he could, the First Sea Lord enquired whether he had anything more to add, and Halton, replying that indeed he had, went on speaking, this time in decisive tones. He soon captured the whole-hearted attention of the assembly. In essence his plan was extremely simple, and yet at the same time it was likely to prove most effective. To begin with, he said, from the radio side they would have to send plain language messages – it was pretty certain that the rebels would intercept them – to the cruiser, addressing it as one of the aircraft carriers. Whilst on passage the cruiser would have to keep off the regular shipping lanes, and keep out of sight of all other ships if possible.

However, this was only the beginning of the plan. The main trump card would be played as the cruiser got nearer the Zembasian coast. At this stage of the operation Rhaman would strongly suspect, from his radio sources, that an aircraft carrier was approaching. It would not matter too much if he did not really believe it, because in any event he would be directly told by the British that a carrier force was near and would take action. Rhaman, of course, would then be left with only two choices; he could either believe the British, or he could completely reject the idea of a powerful force in the offing.

If Rhaman believed that an aircraft carrier was about to operate against him, then he would realise only too well that the revolution was going to fail. Fanatical though the man might be, he was a trained naval officer, and as such would fully realise the devastation that an aircraft carrier could effect. In this case it should not be too difficult to persuade him to surrender, especially if an offer of safe conduct was made. That, then, would be the end of the affair.

But what, enquired the First Sea Lord, what would happen if Rhaman rejected the idea, and would not fall for this bluff?

Then, replied Halton, it would be time to put phase two of his plan into operation. As they all knew, the cruiser was equipped with four Wessex helicopters. At least two of these, preferably three, would take off and make an appearance near the harbour. This should be sufficient to convince Rhaman that there really was an aircraft carrier just over the horizon. After all, although it was common knowledge that many frigates these days carried helicopters, the type they carried was much lighter, and generally only one in number. Therefore the appearance of the three heavy helicopters would imply that the British force – which would remain out of sight just over the horizon – must be quite a powerful one, as aircraft carriers invariably operated with escorting warships.

When he had finished speaking Halton sat down and for a

few seconds there was silence. Then almost everybody started to talk at once. Quickly the First Sea Lord brought the conference back to order. For a start, he said, had anyone else thought of another plan? Could anyone add anything to the proposed plan? Could anyone see any practical objections to this idea?

Where exactly was the cruiser now? asked one of the Rear Admirals. And would she be able to get into a position to launch her helicopters in sufficient time? This was a vital question, agreed the First Sea Lord, as he reached for the fleet operations telephone to find out the answser.

The operations officer, on duty in the large room below the conference hall, quickly plotted the last known position report of the cruiser, and within two minutes was able to give the First Sea Lord an accurate up-to-date fix on the vessel. He was then told to stand by, as in a few minutes time he would have to pass on an important message to this ship. Normally, thought the duty officer – a Commander – things were fairly quiet down here. However, with the First Sea Lord personally giving the orders, he had a growing feeling that this was going to turn out to be a busy day. How right he was!

*　*　*

One thousand miles from Zembesia Captain David Stewart, R.N. was pacing to and fro on the bridge of his cruiser. A heavy Atlantic swell was running, giving the ship, as she thrust through the waves, a distinctly corkscrew-like motion. There had been no messages from the Ministry of Defence during the past twenty-four hours, but the last one, in top secret code, had ordered him to proceed to Zembasia with all possible speed. This message had also given him a brief description of the latest developments in the worsening situation there, and Stewart was heartily glad he was not in the younger Halton's shoes. Once his own vessel reached there he realised, of course, that his own position was not going to be exactly enviable.

The cruiser was crammed full of electronic equipment, radar sets, scanners; she even carried four helicopters, which almost made her a small aircraft carrier. One feature, however, had not been incorporated into this modern ship, and it kept returning as a nagging thought in the Captain's mind. Although covered for just about every other contingency, the cruiser was

116

not adquately equipped to fight a gun battle with a large conventional type cruiser; especially one which mounted eight inch guns. Still, thought Stewart, it would probably not come to anything as dramatic as that. After all, naval battles were completely outmoded in this modern world - or at least that seemed to be the prevailing opinion these days.

His own personal opinion, which coincided with that of many other service officers - for what it was worth, he reflected grimly - was that the British were invariably caught in situations where they were sniped at but could not, under most circumstances he could recall, shoot back. Rumour had it that recruiting officers were horrified, on one recent occasion, when a new recruit had stated that his sole reason for wanting to join the Army was to be aggressive and see action!

On a more serious note, he remembered (only too well, as he had been present), the fiasco of the Suez Canal incident a few years before. It had been a joint services operation which swung into action extremely effectively; then, just after the action had started, the politicians had changed their minds about the whole affair. Britain lost a good deal of her influence and respect in the Middle East through that little effort. Not for the first time Stewart wondered just how far he would be able to go, when he arrived at Zembasia, in taking direct action against the rebels.

One thousand miles to cover, at a speed of twenty-five knots - the upper economical limit - meant that his ship would be arriving at its destination in approximately forty hours. The time was now 2200 hours; therefore, all being well, they should be off the entrance to Toulage harbour by 1400 hours the day after tomorrow. There was no doubt that the presence of a powerful British warship would make some of the more faint hearted among the rebels think deeply about carrying on with the revolution. It would be far more effective than the eagerly awaited *Umled*, out of sight; always provided, of course, that the British ship arrived first.

Stewart wondered again how the *Phoenix* was faring at the moment. He could visualise the tremendous loneliness and great responsibility that her Captain had had to endure these past few days. Command was always a lonely business, even in peacetime. Under operational conditions it was much worse, and caused a strain that few people would really understand.

117

Still, Halton was going to have some company soon, and the two British warships, operating together, would be able to make quite a show of force. He hoped to God that his own vessel would not arrive on the scene too late.

He should, he realised, be getting the latest situation report from the Ministry of Defence very soon. Still, it could do no harm to initiate an enquiry signal. As a Captain taking his ship into an almost certainly hostile area he was entitled to more recent information than that which he had been given up to now. No sooner had he started writing out this message, however, than a rating came on the bridge from the radio room, bringing with him the latest signal from the Ministry of Defence. Eagerly Stewart tore open the buff envelope, took out the message and scanned it. An expression of incredulity spread across his tanned face, and he read it through again, more slowly.

Briefly, the signal stated, the cruiser was going to become an aircraft carrier as far as the radio side of the operation was concerned. Details followed about the various tasks that were to be carried out on the following day. The cruiser's helicopters, it seemed, were going to be extremely busy. It was all a big game of bluff, admittedly, but there was a good chance of getting away with it – if, Stewart realised, his ship could play her unusual part to perfection.

There was one very definite hitch though, which of course the Ministry of Defence could not possibly know about. Only two of the ship's helicopters were serviceable at the moment. 'For want of a nail!' thought Stewart as he picked up the bridge telephone and asked for the wardroom. He wanted the senior pilot and the air engineer officer on the bridge immediately, for consultation. Without them the whole operation would be seriously jeopardised.

As soon as these two officers appeared the Captain quickly explained the gravity of the situation, then began to ask questions. From the air engineer he wanted to know just how long it was going to take to get that third helicopter serviceable; from the pilot he wanted to know just how far away from Toulage they could launch the helicopters. Although the cruiser was going to take another forty hours to get there herself, it was obvious that if she could send off her helicopters when they were well out at sea her presence would be made known sooner in Zembasia. All the while her helicopters were airborne the cruiser would be heading in towards Toulage, and consequently their return flight distance was going to be considerably shortened. Time was the all important factor now, stressed Stewart. They had to help out the *Phoenix* as soon as possible.

The middle aged, bearded engineer Sub Lieutenant Munroe, after giving the Captain a time estimate, asked permission to leave the bridge so that he could re-organise the rectification of the third helicopter. Stewart nodded his assent and watched the short, stocky engineer leave. Munroe had come up the hard way through the ranks to his present appointment, and if anyone could get that helicopter serviceable he could.

Similarly the pilot wanted to get along and brief the aircrew, and said that after he had consulted the senior observer he would let the Captain know the position which would be best for launching the helicopters.

After these two officers had departed, all other senior officers were requested to come to the bridge. The sooner everybody was put in the picture the better, decided Stewart. When he had told the officers about the situation, and the plan that had been devised to meet it, he made a short broadcast to the ship's company over the Tannoy system, knowing very well that if he neglected to tell his crew, wild rumours would quickly spread round the mess decks. In any case, a sailor worked much better when he knew that there was some tangible reason behind all his efforts.

In less than two days Stewart might well need his men to carry out many tasks that normally, in times of peace, they would never be expected to do. From now on, he ordered, the ship would be blacked out. An officer would be continually on duty, with immediate effect, in the radio room. Damage control parties were to bring the ship up to a much higher state of readiness. During the following morning all weapons would be thoroughly tested; it was essential that the cruiser be fully prepared before they entered Zembasian waters.

* * *

As the cruiser was ploughing her way through the heavy Atlantic swell, another section of the Navy back in London – the staff of the operations room – were also being kept very busy. Vice Admiral Halton headed the team there, at his own request, willingly granted by the First Sea Lord. Everything was going according to the plan that he was responsible for initiating. The clicking of teleprinters and the hurrying of messengers, mainly to and from the radio room, gave rise to that hum of activity characteristic whenever there was something big on. It all reminded Halton of wartime days when he had, much against his will at the time, done a spell of duty there after two years in the Atlantic. Although duties in the operations room were equally vital, he had always had the sneaking feeling that a sailor ought to be at sea, and at the present moment wished very much that he could be by his nephew's side.

Streams of messages were being passed to the cruiser in plain language, and Halton hoped fervently that they were being intercepted, and that Rhaman would believe the bluff. Long before these messages to the cruiser had commenced the *Phoenix* had been contacted, in top secret code, and informed of the plan. The destroyer's Captain had had to make an assessment; with his on the spot knowledge this was all important, for the younger Halton was really the only person who could judge the effectiveness of the proposed plan.

Clive Halton had come back with enthusiastic support for the proposed plan, and stated that as far as he was concerned, the idea stood a good chance of success. In any case, he added wryly, there was not much of an alternative. Indeed the sooner the scheme was put into operation the better, for he had good reason to believe that Rhaman was in a nasty and over-confident mood, and that the situation was fast moving towards a crisis. No one knew for certain the exact time of arrival of the other Zembasian cruiser from South America. Should this ship turn up before the plans of the British could be put into operation, all might well be lost.

A pretty young Wren brought Vice Admiral Halton the latest signal from the British cruiser heading south. He gave a brisk nod of satisfaction as he read the message. They had managed to get that third helicopter serviceable, so there now seemed a reasonable chance of bluffing Rhaman into thinking that the approaching British force really did include an aircraft carrier.

In this latest message from the cruiser there was also a new estimated time of arrival off the Zembasian coast. Captain Stewart had certainly worked his ship up to maximum effort; there was now a whole hour substracted from her original estimated time of passage. The First Sea Lord, when apprised of this news, was well pleased. It might be a good idea, he suggested, to let the *Phoenix* know as well, to give her a bit more encouragement.

Halton lost no time in drafting out the signal for his nephew's ship. It would take about ten minutes for it to be coded and transmitted; an acknowledgement from the destroyer could be expected to come through within the next twenty minutes. Meanwhile, he thought, there was just time for a quick cup of coffee and a smoke in the officers' rest room.

It was whilst the Vice Admiral was sipping his coffee – and he could never explain it afterwards – that he began to feel uneasy. There was no logical reason for him to feel like this – but all the same he could not get rid of this uneasy feeling. Cutting short his break, he decided to return to the operations, and as he entered he noticed that a signal was just beginning to come in on the teleprinter from the *Phoenix*.

Halton was surprised to see that the incoming message was being sent in plain language, and for a moment he thought angrily that his nephew should have known better than to so flagrantly breach normal procedure. A few seconds later, though, he grimly understood why. The situation in Zembasia had exploded into open conflict!

He read the unfinished message again before picking up the telephone to report to the First Sea Lord. The teleprinter had suddenly stopped, leaving the room unnaturally quiet.

'From *Phoenix*.: Your message received. In action with . . . .'

Chapter 16

'Good morning. No hostages, no meeting.'

Rhaman stared intently at the signal just received from the

121

Phoenix, then threw it down with a furious exclamation. What the hell was Halton up to now? Surely the British Captain could not afford to risk the lives of his own men, now held hostage by the rebels! Unless of course.... It began to dawn on Rhaman that the prisoners might have escaped – or that they never existed at all. That army colonel – Kualar – was undoubtedly an opportunist, and might well be playing a double game. A visible tremor shook the potential dictator as he realised, like many others before him who had played this dangerous game, that a man in his position could not really trust anyone.

Glancing up, he saw that the officer of the watch was trying to catch his attention. The unfortunate man, seeing the evil mood his leader was in, had been too afraid to make a more direct approach. Rhaman was wanted urgently on the telephone, he said; there was shore call for him, from a Colonel Kualar.

Kualar, in nervous tones, revealed that one of his soldiers, a member of the kidnap party, had just reported back to him. The British sailors had managed to escape.

It was no use cursing this man for being an idiot, decided Rhaman as the colonel made his profuse apologies. He would have him shot the instant he could get his hands on him. There would be no room for bunglers in the new state of Zembasia.

Training his binoculars seawards, Rhaman stared at the *Phoenix* gliding gracefully over the calm sea. Out there was the man who had sworn to topple the régime that Rhaman had decided was best for his country and himself – but no, he determined grimly, one little British destroyer was not going to be allowed to thwart his plans. It had taken years of careful planning to reach the position he was in today, and with his studied act of being just a simple sailor, there had been many frustrations which would certainly have deterred most men. In twenty-four hours the *Umled* would be arriving. If the British destroyer was still in sight of Zembasia, the cruiser would be ordered to engage and sink her.

Rhaman would have dearly loved to take the *Alched* out to sea to fight the *Phoenix* himself, but there was not the slightest chance of being able to do so. With a third of her main armament useless and her steering mechanism out of action – due to the attack by the Canberra – his cruiser was in no fit condition to undertake a sea battle.

Furthermore, if the *Alched* left the harbour there was a

good chance that the mainly pro-government army would take over Toulage. They had already made an attempt to do this, by trying to mount field guns along the water front. A few well placed six inch shells from the cruiser's forward turrets had quickly put a stop to this, but if the *Alched* moved out to sea there was little doubt that the soldiers would try again. It would be quite a simple matter to place a few well camouflaged field guns in warehouses along the water front to greet the Chinese supply ships when they arrived. At least, thought Rhaman, that was what *he* would so, and it would be foolish not to assume that the army was thinking along the same lines.

All the same, he decided, he would still like to get rid of Halton and his interfering little destroyer. Destroyer. Destroyer.... Yes, of course! Why on earth had he not thought of it before? He would send out his own destroyer to attack and he hoped sink the *Phoenix*. Abruptly he ordered the officers of the watch to have his personal launch alongside in five minutes' time.

Captain Tshimbe, the Zembasian destroyer's Captain was at breakfast when a seaman reported that the Admiral's launch was approaching their ship at speed. Hurriedly leaving his meal, the Captain managed to reach the deck a couple of minutes before Rhaman arrived. There had scarcely been time to muster the side party to give their leader the full honours that he was entitled to, and would normally insist upon. Something important was on, for Rhaman - usually meticulous about ceremonials - scarcely acknowledged the salutes, but hustled the Captain below to his cabin, giving orders that they were not to be interrupted.

How long would it take, Rhaman demanded, for the destroyer to get up steam and prepare for going to sea? About an hour, replied the bewildered Tshimbe. From his last meeting with Rhaman the previous day, he had got the impression that none of them would be going to sea for several weeks, as they had to remain in Toulage to keep the situation stable after the rebels succession to power. He was even more astonished when Rhaman began to unfold his more immediate plans. In one hour the destroyer was going to engage and sink the *Phoenix*.

Rhaman went on to outline his simple but deadly method of attack to the now speechless destroyer's Captain. In gun

123

armament, both the destroyers were about evenly matched; the Zembasian ship had six 4.7 inch in three twin mountings, as opposed to the four 4.5 inch singly mounted guns of the *Phoenix*. It must be assumed that the British ship could deliver a quicker and more accurate rate of fire, but, Rhaman continued, Tshimbe was going to have two powerful factors in his favour before any question of a gun battle came about; namely, torpedoes, and the element of surprise.

Quite simply, then, the destroyer would leave the harbour as if on an innocent trip with peaceful intentions, flying the white flag. No doubt the curiosity of the *Phoenix* would be aroused, but there was no reason to suppose that the British would open fire. As soon as the Zembasian came within range, all her torpedoes would be fired at the *Phoenix*. At least one out of the ten should find its target.

* * *

From the bridge of the *Phoenix* Halton had been keeping a close watch on all movement in Toulage harbour. Through his binoculars he had seen Rhaman's launch go over to the destroyer, and about half-an-hour later return to the *Alched*. He was only mildly curious about this event, but soon after the rebel leader had departed things began to get interesting. Picking up one of the telephones, he asked Drew, who was due to relieve him shortly, to come up to the bridge.

'What do you make of that, Harry?' he asked, having allowed the First Lieutenant to study the Zembasian destroyer for a little while.

'I'd say that she was preparing for sea, sir,' came the reply.

'Just what I've been thinking. Now the question is, why should that ship go to sea at the present time?'

Drew suggested that the heavy cruiser, *Umled*, might be arriving much sooner than they expected, and perhaps the destroyer was going out to meet her. If this was the case then the *Phoenix* herself would have to stand out to sea very quickly, for under these rapidly changing circumstances, about the only chance the British destroyer would have against such a large enemy was the use of her greater speed and plenty of sea room. Halton certainly could not afford to allow himself to be trapped in these coastal regions by superior forces.

It was about this time that a further message was received

by the *Phoenix* from London, stating the revised estimated time of arrival of the British cruiser. Its helicopters should be over the harbour at 1000 hours the next morning. Halton lost no time in telling Drew the good news, and at the same time he made a short announcement over the ship's loudspeaker system to let all his crew know what was happening. His message ended on a note of optimism. All being well they stood a good chance of hoodwinking Rhaman and bringing the whole affair to a close.

Next Halton began to write out a reply for the Ministry of Defence, but before he could finish this Drew brought his attention back to the destroyer in the harbour. She would be putting out to sea shortly; it might be worthwhile sending a signal to Rhaman stating that the expected force of British warships was approaching. However, even as this message was being flashed, Halton had a strong notion that this was going to be a waste of time. It was unlikely to deter Rhaman from any action he had decided to take.

From the *Alched* came the flicker of a signal lamp, but then it stopped, almost as if Rhaman had been about to make a reply but then changed his mind. One of the *Phoenix*'s lookouts reported to the two senior officers that the Zembasian destroyer was raising its anchor, and they turned their attention from the *Alched*, training their binoculars round on to the destroyer, just in time to see the anchor break surface. Slowly, almost imperceptibly at first, the destroyer began to move forward, and then her bows began to swing round towards the harbour entrance. There was no doubt at all, now; she was coming out, and with every passing second her bow wave increased as she gathered speed.

Halton was puzzled to note that the crew of the destroyer were not at their normal leaving harbour stations. The upper decks were completely clear of men, although he could see the white caps of many officers on the bridge. Secondly he noticed – and Drew and the lookouts reported it at the same time – she was not flying the normal Zembasian ensign. At her bow and stern ensign staffs fluttered prominent white truce flags, indicating that their mission was peaceful. As they watched a signal lamp began to flash a message to the *Phoenix*.

'Meet me five miles west of Toulage. Have important news.'

At that moment the *Phoenix* was positioned two miles

outside the harbour entrance, which the other ship was just passing, cruising at about fifteen knots in a wide circle. Halton made a quick decision to let the warship proceed, for the present at least. She would not be able to escape from him – the *Phoenix* had a speed advantage of a good five knots. Turning to the duty signalman he dictated:

'Proceed. I will take up station two miles astern of you.'

An acknowledgement followed from the other destroyer. This should be a safe enough distance, Halton considered, as the only armament the Zembasian could bring to bear would be the after twin 4.7 inch turret. If, on the other hand, their opponent tried to make a bolt for it, then with five knots overtaking speed the *Phoenix* could be up alongside her in twenty-four minutes. All the same, he was not entirely easy in his mind.

Taking Drew on one side he said quietly:

'Harry, I don't like the look of this at all. We shall be going to action staions and getting our speed up soon, but first I'll have a word with the ship's company.'

'I agree, sir,' replied his second in command. 'I was about to suggest the same thing. And I'm sure the men would appreciate a word from you.'

Halton nodded, glad of such a staunch right hand man. Picking up the microphone he announced:

'This is the Captain speaking. The Zembasian destroyer which you can see emerging from the harbour has requested a meeting with us five miles out to sea. I have agreed to this, provisionally. We shall take up station two miles astern and follow her for a while.'

He paused for a few seconds to allow the crew to digest this information. Then he continued:

'As you well know, these rebels are not to be trusted. Therefore we shall be going to action stations as soon as I have finished speaking. We shall not be sounding the alarm bells, and I expect the whole procedure to be carried out quickly, quietly and without fuss. It's possible that nothing may happen, but we must be prepared – for anything. That's all. Carry on.'

He gave the necessary helm orders to the quartermaster to bring the ship into the desired position behind the Zembasian destroyer. Even as the *Phoenix* began her curve of pursuit course, heeling gracefully outwards in the steady turn, her crew

126

were hurrying to bring themselves to the highest possible state of readiness at which a warship can function.

All water-tight doors and hatches had been closed and battened securely home. The engine room departments, under the direct command of the senior engineer officer at his action station, had ensured all boilers were connected; in the possible event of 'Full Speed' being ordered, the turbines would be able to come up rapidly to their highest revolutions.

Every member of the crew wore an inflatable life belt, anti-flash gear – consisting of long gauntleted gloves and a hooded headdress which covered the neck, long trousers or overalls, thus keeping to a minimum the area of skin exposed. Bitter experience in both world wars had taught the Navy the deadly effect of flash burns on human skin, especially in confined spaces.

From the bridge Halton could see that all the guns' crews – the four 4.5 inch and four 40mm Bofors guns – were closed up. Ready use ammunition lockers, located around each gun position, had been opened, and live shells were instantly available. The guns were elevated to the correct vertical angle for a range of two miles, the two forward 4.5 inch ones pointing straight at the Zembasian destroyer, following their target gently round as the *Phoenix* completed her wide turn. Drew was busy answering the various telephones as each section of the ship reported that it was ready. As the *Phoenix* swung into position, behind the Zembasian destroyer, Halton gave the helm orders to steady his ship on a parallel course.

'Ship closed up for action, sir,' reported the First Lieutenant, as soon as he had received the last telephone call.

'Thank you, Number One.'

From the time that he had finished addressing the ship's company, Halton noted with satisfaction and justifiable pride, it had taken only six minutes to achieve this state. Two miles ahead steamed the Zembasian destroyer, at a steady twenty knots. So far all was well. In another three miles – nine minutes at this speed – they would be in the designated position for the proposed meeting.

He wondered how his opposite number would want to go about this. There should be a signal from him shortly, and he, Halton, intended to insist that the other Captain come on board the *Phoenix* in one of his own boats; this would automatically put the Zembasians at a disadvantage.

A few moments later a signal lamp began to flash from the other destroyer.

'I am stopping in five minutes. Request your Captain to come on board.'

'Not bloody likely!' exclaimed the British Captain loudly, much to the amusement of the other officers and men on the bridge, who agreed wholeheartedly with this reaction. Without delay Halton dictated a reply to be sent immediately.

'Captain of *Phoenix* will not, repeat not, come on board. If you wish to talk your Captain must come to *Phoenix*. Your safe conduct is guaranteed.'

Now the fat really was in the fire, he thought. If the Zembasian Captain refused his request and continued steaming out to sea, there appeared to be only three courses of action left open to Halton. One – follow the other destroyer; two – return to Zembasia; three – halt the destroyer by persuasion, threat or force. Each of these alternatives was fraught with dangerous possibilities, and he decided that if it came to it, he would flash a message to the Ministry of Defence to seek their guidance.

At that moment the answering signal came. To the British Captain's vast relief it seemed as though things were going to sort themselves out peaceably enough.

'Will stop and send boat.'

'Well, that seems to have settled that little problem, sir,' remarked Drew, with a grin.

'H'm. Things are working out far too smoothly for my liking, Harry, and quite frankly I'm not happy about it. We're going to have to watch our step. I'm certain there's much more to all this than meets the eye,' replied the Captain, his eyes on the other destroyer.

He noticed that the distance between the two ships was decreasing. The Zembasian destroyer was slowing down, and Halton, not wanting to get too close to the other ship, gave orders to reduce speed to fifteen knots. Up ahead the Zembasian destroyer began a turn to starboard, at the same time gradually losing speed. Through his binoculars Halton noted that preparations were being made to lower a boat, and an unusually large number of men were gathered amidships.

128

He gave helm orders to the quartermaster for a gentle turn to starboard in order to parallel the other ship's course. For a few moments his attention was diverted as he glanced down to note the compass reading to establish their next heading. Then Drew suddenly yelled out a terrible warning:

'Torpedoes approaching port side!'

Reacting instantly, but keeping perfectly calm, Halton gave several orders in rapid succession.

'Full starboard rudder,' to the quartermaster.

'Full astern starboard engine,' to the engine room; this would give the rudder a chance to bite.

'All guns train. Commence firing as soon as your guns bear,' to the gunnery officer in the director tower.

Five tell-tale foamy tracks were coming straight from the Zembasian destroyer and tracking very accurately for the *Phoenix*. By putting the helm hard over and getting the starboard engine going full astern, to reduce the radius of the turn that they had already started, there was an even chance that the *Phoenix* would parallel the torpedoes' tracks and considerably reduce the risk of a direct hit. Ideally Halton knew that he should have turned bows on towards the torpedoes – 'combing the tracks', it was termed in naval parlance – but in this case he felt justified, as they had already commenced a starboard turn and had gone through several degrees. If he had gone the other way, port, it would have taken longer, with perhaps fatal results.

In twenty seconds from now he would know whether or not he had been right and quick enough in giving his orders. After that the matter would be entirely academic. Thank God Drew had spotted them when he did! Halton cursed himself for looking at that compass – an entirely natural reaction, everyone else would have said – instead of keeping his eyes on the other destroyer. If the warning had not come in time they would have been caught broadside on to the torpedoes, and at least one, probably more, could have been direct hits.

A quick glance astern showed Halton that the *Phoenix* was coming up to the same heading as the fast approaching torpedoes. Now was the moment to straighten the ship's course. Orders were given to the quartermaster to steady the rudder, and to the engine room, full speed ahead. During the hard turn both the after 4.5 inch guns had opened fire, but as far as Halton could tell had not scored any hits – which was not surprising, due to the rapidly changing azimuth angle of the turn. Loud cheers, mainly of relief, broke out from all over the *Phoenix* as the torpedoes passed down each side of her; three of them were within fifty yards. A hundred yards astern six large splashes indcated that their treacherous opponent had fired a broadside with her six 4.7 inch guns. Accurate shooting, thought Halton – but then, they had had all the advantages of surprise and a steady shooting platform.

'I've had enough of this bloody nonsense, Number One!' he remarked grimly. 'So far that damned ship has had things all her own way, but by God we're going to put a stop to it!'

He gave a quick alteration of heading to 45 degrees starboard. He had been watching the other ship closely, and noticed the flash of her guns. Another broadside was on its way, but when those shells arrived his ship would not be in the position that they were aimed for.

'Well done, sir!' exclaimed Drew admiringly. 'That gunnery officer is going to go wild in more ways than one!'

'He'll do more than that before I've finished,' growled Halton. 'Now – as I was saying. We've got to put this chap out of action, before he gets us. So far we've been lucky – damned lucky – but it can't last much longer. You'll notice that we've been steering straight into the sun, which should have dazzled that lot a bit. In another three minutes I want six depth charges launched, all together. While they're exploding we are going to turn right back at him.'

'Aye aye, sir.' replied Drew enthusiastically, and gave the necessary orders to the two 'Limbo' crews in the rear part of the ship. These three barrelled mortars could launch three depth charges at the same time in any direction.

Halton explained further that in the confusion caused by the six explosions the *Phoenix*'s crew would get her turned round. The next thing the Zembasian crew would see, still looking into the sun, would be the British destroyer racing straight for them. By coming in to the attack on a wide zigzag course, *Phoenix* would, besides spoiling her opponent's aim, be able to bring all her own guns to bear for most of the run in.

As far as Halton could tell the two after 4.5 inch guns had not yet managed to hit the other destroyer. However, he was not really surprised. It was an almost impossible task, in view of the inevitable initial confusion and then the violent evasive action he had had to take. Better keep the brass hats in London in the picture, he thought, and turning to Drew he said:

'Number One, get a signal off to Ministry of Defence at once, please. Better do it yourself. Just plain language – no time for coding now. Tell them what's happening.'

As the First Lieutenant hurried away Halton gave orders for the after guns to cease firing, and at the same time, told the gunnery officer what was going to happen.

'Full starboard rudder. Take her through 180 degrees and then steady up, coxswain. You will be pleased to know that we are going to sort this little lot out,' the Captain added, knowing that he could afford to have this little aside with the coxswain. Chief Petty Officer Gray had had control of the ship ever since they had gone to 'Action Stations', after his narrow escape from the rebels.

Within seconds of giving this order, even before the destroyer began her steep swing round, the Limbos fired their deadly missiles. The sea behind them erupted violently as the six depth charges exploded, with less than two seconds between first and last. For a few moments the view of the other ship was completely blotted out – and conversely, it was hoped, the *Phoenix* had also disappeared. With any luck the Zembasians might think that they had destroyed or badly damaged the British destroyer.

Emerging at top speed from behind the subsiding water spouts, the British destroyer headed straight for her opponent. With her huge bow wave, and stern tucked well into the water, she was an awe-inspiring sight. Halton saw to his astonishment, however, that the other ship had turned about and was heading back towards Toulage. Either the rebels thought that they had sunk or crippled the British destroyer, or else they had suffered some damage and had had enough. In either case Halton was determined, after this further example of treachery, that they were not going to get away with it this time.

He rapidly worked out a cut off vector that would prevent the other ship reaching the safety of harbour without first having to pass very close to the *Phoenix*, and gave the necessary helm order. When the two forward 4.5 inch guns commenced firing the sharp noise startled him for a moment;

up till now they had played no part in the action. The changing pattern of a solid, heavy thump, followed by a blinding flash indicated to him that his ship had just received a direct hit – from the feel of it he knew that it could not be very far from the bridge. A quick look round showed that no one there had been hurt. Young Sub Lieutenant Gordon, who had just answered one of the bridge telephones, turned an anxious face towards him.

'Radio cabin has received a direct hit, sir. There are serious casualties – doctor and first aid party have been sent for.'

Radio cabin.... and Drew was there! It would be bitter to lose one of his best friends and his able second in command – but before his mind could dwell on this awful prospect Drew appeared on the bridge.

'Thank God, Harry! I thought you'd had it down there,' said Halton fervently.

'I was on my way up here when it happened, sir.' Drew, looking pale and shaken, continued: 'Two of the telegraphists have been killed. The chief telegraphist and a radio mechanic are wounded, but not too badly, I think. I went back and gave a hand till the doctor came along. Everything's under control now, but all the R/T sets are smashed. It's a hell of a mess in there, and I'm pretty sure most of our message never got off. One of the telegraphists was killed while he was transmitting.'

'Thanks, Harry. Don't worry about that signal now – we may be able to fix up an emergency set later and get it off.'

Turning his attention again to the Zembasian destroyer, Halton noted with grim satisfaction that the *Phoenix* had scored several hits and was continuing to do so. A small fire had broken out near the base of her funnel, and the rear gun turret was completely out of action – but she was by no means finished. Her two remaining 4.7 inch turrets, forward of the bridge, were still aimed straight at the *Phoenix*, and flashes every thirty seconds or so indicated they were still firing. Her rate of fire had been cut down considerably, however, and many of her shots, even taking into account the zigzag course of the *Phoenix*, were badly aimed, and were not being co-ordinated by a gunnery director. Halton could imagine the awful effect his shells were now having, and decided he would give the other ship a chance to surrender shortly.

In the event, however, Halton never got the chance to extend clemency. Two miles lay between the opposing ships in this running fight, and the Zembasian Captain must have realised that he would never make the harbour entrance with the *Phoenix* on her present course. Knowing that he was cornered, the rebel commander must have been desperate. Suddenly he swung his ship round. Once again he was going to play his trump card - torpedoes. He still had five of them left, and this time was determined to score a hit on the *Phoenix*.

When Halton saw the five torpedoes actually launched from the other destroyer he knew that he was going to be hard put to avoid them all at this short range. Once again he swung his ship round to comb the tracks, but before the turn could be properly completed he saw the torpedoes approaching, fast and accurate. Three shot along the starboard side, passing within thirty yards, but the other two hit the port side of the ship fair and square towards the stern.

For a brief moment there was an almost uncanny silence after the previous din of gunfire. Then came a muffled explosion which sent a huge fountain of water high in the sky at the rear of the ship. This was immediately followed by an unexpected vibration which shook the whole ship as she turned somehow steeply to port.

It was this latter movement that Halton noticed first, when he had recovered from the initial shock of the explosion, which had knocked him off his feet. He had given no helm orders to that effect, and now he quickly took control of the situation. He was determined to finish off the Zembasian destroyer now burning fiercely, before his own ship was finished, and began giving orders in rapid succession.

'Coxswain - get the ship steadied up. Gunnery Control - concentrate all guns on the middle of the target. Engine room - report damage as soon as possible. Number One - stand by to take charge of damage control parties.'

A frantic reply came first from the senior engineer officer in the engine room.

'Sir, one torpedo has sheared off the port propeller completely - you must have felt the vibration of the empty shaft. We've stopped the engine now. The other torpedo has partly penetrated the hull, but hasn't exploded - yet! It's just wedged there. Is it possible to reduce speed at all, sir?'

133

'Sorry, Smythe – not yet. But don't touch the torpedo's warhead. It's safe enough for the moment – I'll get an ordinance artificer down there as soon as I can to disarm it. Tell your department they're doing a damned fine job, and I'm very grateful,' he added. 'Hope to finish off the enemy soon. Let me know at once if we start to take in much water.'

Before the coxswain could give an answering call Halton told him briefly what had happened to the port propeller, adding that he would have to counteract the turning effect by coarse use of starboard rudder. Once the *Phoenix* had steadied up, all her 4.5 inch guns pounded into the enemy. They certainly had the range now, and were unmercifully accurate.

Qute suddenly a terrific flash appeared amidships on the Zembasian destroyer, followed by the deep rumble of a huge explosion. When the smoke cleared her stern, from just behind what was left of her funnel, had completely disappeared. All that remained of her was sinking fast; her bows had reared up into the air, and in a few seconds it was all over. All that remained was a pall of black smoke, and every now and again huge air bubbles broke on the surface of the sea. It was unnecessary for Halton to give the order to 'Cease Fire'. His guns, having completed their deadly task, had stopped of their own accord. No jubilant cheers rang out from the *Phoenix*. Her crew were too astonished and appalled by the sudden ending of their opponent.

The *Phoenix* was now less than two miles from the harbour entrance. Several small boats were putting out from Toulage, obviously with the purpose of picking up survivors. Halton decided to let them get on with it, feeling that the presence of his own ship might easily deter these little boats from coming further.

After standing down from 'Action Stations', securing the guns and receiving the damage control reports, he gave the orders for *Phoenix* to head slowly out to sea. It was time, he felt, to get out of sight of land and take stock of the rapidly changing situation.

Chapter 17

Halton was aware, as the *Phoenix* slowly headed out towards the open sea, that she was in too poor shape to play the lone wolf much longer. Communications - vital to an effective fighting unit - were non-existent at present, although the radio section was trying hard to fix one of the smashed sets, using mainly a combination of spare parts from all the other sets. Speed, too, was essential, but with the port propeller and its integral shaft buckled, there was no hope of rectifying that situation. At best, their maximum speed was cut down to about twenty knots.

Still, on the credit side, they had an effective gunnery control system, and every single gun was serviceable. Also, much to everyone's heartfelt relief, the Zembasian torpedo had been safely removed. Halton had left the First Lieutenant to take charge of the bridge while he went on a short inspection tour of the damage. One of the ordinance artificers was working on the jutting warhead of the torpedo when Halton got to the engine room, and it did not present a pleasant sight. The reason why it had not exploded was due to an almost thousand to one chance; a jammed plunger in the fuse mechanism.

Although the artificer's explanation was couched in casually spoken technical terms, Halton was quite certain that everyone on board the *Phoenix* fully appreciated the awful reality of what could have happened. However, that danger was past now, and there were other things to think about.

Before he went back to the bridge Halton made time to visit the wounded, being cared for in the small sick bay. The doctor reported that all was well; neither of the men who had been in the radio compartment when it received the direct hit were badly hurt, and the only other wounded were three gunnery ratings who had received slight cuts from flying splinters. The dead would have to be buried at sea; the doctor would report personally when all was ready.

Halton was pleased to learn that the cooks had managed,

despite difficulties, to prepare soup, sandwiches and hot drinks for everyone. Indeed, having during his short tour of the ship had a few words with the majority of the crew, he was delighted to find them all in good heart; guns' crews cleaning their guns and getting more ammunition ready, engine room ratings, cooks, communications personnel and many other scattered groups going about their business with cheerful efficiency.

Clearly they were all determined to make the best of a bad job. Perhaps it was this stubborn trait, thought Halton, with a glow of pride, that had, during more than a thousand years, pulled the Navy through many desperate situations which many would have given up as hopeless. The crew of the *Phoenix* had been welded together by their awful baptism of fire, and their Captain realised that he had one priceless asset; his men's high morale.

Heaving himself into the Captain's chair, a permanent fitting on the bridge which was sacrosanct to him alone, he settled down gratefully to the sandwiches and coffee which the wardroom steward had just brought up. Behind, just out of sight below the horizon, lay Toulage, and he decided that this was far enough out. *Phoenix* would now cruise slowly up and down, remaining parallel to the Zembasian coast, for the rest of the evening and the night.

When darkness fell, in approximately one hour's time, they would be able to keep safely in position by their search radar, which fortunately had not been damaged in the recent action. If only the R/T was serviceable, he thought; they would then be able both to hear and see throughout the hours of darkness. Shortly, when he had finished his sandwiches, he would get in touch with the radio section to see if they had made any progress in fixing a set.

'The doctor would like to have a word with you, sir,' reported Drew, who had just answered one of the bridge telephones.

'Thank you, Number One.'

Halton picked up the telephone, knowing already what this message was going to be about. He listened to the doctor reporting that all had been prepared for the burial; the two men had been securely wrapped in their hammocks, and a 4.5 inch shell had been placed at their feet. Halton thanked him for

136

carrying out this unenviable task, and sent Drew off at once to organise the sliding boards and an ensign with which to cover each man.

When Halton arrived on the quarter deck he noticed with gratification that the majority of the ship's company was present, only those on really essential duties were not there. All was quiet; before he left the bridge he had given orders to 'Stop Engines' for a few minutes, and now the only noises were the faint humming of the fans and the occasional shrill cry of seagulls circling overhead. The dead sailors lay on the port side of the quarter deck, covered with white ensigns.

In the brief but solemn ceremony that followed, Halton paid tribute to the dead. Out of sight of land, surrounded only by the lonely wastes of the sea and the sky, the words of the burial service seemed to take on an especially significant meaning. Then, to the shrill, long drawn out pipe of the bosun's call, the two bodies slid gently into the sea with scarcely a splash. After an appropriate silence the 'Carry On' was piped, the ensign was raised from its half mast position, and the ship's company returned to its normal routine. Halton and Drew walked slowly back to the bridge together. The splendour of the tropical sunset, with its rich, deep colours, seemed to provide a perfect finale to what had just taken place.

In fifteen minutes or so it would be completely dark, and the crew would be taking up night cruising stations. Rest was all important to his men, Halton realised, and he was determined that all of them were going to get their fair share. No one knew what tomorrow would bring, but whatever happened, tired men were not going to be efficient. This included himself, and he decided that he and Drew would have to share watch and watch about.

Shortly after Drew had gone below the petty officer radio mechanic reported that a makeshift radio had been rigged up. It could be tuned into any wave length, but for reception only, which was really not much good, for Halton desperately needed to get in touch with the Ministry of Defence in London.

Anxiety must be growing about the situation, with no news at all from the *Phoenix* for several hours. He wondered if the original plan would still be carried out. No doubt the Captain of the approaching British cruiser would be far from happy about bringing his ship into a potentially hostile area with such out of date information. Even if it was assumed by the Ministry of Defence that the *Phoenix* was lost, the Navy would still have to investigate the matter. It was quite feasible, however, that a decision might be made to wait until more ships could be made available for the operation. If this happened it would prove fatal, for Rhaman, with the arrival of the supply ships, could by then have easily taken over the country.

However, by careful use of the radio it might still be possible to glean quite a lot of information about what was going on around. In particular the telegraphists might be able to learn, on the Zembasian frequencies, something about the movements of the supply ships, and possibly the pending arrival of the new cruiser *Umled*. Halton issued detailed instructions as to what they were to listen to and asked to be kept informed of developments.

Captain Morrison, Her Majesty's late Naval Attaché to the Republic of Zembasia now resident on board H.M.S. *Phoenix*, had proved to be quite an asset during his temporary stay. In a quiet, unobstrusive manner, without any of the direct interference that some officers of his senior rank might have been tempted to use, he had made it absolutely clear that his sole function was to help out in any way he could. Halton learnt from the surgeon lieutenant, long after their action with the Zembasian destroyer, that Morrison had given him considerable practical help and encouragement with the wounded men, and this sort of charitable action was characteristic of the way the ex-Attaché made himself useful. This, coupled with his cheerful, friendly manner to both senior and junior alike, had caused him to be willingly accepted by the ship's company as one of themselves – a rare compliment to a stranger.

There was one tangible way he could offer his services, Morrison decided, and that was to take charge of the bridge for much of what should be a comparatively calm night. If Halton agreed to this, the destroyer's two senior officers, who had borne the brunt of all the action and the subsequent heavy responsibilities, would be able to snatch a few hours of much needed sleep.

Night had now fallen completely, with the abruptness

138

characteristic of tropical latitudes, and the destroyer steamed slowly on her way across the calm sea at an economical speed of ten knots. Halton needed little persuasion to accept Morrison's offer, and went below to his cabin in the comfortable knowledge that he had left his ship in safe and capable hands.

For several hours all was quiet. As the *Phoenix* patrolled up and down the Zembasian coast with Morrison giving routine helm orders and the watch keepers quietly taking over their duties, the ex-Attaché was in his element. This was the real Navy, he thought, recalling with nostalgia his early days in the service when he had been a destroyer officer. Now that he was a full Captain and stood a good chance of becoming an Admiral he realised, with genuine sadness, that his days at sea were going to be extremely limited. Out there, surrounded by the sea and the dark blue, starry sky, was a totally different world from which a man could derive peace and a rich sense of purpose. If a sailor from many centuries past arrived here suddenly, Morrison mused, he would still find his natural element, the sea, just as before, with its many changing moods....

His thoughts were interrupted by the arrival of one of the radio mechanics on the bridge.

'Excuse me, sir, but I thought that I had better let you know that we have managed to get the radio tuned into Zembasia,' the latter said quietly.

'Thank you,' replied Morrison; then sensing that the rating had more to report, he went on, 'Anything out of the ordinary happening?'

'Yes, sir. For the past hour or so they have been playing patriotic music, and there's an announcement every few minutes that their leader will be speaking to the world at midnight. It's now five to twelve, sir. We thought you would probably want to hear the broadcast.'

'Quite right,' approved Morrison, and handing over command of the bridge to Thomson, the gunnery officer who was taking his turn as officer of the watch, he went below to the radio compartment just in time to hear Rhaman's voice saying:

'Today one of our warships, sailing on a peaceful mission, was treacherously attacked without warning and sunk by the British destroyer *Phoenix* inside Zembasian territorial

139

waters. There can be no excuse for this vile attack, which has caused the death of many innocent sailors.

'We cannot and will not tolerate this terrible act of piracy. Today we mourn our brave sailors, but tomorrow – and let the interfering British take careful note of this – we will wipe this scourge from the sea.'

The rest of the would-be dictator's speech was devoted to asserting that he was the country's chosen leader, elected by an overwhelming majority in a democratic vote, and that very soon Zembasia was going to become the leading power in Africa. Britain, and for that matter any other imperialistic country which attempted to intervene in Zembasian affairs, would soon regret doing so.

Speaking with all the skill of the powerful orator, Rhaman's impassioned speech was bound to make an impact on the world in general and the continent of Africa in particular. Other potential revolutionaries would no doubt be inspired into following his example of ousting the established government. If the rebellion proved successful – and the way things were going at present, this seemed quite a strong possibility – that much quoted phrase, 'the winds of change' looked like developing into a howling hurricane.

* * *

Apart from Captain Morrison there were many other interested listeners to Rhaman's speech, and foremost amongst them in London was Vice Admiral Sir Walter Halton, on duty at the Ministry of Defence. Radio contact with the *Phoenix* had been lost for almost twenty-four hours, and this long silence had given rise to considerable anxiety and concern in both the government and naval headquarters. A tense atmosphere had developed following the destroyer's last unfinished message, and speculation was rife as to what had happened to her, and what was going on at the present time in Zembasia. Communication with the loyal element of the republic's government had, in the event, proved to be fruitless, as the latter had not been able to witness the sea battle. However, it was established that unless the *Phoenix* and the British cruiser could get there soon and give a hand, the loyalist forces were in grave danger of being overwhelmed.

When Rhaman had finished speaking one of the first to

contact the Ministry of Defence was the Prime Minister. There was no doubt about it, he told the First Sea Lord, this speech by Rhaman had put Britain in a very bad light. Of course he realised, he went on hastily, that a British warship would not commit an act of piracy. Obviously all the facts were not known; nevertheless, Rhaman had achieved a major verbal triumph and he – the Prime Minister – was going to have to make a public reply to the nation and the world within the next twenty-four hours at the most.

Accusations that a British warship had committed an act of piracy on the high seas could not go unanswered, and it might be wise to consider recalling the cruiser that was hurrying to the troubled area. The arrival of an even larger British warship in Zembasian waters might well cause the situation to deteriorate; therefore, the Prime Minister concluded, although he wanted to allow the Navy as free a hand as possible, he must be given some pertinent facts and answers from the Ministry of Defence before making his broadcast on the following day.

The First Sea Lord passed on this information to Vice Admiral Halton in the operations room. It appeared at once to the latter that neither his senior officer nor the Prime Minister had paid much attention to one very pertinent factor that had emerged from Rhaman's speech. Out there in Zembasia, the British were still effectively represented, and could clearly bring pressure to bear. His nephew's ship had engaged and sunk the Zembasian destroyer. This action, he realised, could only have been brought about through extreme provocation on the part of the Zembasian ship. No British naval Captain would institute any high handed action that could be possibly construed as piracy, and thus involve his country in a serious diplomatic incident.

Selection and maintenance of the aim – the first and cardinal principal of war; this well worn phrase was running through Halton's mind. That was it, then, he decided. They would press on with the basic plan he had devised. Of course there would have to be a certain amount of modification. For a start, the cruiser could not be allowed to sail blindly on into these dangerous waters. Blindly, blindly.... This was the key word to the whole situation! There was absolutely no need at all for this type of cruiser to enter Zembasian waters in such a manner anyway. One of her helicopters could be launched, long before the ship herself came anywhere near the danger zone, to fly on ahead and make contact with the *Phoenix*.

While it was obvious that there was little chance of making radio contact with the destroyer, the helicopter could get the latest situation reports by means of visual signalling. This information could be instantly radioed back to the cruiser, which in its turn would pass it on to the Ministry of Defence. Thus both the cruiser and the operations room would be linked, able to make decisions in the light of really up-to-date information, and take the appropriate action. Ever since the start of the emergency soldiers and transport aircraft of the Strategic Reserve had been put on stand by, but with the major communications breakdown, Halton had not been able to pass them any information. Once the airborne link had been established by the cruiser's helicopter, he would be able to judge the situation, and give the stand-by detachment commander his orders.

In addition to the advantage of the re-establishment of communications, the Admiral realised, with an insight derived from his many years of experience, that another important asset would derive from the plan. When the helicopter suddenly appeared – by then it would be daylight – it would immediately be noticed by the Zembasians. Its presence could only mean to them that another British warship, or perhaps more than one, was getting near their coast. This fact was bound to cause dismay amongst the rebels, while giving much needed encouragement to the hard pressed government forces. Last, but by no means least, the crew of the *Phoenix* would receive tangible evidence that help was at last not far off.

* * *

Another interested listener to Rhaman's broadcast, but much nearer to the source than London, was Captain Stewart, Captain of the British cruiser that was heading towards Zembasia. At just after midnight the navigating officer carefully worked out their position. They had, he informed his Captain, three hundred miles to go to reach their destination. If they could maintain a relatively high speed of thirty knots, provided nothing slowed them down they would arrive in ten hours' time.

Fuel consumption would be high at this sustained high

speed, and Stewart realised that shortly after their arrival they would have to take on more oil fuel. Still, he had been told by the Ministry of Defence that this was a vital mission, and his first priority was to get to Zembasia as soon as possible. Consideration of fuel, always a nagging thought to a Captain when it was running low, would have to come later. In any case Naval headquarters knew his position and would doubtless arrange for one of the far roaming fleet auxiliaries to rendezvous with the cruiser.

Stewart was not greatly surprised when, about twenty minutes after Rhaman had finished speaking he was informed by the officer of the watch that new instructions had just been sent by the Ministry of Defence. Originally the broad plan had laid down that he was to put on a show of strength, with as many helicopters as possible, over Toulage well in advance of the actual arrival of his ship. Now the order was to launch a helicopter – at maximum range – to act as a communications link between the destroyer, the cruiser and London.

Word had spread quickly round the cruiser about Rhaman's broadcast and the sinking of the Zembasian destroyer, and all of the ship's company were keen to get to the aid of one of their own ships. God knew, thought Stewart to himself, what they were going to find when they got there. The *Phoenix* must have been really pushed to go into such an action. However, if there were many serious British casualties the cruiser was far better equipped medically than the smaller ship, and would be able to take good care of them.

When the senior pilot and senior observer arrived in his day cabin – Stewart had sent for these two aircrew officers shortly after he received his new instructions – the Captain informed them of the changed position, saying that they were now going to launch a long range reconnaissance flight before dawn. By then the ship would only be about 120 miles from Zembasia, and if the helicopter flew at 90 knots, visual contact should be obtained with the *Phoenix* in less than an hour and a half. It would be wise, commented the senior observer when he heard about the visual signalling, to take along one of the cruiser's signal ratings in the helicopter. Not many aircrew these days, he explained, were in practice with visual morse signals. Just as well to get a small detail like that taken care of now, replied Stewart, pleased that the observer had admitted something of which he himself had not been aware. They certainly could not afford a breakdown in signals once they had got in touch with the *Phoenix*.

Provided that there were no strong head winds, the senior observer went on, the Wessex helicopter could afford to spend forty minutes in the vicinity of the *Phoenix* before returning to the cruiser. On the return flight, two hours after take off, the distance would have been cut down considerably, to about sixty miles.

Both the pilot and the observer volunteered to go on this important flight, but since they could not both be spared, Stewart decided to let the observer fly, and retain the pilot.

* * *

Perhaps the least surprised listener to the broadcast made by the rebel leader was Captain Dogmar of the Zembasian Navy. At midnight his ship, the heavy cruiser *Umled*, was approximately one hundred miles west of Toulage, steaming towards the port at a carefully calculated sixteen knots, so that her arrival would coincide with dawn in the Bay of Zembasia. Dogmar's orders were straightforward enough. He was to seek out the British destroyer which had been prowling around these waters for the past few days, and sink her.

With his nine eight inch guns, which had recently been thoroughly overhauled before the Zembasian Navy had taken over their biggest and most modern warship, Dogmar knew that the British destroyer would not stand the slightest chance when the two ships met. Once the sinking had been accomplished, the *Umled* would make a ceremonial entrance into the harbour. With the addition of this powerful fighting ship to help dominate the harbour, Rhaman's revolt would be given fresh impetus. Soon after the cruiser's arrival, to consolidate the whole affair, the Chinese supply ships would also be entering Toulage. Then, thought Dogmar to himself – not for the first time – he was likely to get his much coveted promotion to Commander in Chief of the new republic's Navy.

Rhaman, by use of a carefully kept secret radio frequency, had been able to keep in touch with the *Umled* ever since she left South America. Although the existence of the cruiser was common knowledge, few knew her exact position, and Rhaman was determined to keep it that way. This was one of the trump cards in the rebel leader's hand, and he knew that he must play it carefully, and at just the right moment.

It would be much too risky to bring in the *Umled* at night. She lacked the sophisticated radar equipment necessary to enable her to fight effectively in the dark, should the *Phoenix* try to interfere. In daylight however, it would be an entirely different proposition. No mere destroyer would willingly attempt to engage a heavy cruiser. Up till now, thought Rhaman grimly, his deadly opponent, Halton, had had things far too much his own way. In the morning the British commander was going to have the surprise of his life!

Chapter 18

For a few moments, after Rhaman had finished speaking, Morrison wondered whether to wake up Halton and tell him what had happened. Then he decided that this news could wait; the destroyer's Captain needed his rest. An hour before dawn, if the night continued to remain quiet, he would have both the Captain and his second in command called, and hand over the ship again. Six or eight hours' uninterrupted sleep would ensure that when they came back on the bridge the two men would have all their wits about them. Somehow, Morrison felt, tomorrow was going to be one of those days, when they would all need to be very much on the alert.

Although the ex-Naval Attaché could not possibly have known all the reactions to Rhaman's broadcast, he did appreciate that the rebel leader had just done the British a good turn. The Ministry of Defence would have confirmation that the *Phoenix* was still very much an effective unit of the Royal Navy. Some time around noon the next day, according to their last two way contact with London, the British cruiser would be arriving, and the destroyer's lonely vigil would be over. It was, however, thought Morrison, the other possible arrivals to Zembasia that they were more concerned about for the moment. So far there had been no news nor sign of the Chinese supply ships, nor, thank God, the new Zembasian cruiser *Umled*.

If their own cruiser managed to get there first then the two British warships, operating together, would easily be able to intercept and thwart the arrival of the Chinese supply ships. Rhaman, without the essential supplies and specialist personnel that they were carrying, would not be able to sustain his revolt for much longer. On board the cruiser was a contingent of Royal Marines who should be able to recapture the all important airfield, taken by the rebels soon after the British had evacuated their civilians, and hold on to it until reinforcements could be flown in by the R.A.F.

Should the *Umled* arrive later, and if she chose to fight, then the two British ships should prove a match for her. The Zembasian cruiser, although she carried a heavier armament than both the British ships combined, would have to dissipate her fire power upon two targets that would be carrying out hard evasive tactics. Morrison also knew, from naval reports, that the six inch guns in 'Tiger' class cruisers were semi-automatic, and accurately aimed by radar. This ship could produce such a volume of fire that should, combined with the lesser effort of the *Phoenix* from another direction, prove enough to put the *Umled* quickly out of action. Although the rebels would fight with all the zeal of fanatics, their steadiness and accuracy under heavy fire was unlikely to compare with that of the British.

Throughout the hours of darkness, in conjunction with the visual lookout that was being maintained, the destroyer's search radar had been constantly probing far beyond the range of human eyes. Halton had given orders for this, in case any of the Chinese supply ships tried to slip past them into Toulage. They were not far enough out to sea, fortunately, for the radar screen to be cluttered up with any responses from the busy shipping lane that lay further out from the Zembasian coast.

Now, interrupting Morrison's speculations about the *Umled*, a radar rating appeared on the bridge to report that a blip had suddenly appeared on the screen, at almost maximum range. Furthermore, the rating went on, the response was almost certainly that of a large ship steering straight towards them.

146

Having scanned the radar screen and confirmed to his own satisfaction the rating's report, Morrison gave orders for Halton to be called. With a contact such as this he knew that the destroyer's Captain would have to be informed at once. Glancing at his watch, he saw that the time was 0445 hours; Halton would have been called soon anyway.

Within five minutes the Captain came up on the bridge, looking spruce and alert. Having sincerely thanked Morrison – the Naval Attaché had stood almost a double watch – he went to look at the radar screen, while Morrison briefly related the content of Rhaman's broadcast. Halton smiled wryly at being accused of piracy, but as Morrison had earlier on, commented that Rhaman had certainly done them a favour in letting the Ministry of Defence know that all was well with the *Phoenix*. Then he went on:

'Well, sir, that contact is almost certainly heading straight in towards Toulage, and at the moment we are right in its path. I estimate it has a speed of about fifteen knots. If it continues at that rate it will have the harbour in sight at dawn.'

'What do you think it is?' Halton lowered his voice. 'In my view, there can be only two possibilities. It could be the *Umled,* or alternatively it could be the first of the Chinese supply ships arriving. God help us if it *is* the *Umled* – we shall have to get out of the way fast! The main snag is, though, that if we assume it's the *Umled* and do get out, it might well turn out to be one of the Chinese ships, and if we give it too wide a berth now, with that damned propeller gone, we wouldn't be able to catch it up in time to stop it getting into Toulage. It seems to me we've got to take a chance; stay where we are, until we know what it is, or until daylight breaks.'

Morrison nodded. In one hour's time it would be broad daylight, and if the radar contact held its course and speed, the oncoming ship would be quickly identified. If it was burning lights they should be able to see something in about twenty minutes time. Even with normal navigation lights though, night identification, with a few obvious exceptions like well lit up liners and small fishing craft bobbing up and down, could prove extremely difficult.

One distinct advantage which the *Phoenix* had over the unidentified ship was that she was steaming under complete

147

blackout. This, combined with the long, low outline characteristic of destroyers, almost certainly ensured that she would not be seen first by the other ship. It might mean a gain of only a few minutes, but this asset could be vital, as had been proved in the Second World War by submarines shadowing convoys on the surface.

Drew joined the small group on the bridge looking, like his Captain, very much better for the long sleep he had been allowed to have. Assuring Morrison that he would be called when the situation began to resolve itself, Halton managed to persuade the Naval Attaché to go below and get his head down. After bringing Drew up to date with the events of the night, and in particular with the significance of Rhaman's broadcast, Halton proceeded to explain his proposed plan of action.

If the unidentified contact turned out to be a Chinese supply ship, it would be a comparatively straightforward matter; they would intercept it at once. If the ship could not be persuaded to heave to peacefully, a boarding party would be put on her. Those supply ships must be prevented at all costs from getting to Toulage.

Should the contact turn out to be the *Umled*, however, the *Phoenix* would have to avoid, if possible, getting too near the big cruiser. Rhaman might not want to risk his latest warship chasing a destroyer round the coast of Zembasia. Once safely inside the harbour, the cruiser, with its eight inch guns and numerous crew, would be in a position to dominate a large area of the town and the narrow entrance from the sea to Toulage.

When the Chinese supply ships were sighted, or made radio contact with the rebels, Halton continued, that would be the time for the *Umled* to come out and escort them in. If the British warships tried to stop these merchant ships she could effectively intervene, and even if she was destroyed herself – which would certainly be a disaster for the rebels – her sacrifice would have been justified. In the heat of the battle against such a large opponent the British warships, with all their efforts concentrated in fighting, would not be able to stop the supply ships from getting to their goal. Not for the first time Drew appreciated his Captain's ability to put himself in his opponent's place and then make his plans accordingly.

Meanwhile, Halton said, returning to the immediate problem in hand, the ship's company would go to 'Action Statons' just before dawn. This would be at 0545 hours – in another half-an-hour. At the same time the engine room must stand by to make as much speed as possible at a moment's notice. With only one propeller – Halton had already checked with the senior engineer officer – this could only be, at best, just over twenty knots. It was damned bad luck that they should be without that propeller, just when it was needed most.

Leaving Drew in charge of the bridge, to supervise the coming 'Action Stations' and get the ship's company thoroughly prepared before daylight came, Halton concentrated his own attention mainly on the radar screen. Slowly the unknown contact crept down the screen. At a range of fifteen miles Halton decided to turn his ship directly towards the contact. On a reciprocal heading, at a relative velocity of thirty knots, the two ships would come together in a half-an-hour. This would coincide, within a few minutes, with dawn.

However, before actual daylight came Drew and the bridge lookouts should be able to sight and identify the oncoming ship. If she was burning navigation lights it should be possible to spot her at about ten miles. By heading straight towards the unidentified ship, apart from cutting down the time to sighting, the arc of search for the lookouts was narrowed down to virtually dead ahead. Unfortunately the sky had become rather overcast, and patches of low cloud blotted out the moon intermittently cutting down visibility.

Once again the crew of the *Phoenix* went quietly to their action stations. Drew, up on the bridge, received the flow of reports as each section came to the ready. When the contact was ten miles away, with no visual sighting report, Halton decided to go back on the bridge. He left the operator instructions to keep him informed of the contact's range at one mile intervals, and any alteration of heading.

Taking his customary quick look round, he noted that all was in order. It was still dark and, after the artificial warmth of the radar compartment, quite cold. Streaking past each side of the ship were the tips of phosphorescent waves, the scattered remains of the bow wave, as the destroyer cleaved her way through the calm sea. Apart from the familiar swish of the water against the thin hull plating, and the low hum of the turbines, all was quiet up there in the open air. At first no one noticed Halton's arrival; Drew, the officer of the watch and the lookouts were all busy searching ahead with their binoculars. Then the First Lieutenant, lowering his glasses for a moment, saw his Captain and said:

'Nothing doing, sir. We've not spotted her yet. Any idea how far away she is now?'

Before Halton could reply, the radar operator reported, 'Nine miles, sir – still heading straight towards us.'

Halton made the necessary acknowledgement. Then he said, 'Well, there's your answer, Number One. We should be seeing something shortly.'

Nine miles – eighteen minutes at the closing speed. Peering into the darkness ahead, like most of the other personnel on the bridge, Halton could not see any sudden interruption on the almost indeterminate horizon. Resting his eyes for a brief moment, he noticed a very slight paling of the dark sky above – the pre-dawn flush was coming. Visibility was not all that bad, he thought to himself. They should have seen that ship by now, especially if she was burning lights.

Lights, lights.... his mind was beginning to work quickly. A merchant ship would almost certainly have navigation lights, especially if she was nearing a strange coast. On the other hand the *Umled*, whose Captain must know these waters, would not want to announce her arrival, especially if her Captain had had radio contact with the rebels – which was almost a certainty – and knew that a British destroyer was patrolling off the coast. Quickly he made up his mind. The unidentified ship could only be the *Umled*; he must act accordingly.

'Full starboard rudder. Take her round ninety degrees and then steady on that heading.'

The coxswain acknowledged his Captain's order and the destroyer, heeling gently outwards, commenced her turn. Drew and the lookouts, informed of the alteration of heading, trained their binoculars slowly round to maintain the relative bearing on the spot where the unidentified ship should appear. As the destroyer steadied on her new heading, eight miles range was called by the radar operator, but there was still nothing in sight.

Halton, having decided that the radar contact *must* be the *Umled*, gave orders to the engine room to bring their speed

150

up to twenty knots. At the same time he told Smythe – the senior engineer officer was in direct command of his department – to be prepared at short notice for smoke screen operations. It was extremely important for Drew as second in command to know exactly what Halton's intentions were in case anything happened to the Captain. Taking the first lieutenant quietly on one side, so as not to distract other bridge personnel from their duties, Halton explained the situation and his plan of action.

For the next twelve minutes the *Phoenix* would continue on the new heading, and this should take her four miles out of the direct track of the *Umled*. (Drew agreed with his Captain's reasons for deciding that the unidentified contact *was* the new Zembasian cruiser.) At some time during this run of twelve minutes, with dawn rapidly approaching, they should be able to sight the ship. Even if they did not, however, this would not affect the next part of the plan, unless by some remote chance it turned out to be one of the Chinese supply ships. Should this be the case, the *Phoenix* would simply turn about and carry out an interception.

Assuming that it proved to be the *Umled*, at the end of this twelve minute run the *Phoenix* would turn ninety degrees to port and head out to sea. In any case, when the twelve minutes were up she would be committed to turn one way or the other, to miss the long peninsula that jutted out into the South Atlantic. A starboard turn would take them back, if they followed the coast far enough, to the harbour entrance of Toulage. Then, once the *Umled* had spotted them, the *Phoenix* would be trapped and forced into a fight which, with the land so close behind her, would be very much in favour of the cruiser. On the other hand, with a port turn to the sea there was a slender chance that the *Umled* might miss seeing them altogether. Even if she did, the *Phoenix* would have the advantage of the open sea ahead in which she could carry out evasive action, rather than be hemmed in by the peninsula.

A sudden shout from the officer of the watch revealed that the radar contact had at last been spotted. Halton, like all the other men on the bridge, swung round with his binoculars towards the relative bearing of the sighting. It was now almost daylight and there, right in the middle of his glasses, was a cruiser just emerging from a patch of localised sea mist. Not surprising that she had not been spotted before, thought Halton, as he studied the ship carefully. Three large gun turrets, two forward and one aft; flush decked, and with two narrow funnels close together. Having closely studied the photographs and outline drawings in 'Jane's Fighting Ships' he knew for certain that this was the *Umled*.

Glancing at his watch Halton noticed that eleven minutes of the pre-determined twelve had just elapsed. Excited chatter had broken out amongst the bridge personnel as the lookouts spotted and recognised the large cruiser. An approximate range of six miles was reported, on Halton's query, by the radar operator. Drew had also noted the time, and after a terse comment about the *Umled*'s appearance, reminded Halton that they should be turning to port in the next few seconds. Halton nodded, and gave the appropriate helm orders. This time it was going to have to be a very gentle turn, Halton warned the coxswain; a sudden movement would be noticed more quickly by lookouts on the cruiser. Every minute they could gain without being spotted by the *Umled* would put them that much nearer to the comparative safety of the sea.

Slowly the destroyer's bows came round and then, when the sea was dead ahead, steadied on the new heading. So far so good. Halton was almost certain they had not been spotted for the moment. Maintaining what was now a reciprocal course, the *Umled* was heading steadily in towards Toulage. Her light grey hull showed a few reddish rust streaks, evidence of her long passage from South America, Halton noticed, keeping his glasses trained on the large cruiser. With any luck at all her lookouts and officers would now be studying the coast ahead, looking for the buoy-marked channel that led to the harbour entrance.

Hugging the high coast of the long peninsula, approximately one mile off to starboard – as near as she could safely afford to be – the *Phoenix* was not standing out as a stark silhouette. On board the *Umled* all still appeared to be quite normal; her powerful eight inch gun turrels remained trained fore and aft, and as yet there had been no alteration of speed and course.

* * *

Captain Dogmar, on board the *Umled*, was uneasy. Although

nothing much was expected to happen that night, it might be a different case in the morning. If only the hastily installed radar had been serviceable he might have felt a good deal more relaxed. A few more days, he thought angrily, perhaps even hours, spent at the South American base where they had collected his ship would almost certainly have ensured this.

Right in the middle of the *Umled's* necessarily lengthy acceptance trials Rhaman's message had arrived instructing Dogmar to take over the ship and return immediately. This news had been conveyed to him very discreetly by Zembasia's resident Military Attaché, who was another of Rhaman's trusted supporters. If the naval commander in chief, now securely locked up below, had got wind of what was taking place in his country, the *Umled* would have been sailing on an entirely different mission. As it was they had only just managed to clear the port and at the same time take over the ship before the Zembasian revolution became world news.

Like so many others, Dogmar had listened to his leader's broadcast, but to him, not unnaturally, the event was certainly not startling news. Long before his broadcast Rhaman, using his top secret frequency, had made contact with the *Umled* and passed on all the latest information concerning the progress of the revolution. During the night several messages had been passed to and from Toulage. In answer to repeated questions from Rhaman, Dogmar was forced to admit that it was impossible to pick up a sighting of the British *Phoenix*, as he was sailing blind without radar. This had evoked an angry response from the rebel leader, who would never accept excuses from his subordinates, no matter how genuine they were. Dogmar was told to slow down and delay his arrival in the Bay of Zembasia until dawn.

Staring into the darkness from the vantage point of his high bridge, Dogmar was feeling distinctly nervous. Apart from the tremendous responsibility of commanding an unfamiliar 12,000 ton cruiser – prior to this hasty appointment he had never commanded anything except a small destroyer – he knew that his ship was the lynch pin of the revolution. If the *Umled* failed to reach Toulage on time Rhaman stood little chance of seeing his grand scheme come to fruiton. The much more lightly armed *Alched*, now partially disabled after the bombing attack, could no longer be considered as an effective

153

deterrent. The surprise appearance of the *Umled* would give fresh impetus, desperately needed, to the revolution.

Somewhere out there in the darkness that shrouded them like a heavy cloak was a British destroyer. This ship, whose commander was obviously no fool, judging by the havoc that he had already created, was almost certainly in radar contact with the *Umled*, and Dogmar expected at any moment to see torpedo tracks which would put an end to all Rhaman's hopes and plans – and to himself, his crew and his ship.

No one had informed Dogmar that *Phoenix* no longer carried torpedo tubes – a strange omission, for Rhaman was a stickler for detail. The Captain had not had time to obtain the latest 'Jane's' before sailing and so, professional seaman that he was, he had taken all normal precautions for their last night at sea. Lookouts had been doubled, a high state of readiness, just short of full manning for 'Action Stations', was being maintained and no external lights were visible as the cruiser steamed comparatively slowly towards her destination.

Presently the pre-dawn pale flush began to lighten the dark sky. Soon it would be full daylight, and Dogmar would be able to shake off this unpleasant feeling of being a blind fugitive in the dark. In the daytime, with no other comparable warship within several thousand miles, the *Umled* could destroy anything afloat. Should the *Phoenix* be in sight then, nothing could save the small British ship which had interfered so persistently with the revolution.

Glancing round the bridge, the Zembasian Captain noticed with extreme displeasure that the officer of the watch and most of the lookouts were concentrating their searching ahead, looking for buoys or landmarks that would lead them home. He reprimanded the officer sharply ordering him to organise all the lookouts into a proper search pattern. Dawn was flooding in rapidly now, and visibility improving perceptively every minute. Below decks the rest of the ship's company were being roused; after the long hours of quiet the *Umled* was stirring and coming to life again.

A radio message was coming through from Rhaman's headquarters; one of the rebel army patrols had reported seeing the *Phoenix* moving slowly along the peninsula towards the sea. Quickly the bridge lookouts and Dogmar trained their binoculars round to port in the general direction of the peninsula. Within a few minutes they had spotted the British destroyer. Alarm bells rang out their urgent message, and Dogmar, with grim satisfaction, brought his ship to 'Action Stations'. Now the British was going to pay for their arrogant stupidity in becoming involved in the revolution!

* * *

One thousand feet above the dark wastes of the South Atlantic, Lieutenant Commander Brian Saddler, the senior observer of the British cruiser's air detachment, was studying the instruments of the Decca navigation equipment installed in the Wessex helicopter in which he was flying. Ten minutes before, at exactly 0430 hours local time, they had taken off from the small flight deck at the rear of the cruiser. The heavily pitching flight deck was a mere postage stamp compared with the large aircraft carriers to which Saddler was accustomed, and the young pilot, a marine lieutenant, was hindered by the darkness, but somehow he had managed to get the large helicopter airborne.

If their mission had not been so urgent no one in their right mind would have authorised such a hazardous take off under these conditions, especially at night. Saddler was fervently thankful that young Bob Stannard had got them into the air safely. What the signal rating from the cruiser – it was his first flight ever – felt about all this was anyone's guess, thought Saddler. Still, they had managed it, and were well on their way to the *Phoenix*. When they had to return to their ship it would be broad daylight, and landing would be a great deal easier.

One hundred and fifty miles from the position from which they had been launched lay the the centre part of the large bay of Zembasia. At their present speed they should reach there in an hour and a half. Dawn was at 0600 hours, but with the advantage of their height, it would be daylight about a quarter of an hour earlier than down at sea level. As it was going to be a completely unfamiliar landfall for all of them, this was just as well.

For an hour the helicopter flew on steadily, and during this period covered a distance of 110 miles, helped along by a gentle tail wind. Only forty miles to go; in twenty five minutes at the latest, Saddler told the pilot and the signalman, they

155

would be arriving in the Bay of Zembasia. Dawn was coming up fast, and soon they would be able to dispense with interior lighting.

To make sure of a good landfall Saddler told the pilot to alter heading ten degrees port. He had decided to use the old homing method; aiming deliberately to one side of the target, then when they crossed the coast, turning starboard to follow the coast until they came to the point they were aiming for. This would ensure their successful location of the target point, and would save wasting time looking for unfamiliar landmarks. Ten degrees off to one side of their original track, for a distance of forty miles, would put them just over six miles north of the centre of the bay. Glancing at his chart, Saddler estimated that their new landfall should be the tip of the peninsula. He passed this information on to the others, telling them exactly what to look out for. He knew that three pairs of eyes searching ahead stood a better chance than one of spotting a pre-described target.

Two minutes after the helicopter had taken up its new heading Stannard, the pilot, suddenly asked the observer to take a look out of the side window. There below them – fortunately there was a large break in the low lying stratus cloud – was a a large merchant ship ploughing her way steadily through the sea. Quickly Saddler marked the position and time on his chart, and after watching the ship for a few moments, noted its heading.

There was no doubt about it, he told the pilot, this ship was heading straight for Toulage. From its bow wave and wake he estimated that she was making a good fifteen knots, and with approximately thirty miles to run, should arrive there in about two hours. With the time that they had gained through the tail wind, it might be worth doing an orbit round the ship to try and identify her. Stannard brought the helicopter round through 180 degrees and, during the long turn, dropped down to one hundred feet. Flying along the merchant ship's side, and a little more than a hundred yards away from her, the helicopter crew were able to study her in detail.

Fifteen thousand tons, and deeply loaded, noted Saddler. No visible deck cargo, and wearing the Chinese Republic's flag, added the signalman. This last piece of information was vital. It was just as well the signalman, who was used to recognising wind-whipped flags, had come along on this trip, Saddler realised. Both he and the senior pilot had been carefully briefed, prior to this mission, on the Zembasian situation, and knew of the potential threat of Chinese intervention. When they got to the *Phoenix*, Saddler told the pilot, one of their first communications must be to let the destroyer's Captain know about this merchant ship hurrying towards the trouble spot.

Resuming its original course, the helicopter continued on its way to Zembasia. Soon, ahead lay the blurred outline of the mainland; the details would shortly become very clear. Slightly to their right was the seaward end of the peninsula they were expecting to see, and when they got overhead Stannard asked Saddler, in anticipation of their pending landfall, what sort of search pattern the observer wanted to set up to look for the *Phoenix* if she was not in sight. It would be advisable, Saddler replied, to start climbing gently now – less fuel would be used – up to 2,000 feet. From that height they would be able to see any ships in the bay, and the *Phoenix*, with her destroyer's characteristic outline, should be easily identifiable.

Turning to the signalman, Saddler told him to make ready with Aldis lamp and message pad. He had barely finished speaking when a tap on the shoulder from Stannard made him look out quickly. There, just below them, lay the *Phoenix* – but it was not at the destroyer Stannard was pointing. Approximately five miles dead ahead was a large cruiser. As the three men watched, they saw to their horror that the cruiser's turrets were training round until they pointed straight at the British destroyer. Then her eight inch guns erupted in tongues of orange flame as she opened fire with a full broadside.

Chapter 19

Everything was moving far too smoothly, remarked Halton

uneasily to Drew, as the *Phoenix* steadily headed out towards the open sea. The atmosphere on the destroyer's bridge was, not surprisingly, tense. Less than five miles away, on their port side, the Zembasian cruiser *Umled* held her parallel opposing course towards Toulage. At any moment the early morning stillness could be shattered by naval gunfire. However, whatever happened in the next few minutes, the *Phoenix* would not be caught napping. Anticipating action, Halton had already given careful instructions to the coxswain and senior engineer officer.

Nevertheless gnawing doubts kept flooding through the destroyer Captain's mind. He was very conscious of the fact that two hundred British lives depended upon his doing the right thing at the right time. On reflection it might have been wiser to take his ship away from the danger zone the previous day, while there was still time. With only one propeller in action, he had had every excuse; no one could have criticised such a decision. And yet if he *had* done that, the entrance to Toulage would have been left wide open for a long period- - long enough to have allowed the rebels to consolidate their position. In the event the Chinese supply ships had not turned up, but at the time he had made his decision Halton could not have foreseen this. It was always the same, he thought, recalling other dangerous situations he had been in; this waiting period, when every minute seemed as long as an hour....

A warning shout came suddenly from Drew. The waiting period was over.

'*Umled* has just spotted us - her turrets are beginning to train round.'

'Thank you, Number One,' replied Halton calmly, and deliberately keeping his voice low he went on to give his orders.

'Port hard - turn through ninety degrees and then steady on that heading, coxswain.'

'Aye, aye sir.' The immediate response from Gray was equally steady.

'Full speed ahead - give us all you can.' With only one propeller turning, Halton was aware of the difficulties of his engine room department.

'Gunnery director - forward guns to open fire as soon as they bear. We are within range.'

158

Heeling heavily outwards in her turn, the *Phoenix* came round fast and took up her new heading. By deliberately pointing straight towards the hostile cruiser Halton had, with one quick command, put the *Umled* under a double disadvantage. First he had reduced her target area from the destroyer's length of 360 feet to her beam of a mere 40 feet. Secondly, the cruiser's range finders would not be so accurate in determining the exact range, with a target that was rapidly changing the distance between them. These two important factors would almost certainly ensure that the powerful eight inch guns, when they first opened fire, were going to miss their target.

The officers and men gathered on the bridge of the *Phoenix* saw the guns of the *Umled* sparkle into life. Then came an eerie whistling roar, something akin to the noise of an express train rushing by, as the eight inch shells hurtled over the destroyer. Halton and his crew ducked instinctively, though this was a futile gesture to a danger that had already passed. Both he and Drew looked astern and as Halton had anticipated, nine large fountains of water arose slightly less than a half mile behind them. This was damned good shooting, he commented grudgingly to his first lieutenant. If the *Phoenix* had not taken rapid evasive action there was little doubt that at least one of those shells would have been a direct hit. Finally came the dull rumble, caused by the much slower travelling sound waves, of the cruiser's guns.

Two loud explosions made the *Phoenix* tremble as both the forward 4.5 inch guns opened fire; a tonic to the crew, realising that they were hitting back at the enemy. Both the shells fell just in front of the cruiser's bows, and an idea suddenly occurred to Halton. If his gunners concentrated their fire on the front area of the cruiser, it should be possible to score at least two or three direct hits. These would force the cruiser to reduce speed immediately, thus allowing the *Phoenix* to make her escape.

Quickly he gave orders to the gunnery officer, and then informed Drew of his intentions. The performance of the unexpected was the only real chance his ship had now against such a superior enemy; they were speeding towards the *Umled*, which now lay only four miles ahead, but this could not continue – it would mean almost certain destruction.

159

Picking up the engine room telephone, Halton gave instructions for an immediate smoke screen to be laid. Down below, the senior engineer officer, who had been standing by for just such an eventuality, relayed the order to the waiting engine room artificer, and soon thick, black, oily smoke was belching out of the *Phoenix*'s funnel and streaking astern, to lie like a heavy cloud on the sea. Into this the destroyer would retire to seek a temporary respite – but Halton had decided to carry out the manoeuvre in a completely unconventional manner. As far as he knew, what he had in mind had not been done before, and it was going to surprise both the enemy and his own crew.

'Direct hit – right on her bows, sir!' reported Drew, with obvious satisfaction. Sure enough a jagged hole had appeared just above the *Umled*'s waterline, right at the front, marring the smooth upward sweep of her bows. If only they could keep up this standard of shooting without being hit seriously themselves, a few more well placed shells would certainly force the cruiser to cut down her speed. For every eight inch shell fired by the enemy, the *Phoenix* could get off five, for her lighter guns were much easier to handle

Another broadside arrived from the *Umled*, and this time the shells landed just ahead of the destroyer, blotting out the cruiser for a moment. Straddled, by God! thought Halton desperately. The enemy was getting his range problems sorted out accurately; one over, one under, and then, with the extremely accurate range that would have been computed from these shots, the third broadside should land right on the target. Just as Halton was about to give orders which should upset the enemy's calculations, one of the lookouts shouted suddenly:

'Helicopter coming in from the port beam, sir! Looks like one of our Wessexes.'

'Check on that, Number One. Tell the Bofors guns to stand by, just in case,' ordered Halton quickly; then switching on the ship's loudspeaker system he made a brief announcement.

'This is the Captain speaking. Stand by, everybody – we are about to go full speed astern. We are going backwards into the smoke screen for cover.'

He then gave orders to the engine room. To bring a ship of 2,500 tons to a dead stop, from a speed of over twenty knots, and then start going astern was going to take time, distance and effort. It was the latter that was immediately obvious as, with the propeller now turning over in the opposite direction at full revolutions, the *Phoenix* began to shudder under the forces of deceleration. Everyone grabbed at something with one hand, to avoid pitching forwards on their faces.

Halton knew that those aboard the *Umled* would be expecting the *Phoenix* to make use at any moment of the thick smoke screen she had been laying. The Zembasian Captain would be expecting the destroyer to carry out a turn through 180 degrees to do this, and was probably waiting for a sight of the full side of his opponent when she turned, presenting a bigger target to his guns. Halton, however, by carrying out this unusual manoeuvre, was presenting his opponent with the same small target area as before; just the narrow beam of his ship. Furthermore, by coming to a stop and then reversing, the range changes would not be consistent. All this should throw the *Umled's* gunners into confusion, and at the same time enhance the *Phoenix's* chances of avoiding the huge destructive potential of her enemy.

Now that his ship was committed to the planned course of action, Halton had time for a brief moment to turn his attention to the helicopter that had suddenly arrived on the scene. Thank God it had turned out to be British, he thought. The *Phoenix* had enough on her plate without the unwelcome interference of an enemy aircraft! This Wessex had undoubtedly come from the British cruiser, and its mere presence meant that a superior force could not be very far away now.

'She's identified herself, sir,' reported Drew, adding, 'No chance of radio contact, but thank the Lord they've come prepared with an Aldis lamp.'

'Thank you, Number One. Get a signal off quickly, please. Tell him to stay well clear of us until we get behind the smoke screen. We might be able to make use of him then.'

So saying, Halton turned once again to the more immediate business of fighting his ship. Nearly all the forward way of the destroyer was off now, and in a matter of a few seconds they would be going astern fairly fast into the comparative safety of the thick smoke. Another broadside from the *Umled* landed ahead of them; just about the position, remarked Drew, that the *Phoenix* would have been had she continued on her previous course. Two more shots from the destroyer had meanwhile scored direct hits in the forward part of the *Umled*, one of these shots, the gunnery officer reported with almost certainty, had landed just on the cruiser's waterline. Thomson must be right, thought Halton; the bow wave of the *Umled* had been reduced considerably since the action began. Now there might be a real chance of getting away without damage.

Thick black smoke engulfed the *Phoenix* as she slid into the smoke screen. For the moment at least, she was completely out of sight of the enemy cruiser. When they had backed a little further into the evil smelling stuff, whose acrid sulphur fumes brought tears to their eyes and caused outbursts of coughing amongst those members of the crew in exposed positions, Halton intended to turn the ship round through 180 degrees and leave the smoke behind. With the smoke screen between her and the *Umled* – it should persist for another five to ten minutes – the destroyer would be free to move in any direction. At the same time they could make good use of the helicopter for spotting the *Umled*'s movements.

Drew said: 'The helicopter has just reported, sir, that on the way here they passed over a Chinese cargo ship heading this way. They estimate that it should be here in about two hours.'

'Thank you, Number One.' Halton nodded, then continued, 'Can't honestly say I'm surprised – we've been expecting this for some time now. Somehow, although God knows how at the moment, we've got to stop her from getting through. The others won't be far behind, and if they get into Toulage we'll all have been wasting our time.'

'Helicopter reports that the *Umled* is coming straight towards us, sir,' reported the young signal rating urgently, the Captain having earlier taken the precaution of detailing a signalman specifically to liaise with the helicopter. Halton wanted to know whether the helicopter was able to make an estimate of the cruiser's speed. This information was vital, for from it he could deduce whether or not the *Phoenix*'s shooting had been effective. If she had failed to weaken the cruiser's bows her own situation would become critical.

Deciding that his ship had gone back far enough into the smoke screen, Halton gave his order for 'Full Ahead', and immediately told the coxswain to put the helm hard over. Slowly at first, the *Phoenix* began to come round, and then

162

as the rudder really began to get a firm grip, her turning momentum rapidly increased. Judging this movement to a nicety, the experienced Gray put on opposite rudder to counteract the swing, just in time to ensure that the destroyer headed straight down the line of smoke.

For the time being at least Halton had decided to keep laying smoke, which would add to the confusion of the *Umled's* gunners, and he gave orders to the coxswain to adopt a mean course zigzag pattern. This would worry the enemy even more, for when he broke through the first already thinning smoke screen, he would be faced with an even thicker layer of smoke.

The helicopter reported that the *Umled's* estimated speed was reduced to sixteen knots. At last the *Phoenix* now had the advantage of speed; even operating with only one propeller it began to look as though she would have at least a five knot edge over her opponent. Such an edge could get her safely out of the danger zone, and equally important, she should manage to get to the Chinese ship before the cruiser could stop them intervening and make her alter course.

The smoke-begrimed battle ensigns, which had been hoisted automatically when the *Phoenix* went to 'Action Stations', fluttered proudly at the foremast, small mainmast gaff and the quarterdeck ensign staff. Catching a glimpse of them just for a moment, as the destroyer gathered speed, Halton felt a quick thrill of pride. Under the distinctive White Ensign many battles for just causes had been fought all over the world, and now the *Phoenix* was playing her part.

All guns' crews were standing by. Up till now only the forward 4.5 inch guns had been firing, but soon the two aft 4.5's would go into action as well. The four Bofors guns were manned, but being essentially short range weapons, had not yet been required. If the enemy got close enough for them to be used, the *Phoenix* would be in serious trouble.

Flying near the British destroyer at almost sea level in order not to give position away, the helicopter had passed on all the latest information. Now Halton knew for certain that his counterpart cruiser would be arriving in less than four hours time, and the knowledge was enormously encouraging. A detachment from the Strategic Reserve was standing by, and should it prove necessary, could be flown to Zembasia within a matter of hours. In turn Halton had passed on his own information, in the compilation of which Captain Morrison had been of tremendous assistance. Within minutes the Ministry of Defence was receiving an up-to-date picture, including the very important information that the potential threat of Chinese intervention was fast becoming a reality.

Every half minute, almost to the exact second, came the deep rumble of the *Umled*'s guns. The Zembasian cruiser was obviously not prepared to give up her prey so easily. So far the destroyer's crew had seen, through the thick smoke screen which now lay heavily astern of them, only the occasional splash of an isolated shell bursting in the sea. Nevertheless, this random shooting was decidedly uncomfortable; it would only take a few direct hits – even one, if it found a vital part – to cripple the *Phoenix* and cause heavy casualties. Her only hope lay in her speed advantage, gained by the accuracy of the forward guns. It was doubtful if the *Umled* would pursue them for long, thought Halton, once she realised that the destroyer was getting further and further out of range.

Ahead of the *Phoenix* loomed the Zembasian peninsula, getting closer every minute. Halton knew that he would have to alter course drastically soon. He estimated, from the depths marked on the chart, that they could go to within a half mile. If they went in to a quarter of a mile the water was still fairly deep, but the *Umled*, with her much deeper draught, would never be able to go in so far. However, Halton doubted very much if the Zembasian Captain would be ignorant enough to run his ship aground in her home waters.

A quick glance at the automatic depth gauge revealed that water was beginning to get shallower. Shortly he was going to have to give the order for a hard port turn, through ninety degrees, and head out to sea. However, having carried out this manoeuvre, *Phoenix* would have broken cover from her protective smoke screen, and would then, for at least fifteen minutes, be running the gauntlet of the *Umled*'s guns, until she was out of range. Halton told the signal rating, standing by for his orders, to let the helicopter know that they were about to turn port hard. The helicopter was to get well out of the way, and at the same time have a quick look at the *Umled* and report her position and speed.

Just before Halton gave his helm order the helicopter

reported that the *Umled* was steadily dropping further behind. According to radar the distance between the two ships was four miles; this was to the *Phoenix*'s advantage, as the 4.5 inch guns would still be in range. Therefore Halton passed the necessary order to Thomson that they were to come out of the smoke screen with all four guns firing. The guns would keep firing continuously, as they steamed out of the bay, until it was obvious that the enemy was beyond their range. This constant rapid fire would continue to jar the enemy cruiser – with luck a few more direct hits might be achieved – and the morale of the *Phoenix*'s crew would remain high in the knowledge that they were still hitting back.

'Port hard – steady on 270 degrees. All guns' crews stand by to open rapid fire as soon as you can see the target. Engine room – stop making smoke now. Tell the helicopter to keep clear for the moment and then take up position on our starboard side.'

Halton's orders came out crisply but calmly; there must be no misunderstandings at this critical point. His last order had been given to the signalman liaising with the helicopter, and thinking of the latter, for a brief moment, Halton realised that it had been on the scene for quite a while now. He wondered just how much longer he could expect it to stay. As the *Phoenix* was completing the last part of her turn, towards the open sea horizon, he told the signalman to find out the helicopter's remaining fuel endurance.

Emerging from the smoke screen at right angles to her former track, the *Phoenix* presented an awe inspiring sight as she raced seawards. All her 4.5 inch guns were firing rapidly at the *Umled*, which had obviously been taken by surprise by this sudden appearance of the British destroyer. Almost immediately, however – albeit far more slowly than her smaller opponent – the bows of the cruiser began to swing to port, and Halton realised that the enemy was coming round to a parallel course from which, although he could not now match the *Phoenix*'s speed, he would be able to bring his full broadside into action for a considerable time. Just after the cruiser had completed her turn she opened fire again, and this time her shells fell uncomfortably close.

Every so often Halton gave orders for evading turns, judging the fall of the *Umled*'s shells. (If he carried out too many alterations of heading they would not be able to gain so much distance on their enemy.) Soon it became apparent that the distance between the two ships was gradually increasing, for the destroyer's 4.5 inch shells began to fall short of the target. At least three British shots, in this second phase of the battle, had been direct hits, including one right on the cruiser's bridge. It seemed that the *Umled* faltered for a few moments, and Halton wondered if any serious damage or casualties had been inflicted.

He had just given the 'Cease Fire', and was making a remark to Drew, when the signalman reported that the helicopter had sent an important message. From its height advantage, a minute or so before climbing about three hundred feet to get a better view of the *Umled*, its observer had spotted the Chinese supply ship heading in their direction. Soon its masts would be seen by both warships, but for the next few minutes only the British had this vital information. However, before Halton could take advantage of the news, disaster struck. The *Phoenix* shuddered violently like a creature in torment as three heavy shells plunged into her fragile hull.

Chapter 20

Throughout the entire action Captain Dogmar, on board the *Umled*, had met with ever growing difficulties. For a start, a message had come from Rhaman stating tersely that he, Dogmar, was not to risk any damage to his ship. This was a ridiculous order, Dogmar told himself angrily. How on earth was he supposed to fight the British destroyer without involving any risk at all? It was all very well in theory – obviously eight inch guns could considerably outrange the smaller guns of a destroyer; in practice his crew were not used to handling the heavy armament and complicated equipment of this ship. Therefore, when they first sighted the *Phoenix* he decided to go in close and finish her off quickly by the sheer weight of his broadside, knowing that it was unlikely the British guns would be able to inflict much damage on his heavily armoured-plated hull.

Initially, when the *Phoenix* had turned directly towards his ship, Dogmar had been taken completely by surprise. For a few minutes he wondered if the British Captain had gone mad, and was going to try to ram him. Then he realised too late that his opponent meant to hide behind the smoke screen. Soon afterwards came the damage control report from the bows – the first two bulkheads had been stove in by the British shells, combined with water pressure – and he had had to reduce forward speed considerably. From that point on, whether he liked it or not, he was committed to Rhaman's policy of playing it safe.

The appearance of the helicopter had been a nasty shock, indicating at it seemed to that a heavy British force was somewhere in the immediate vicinity. Dogmar knew that if he was foolish enough to be led into a trap by the British destroyer, not only might his ship be lost, but the revolution would fail. Then, right in the midst of an exchange of important messages with Rhaman concerning the possibility of an immediate return to Toulage, there had arrived a direct hit on the cruiser's bridge. Temporarily, at least, all his radio sets were put out of action, and Dogmar bitterly realised that he would have to break off the engagement and return to Toulage.

When the Zembasian Captain saw that his guns had scored three direct hits on the *Phoenix*, however, and realised that she must be badly damaged, he was determined to finish off his opponent. At this critical point a lookout reported masts on the distant horizon. It was too far to be able to make out exactly what vessel the masts tops belonged to, but coming from that direction was another helicopter; the first had already flown back that way. This, decided Dogmar, must be the trap into which the British were trying to lure him.

If there was an aircraft carrier out there, which seemed likely, she could be expected to launch an air strike at any moment to save the British destroyer from being sunk. Quickly the Zembasian Captain made his decision. The potential odds were too much against him to warrant the risking of the cruiser on which the cause depended. Abruptly he gave the orders that would bring his ship round on a heading for Toulage, feeling that a certain amount of honour was his for leaving the British destroyer in a sinking condition. That would serve as an example to deter others from meddling in Zembasian affairs!

* * *

Halton, like everyone else on the bridge, had been knocked off his feet by the blast from the explosions. Slowly, still dazed, he raised himself and gazed around as other men stirred and began to clamber to their feet. Realisation came to him that his ship had been badly hit, and his mind came quickly back into sharp focus.

The *Phoenix* had indeed suffered severe damage. From behind the funnel almost to the extreme stern was a tangled mess of metal plating. Both the rear 4.5 inch guns had been twisted almost out of their mountings, and their barrels pointed grotesquely to the sky, surrounded by the bodies of the men who had been working with them. One shell had penetrated into the engine room, leaving a huge jagged hole in the thin deck plating. Halton dreaded to think of the damage and casualties it must have caused below. Minor fires had broken out, but as far as he could tell these seemed to be already well under control. Amid the groans and cries of wounded men, Halton staggered to the microphone of the ship's loudspeaker system and began to give his orders.

'This is the Captain speaking – pay attention everybody. Doctor and stretcher bearers to aft guns' crews immediately. Damage control parties close up and report to the First Lieutenant on the quarter deck.'

A quick aside to Drew, also fortunately unhurt, sent the latter hurrying off while Halton continued speaking.

'Keep calm, men. There is no immediate danger, so let's get the ship back in business again. I shall keep you informed of all developments. That is all.'

Reaching for the engine room telephone, he found Smythe, the senior engineer officer, ready with his report.

The shell which had penetrated through to the engine room had, miraculously, made a direct hit on the useless port engine. There was no one working near at the time, and consequently there were only a few minor casualties. The starboard engine was still fully serviceable.

Halton could hardly contain his relief; he had been fully

prepared to hear shocking news. However, before ending this initial report Smythe struck a note of caution. Flooding had been reported, and he was going to investigate. He would let the Captain know as soon as possible what the damage was.

Next came an anxious message from the helicopter enquiring after casualties and damage. Fuel was running low, but could they, before they departed, do anything more for the *Phoenix?* Yes, Halton replied urgently. On its return flight to the ship could the helicopter first fly in the direction of the Chinese ship? The masts of the latter had just appeared over the horizon, and might be taken by the Zembasians for another British warship. Their suspicions might be further increased if the helicopter and the destroyer both began to head for those masts. By economising on fuel, the helicopter observer replied, they could also simulate a return flight from the Chinese ship, which would no doubt heighten the Zembasians' suspicions. As he watched the helicopter swing away, Halton's attention was attracted by an exclamation from Drew, standing beside him.

'Good God, sir – look!'

Looking in the direction the First Lieutenant was pointing, Halton saw that the *Umled* was turning completely round away from them. She had obviously decided to break off the action! Relief flooded through him, though he maintained his outward calm. One or two more hits from those deadly eight inch shells would have blown his ship apart. As it was, the damage sustained by the *Phoenix* from the three earlier direct hits was turning out to be more serious than it had been first thought.

Two huge holes in the bottom of the destroyer – two of the three shells had penetrated right through the hull – were letting in water much faster than the remaining pumps could cope with; only two of the four high capacity pumps were working in any case. The ghastly truth was that the destroyer was very slowly sinking. There would be engine power for another twenty minutes approximately, the engineer told him. Once the water reached the boilers, that was it; and with the pumps out of action, the *Phoenix* would settle down quickly.

Twelve of the crew were dead and another twenty wounded, some badly, according to the doctor's latest report. The young surgeon lieutenant had carried out an excellent job in extremely difficult circumstances, greatly assisted by the indefatigable Captain Morrison. Working under a hastily set up awning on the quarterdeck – the small sick quarters and surgery compartment had been compltely wrecked – the two officers had sorted out the living from the dead.

The cruiser which had caused all this havoc was now gradually receding from sight towards the Zembasian coast. Halton glanced at his watch. It was nearly 0700 hours. Less than an hour before, his ship had been a very effective fighting unit of the Royal Navy; now many of his men were dead, and in twenty minutes time his ship would be no more.

He knew that he must move quickly to make the best possible use of the short time he had left to him. Twenty miles from land, and ten from the oncoming Chinese ship; to save his crew and at the same time stop the Chinese ship it was necessary to head towards the latter as fast as possible. If he turned towards the shore, the *Phoenix* would sink with at least ten miles to go. All three of the destroyer's boats had been so badly damaged as to render them unusable. There would be little chance of any of the wounded surviving, and even if the British cruiser came along in about three hours' time, there could be no guarantee that she would be able to spot the rest of the crew. As Halton knew from experience, a few heads bobbing on the surface were difficult to pick out even if it was known that they were there.

As soon as he had given orders to Gray, in the steering compartment, to head straight for the Chinese ship which was now clearly visible, Halton explained his plan to Drew and Morrison. They were going to go right alongside the cargo ship and take her over. As soon as the initial boarding party, under the command of Drew, had got a firm foothold, the rest of the destroyer's crew would be quickly transferred across. Although it was impossible to save the *Phoenix* from sinking, further loss of life could and must be avoided. Having said this, the destroyer Captain's next order took everyone by surprise. Turning to the signal rating he said:

'Haul down the ensign and hoist the Zembasian flag. Quickly!'

The startled rating, to his credit, carried out his Captain's unusual order without question. Fortunately, due to their recent official visit to the country, the Zembasian flag was readily available at the top of the signal locker. Drew looked at Halton with a bewilderment that was clearly shared by the rest of the bridge personnel.

'All right, Number One, I haven't gone off my head!' Halton assured him, with the merest trace of a smile. Then he continued. 'There is a very good reason for this. I think I'd better have a word with the ship's company.'

He switched on the loudspeaker system and commenced his short broadcast.

'This is the Captain speaking. We are heading straight for the Chinese ship, as you can all see, and we are going to board her. I shall be running up alongside her, and the boarding party, to be detailed off by the First Lieutenant, will get on board her as quickly as possible. The rest of us – wounded first, of course – will transfer to her without delay, before the *Phoenix* goes down.

'We are flying the Zembasian flag deliberately so that the Chinese will think we are a welcoming committee, and not try to avoid us. Just before we go alongside we shall fly our own colours. There is a lot to be done in the next quarter of an hour, and I want all personnel not on essential duty below to come up on the main deck immediately. Carry on.'

In an orderly manner the ship's company carried out their duties. The wounded were gently moved forward to the fo'castle; Halton intended using this highest deck, near enough level with the deck of the merchant ship, as a jumping off point for the operation. The boarding party began to assemble there, and Thomson, the gunnery officer, and the chief gunner's mate supervised the issue of small arms to all who could carry them. Down below in the engineroom, only the senior engineer officer remained with a handful of men. Smythe and his staff were fighting a losing battle in trying to stem the incoming flood, but had received strict instructions from the Captain that the engine room was to be abandoned and steam pressure released well before the water reached the boilers.

So far the Chinese ship had not given any signs of recognising the *Phoenix* for what she really was. If the merchant ship had altered course away from her, there was no doubt that the destroyer would have sunk before she could catch up. In case this happened Halton had ordered No. 1

gun's crew to be ready to open fire. Their first shot was to be aimed as close to the merchant ship's bows as possible; it was unlikely that the Captain, with his highly explosive cargo, would ignore this international signal for heaving to.

Down on the fo'castle Drew had everything well under control. Hawsers and boarding nets were neatly laid out ready for instant use, and the boarding party was fully armed and ready to go.

A half mile ahead lay the Chinese ship, which had slowed right down to welcome the warship, which she obviously thought was an ally. Quickly the distance between the two ships narrowed until, coming to the end of a 180 degree turn in order to achieve a parallel course, the *Phoenix* steadied up only two hundred yards astern of the slow moving merchant ship.

'Now,' Halton rapped out, 'haul down that damned flag and hoist our own! Number One, stand by to board. We shall be going straight alongside.'

Even if his engines failed now, he knew that the *Phoenix* had sufficient headway to bridge the gap. As he steered the destroyer up alongside the merchant ship, whose crew were gathered on the nearest side looking very puzzled, Halton ordered 'Full Astern' to bring his ship to a stop. There were loud screeching noises, and sparks flew as metal rubbed against metal. Halton, normally one of the most careful of ship handlers, had not bothered with any finesse in this last vital manoeuvre.

Drew, closely followed by the rest of the boarding party, was able to get across easily to the other ship, and as soon as they were firmly established there Halton gave orders for Smythe to stop engines, release steam pressure and get up to the fo'castle as quickly as possible. The coxswain and all the bridge personnel were ordered forward, and just before he left the bridge for the last time, Halton took one final glance round.

From the funnel burst great volumes of hissing steam. Further aft the deck was deserted, but on the fo'castle firm links had been established with the Chinese ship. All the wounded had been evacuated, and only a dozen or so of *Phoenix*'s men stood patiently awaiting their turn to go across. The reliable Drew had carried out his part of the operation to perfection.

172

As Halton made his way forward he felt the ship shudder. The water had reached the boilers already; it would not be long now before she went. It seemed somehow fitting that Gray, the coxswain, senior rating of the destroyer, should be waiting for the Captain as he reached the fo'castle. With a friendly nod, which meant more than words between the two men who had shared so many grim experiences together, Halton motioned Gray to board the merchant ship before him. It was a Captain's duty to be the last person to leave a sinking ship.

When Halton came on board the Chinese ship a ragged cheer broke out amongst his own crew, who were mainly gathered in a group just below the high bridge. Looking down from the bridge, Drew made a cheery gesture that was half wave, half salute. Groups of Chinese sailors stood sullenly, watched over by armed guards and obviously bewildered by the unforeseen happenings of the past few minutes.

Halton, escorted by some of his own men, quickly made his way up to the unfamiliar bridge. There Drew made his report, while on the other side of the bridge, under guard, stood the Chinese Captain and his officers, who were obviously protesting. Halton was pleased to learn that there had been no bloodshed at all. Everything was well under control; Smythe and his engine room ratings had gone below immediately and taken control of the radio compartment before the Chinese operators could do any damage, and were hoping to be able to use the equipment.

Before Drew could complete his report all attentions were diverted by a sudden shout from one of the the lookouts.

'She's going, sir!'

Lying barely a hundred yards astern the destroyer's bows were beginning to rise up. For a few moments there was an awed hush as the gallant little ship slid slowly, stern first on an even keel beneath the waves, carrying the dead with her. Sadly the crew watched her go, and then, quite suddenly it seemed, she disappeared completely, leaving behind a turmoil of huge bubbles and whirlpools.

Seagulls wheeled and screeched above the spot. Halton's ship was irrevocably lost.

Chapter 21

An excited telegraphist appeared on the bridge within a few seconds of the *Phoenix*'s disappearance to report that contact had been made with the British cruiser. The chief telegraphist and chief radio electrician had worked wonders with the entirely strange radio equipment, Halton realised, and he told the telegraphist so before saying that he wanted a message sent off quickly. The cruiser's Captain must be informed briefly of what had happened and asked to give his estimated time of arrival.

'Mast tops in sight on the port quarter, sir!' shouted one of the lookouts.

Both Halton and Drew swung round with their binoculars. From this bridge, a good twenty feet higher above the sea than a destroyer's bridge, Halton estimated the range to the masts to be fifteen miles. He knew that they could not belong to the British cruiser; she was at least ninety miles away. These masts were those of a cargo ship, he decided, and she was heading this way. It could only be another of the Chinese ships making for Toulage.

Somehow the other ship would have to be prevented from getting to her intended destination – although it was difficult to see how this was to be done. It had been a fairly straightforward matter for Halton to take this ship, with his guns to back him up if all else failed, but the second merchant vessel was an entirely different proposition. When she got nearer her suspicions would be aroused, seeing one of her sister ships just lying there, and she would no doubt signal to ask why. None of the *Phoenix*'s crew knew any Chinese, and it was unlikely that any of the Chinese sailors could be made to co-operate; even if they did show willing it would be foolish to trust them. There was no doubt that the oncoming ship would promptly inform the other Chinese ships of the situation, and they would immediately take alternative routes into Toulage. It would be a hopeless task then for the British cruiser to try and intercept the scattered ships. As Halton turned over these problems in his mind, a message was handed to him from the cruiser.

'Forced to reduce speed, heavy weather, estimated time of arrival now 1300 hours.'

Drew and Morrison knew from Halton's expression, as he drew them aside, that something was wrong. Explaining what had happened, he went on to point out the seriousness of the situation. The time was now 0800 hours, and it would be at least five hours before they could expect any help; time and to spare for the rest of the Chinese ships to get into Toulage and unload their deadly cargoes.

From what Thomson had reported – he had made a quick inspection of the cargo – these ships were carrying missiles that could be speedily set up and put into operational use. Apart from the more complex medium range intercontinental ballistic missiles there were, loaded carefully at the tops of the cargo holds, smaller surface to surface and surface to air missiles. These would be obviously landed first, and could be in operation within two or three hours, at most. Any ship or aircraft that approached Zembasia without Rhaman's permission, could then be destroyed at once, and with such effective protection for his base, Rhaman could go ahead and set up the more complex ballistic missiles. Having done so, he would, besides being the established dictator of his own country, become the absolute power in all Africa. No other country in that continent could hope to match such a nuclear arsenal, Halton concluded. Even if only one ship managed to get through, Rhaman would still have a considerabe advantage over all his immediate neighbours.

As the destroyer's Captain finished speaking, Gray – the coxswain and his quartermasters had taken over the wheel and engine-room telegraphs – requested a course to steer. At the present moment they were on a heading for Toulage at the slow speed of five knots, and now, in a split second decision, Halton gave orders to continue on course. He then tried the engine room telegraphs. Ringing down for 'Full Speed Ahead' he was agreeably surprised. Smythe could obviously understand the orders from the bridge, for there was an instant reaction; the slow throb of the large diesels – they had only just been ticking over for the past few minutes – increased to

175

the characteristic muffled roar, and the water immediately astern began to be churned up by the faster moving propeller. Up forward, a bow wave was beginning to form as the ship surged ahead. Twenty six miles to Toulage. At this speed of sixteen knots, Halton estimated, they should take an hour and forty minutes, arriving there at 0945 hours.

Approximately twelve miles astern was the other Chinese ship, following the same track. Studying her closely through his binoculars, Halton reckoned that her top speed would be about the same. If they could keep up this speed, then the distance between them should remain equal – an important factor if the plan he had quickly worked out during these last few minutes was to succeed. However, before he could tell his senior officers exactly what he had in mind, the radio room telephoned to report that Rhaman was about to make an important speech.

'Number One, I want you to stay here and take charge,' Halton told his First Lieutenant. 'Keep her on 120 degrees – that should get us to Toulage and hold this speed. I don't want that other ship catching up with us. Captain Morrison, I want you if you will, sir, to come below with me and hear what Rhaman has to say. I'll keep you informed of what is happening. Meanwhile get all those Chinese into one compartment – the saloon will do – and keep them under guard.'

The two senior officers entered the radio compartment just as Rhaman began to speak.

'Zembasia's greatest warship, the *Umled*, has just entered harbour, and fully supports our cause. She was intercepted on the way by the British destroyer *Phoenix*. That destroyer now lies at the bottom of the sea, sunk with all her crew. This is the same ship which has repeatedly tried to interfere in Zembasian affairs, despite all my warnings. Let us hope the British have now learned their lesson.'

Halton and Morrison exchanged glances at this somewhat exaggerated report of the recent engagement.

'This morning', Rhaman continued, 'within the next few hours, in fact, ships from a friendly country will be arriving, loaded with supplies and weapons that will make us the greatest country in the whole of Africa. Those misguided few who still endeavour to support a decadent capitalist government have not the slightest chance now of stopping us. If they

176

will lay down their arms immediately we shall show them mercy, but if they do not take this opportunity, we shall wipe them out completely.

'Bearing in mind this fact, the *Umled* will shortly be leaving Toulage to visit all our coastal towns. Each town will be asked the same question; are you for us or against us? Those which are foolish enough to resist will be reduced to rubble by the *Umled*'s guns in a few minutes. I say to you, join us! The success of our revolution is assured!'

On this heroic note Rhaman ended his speech. For a few moments there was a silence in the radio compartment, as the British sailors digested the import of his message. This man was obviously prepared to go to the most ruthless lengths to get his way. Thousands of loyal Zembasians, including women and children, would perish under the power of the *Umled*'s guns. It would be a terrible decision for even the staunchest supporters of the government, to continue the fight which would result in the deaths of countless innocent people. Tanjong, the loyal Vice President, might have to reconsider his position completely, especially now that the chances of British help arriving in time looked so slim.

Just before he left the radio compartment Halton dictated a brief message to the chief telegraphist, for immediate transmission to the British cruiser:

'Am taking this ship in to block harbour entrance.'

This then, he told Drew and Morrison when they were back on the bridge, was his plan. The entrance to Toulage harbour was narrow, and one medium sized vessel like the Chinese merchant ship could block that entrance completely.

But even if they got to the entrance without raising any suspicion, how were they going to maintain such a position, asked Morrison? And how long, added Drew, was Rhaman going to let a bloody great merchantman sit right in the middle of the entrance, stopping all traffic? Surely he'd get a tug to shift her, or try to board her, which wouldn't be difficult in view of the large number of Zembasian soldiers at his disposal, against which the British crew would not stand very much chance. And another thing, Morrison pointed out, what about the *Umled*? If she came out of the harbour before they got there, she might ask awkward questions, in which case the game would be up with a vengeance!

If Halton was at all disappointed by these objections he showed no sign. There was no doubting the personal bravery of the other two officers, who had backed him up unwaveringly during these past few terrible days. Before he could explain, however, a signal arrived from the cruiser, asking him to repeat his last message. Clearly Morrison and Drew were not the only ones who had doubts about his audacious plan!

'Stand by to reply,' ordered the destroyer's Captain, and then went on to his brother officers: 'The position is, when we really come down to it, that there is no alternative action we *can* take. We must block that entrance at all costs, and prevent those ships getting in and the *Umled* getting out. Regarding the *Umled*, I'm fairly certain that, after her run across the Atlantic, she must be low on fuel. Therefore she's going to have to refuel before she comes out again and that's going to take time; time enough for us to get there before she can leave. I think we all appreciate that if she does get out, especially to those coastal towns, then the loyalists have had it.'

Morrison and Drew nodded, listening intently.

'At the moment,' Halton continued, 'we're nearly an hour ahead of the nearest Chinese ship, and if we can keep up this speed, we shall get to Toulage before any of them. It seems fairly certain that Rhaman hasn't got an exact E.T.A., although he's obviously expecting the ships sometime this morning. Therefore I don't think we shall have any trouble in getting to the harbour undetected.

'When we reach the middle of the entrance we shall drop anchor, and there we'll stay until our cruiser turns up. As long as we remain there no ship can enter or leave that harbour. Rhaman's plan depends entirely on the *Umled*'s getting out on her terrorist mission, and on the Chinese ships getting in to unload their missiles.'

Morrison and Drew agreed wholeheartedly with the reasons behind Halton's plan. There was no doubt that if they waited for the cruiser to arrive it would far too late for any effective action to be taken.

Mention of the cruiser reminded Halton that the chief telegraphist, who had been waiting discreetly out of hearing during the senior officers' conference, must be given a reply to send to the cruiser's last message. Perhaps the original one had been too brief. Turning to Morrison with a wry smile, he said:

'Come on, sir, you're the diplomat around here! Will you draft out a signal for the cruiser? Tell them as briefly as you can what we're going to do, and why it's the only thing possible. I'll be glad if you'll go with the telegraphist and wait for the reply. Meanwhile Drew and I had better check on what's happening on the bridge.'

Stepping outside from the wheelhouse, the two officers were met by Thomson, who had been in charge during their absence. He reported that everything was under control; it was just coming up to 0900 hours, and the ship was maintaining a steady sixteen knots. The wounded men had been placed in comfortable bunks and the doctor reported that all of them stood a good chance of recovery. The Chinese, he concluded, were being kept under close guard in the saloon.

Toulage now lay twelve miles ahead. The hot sun had quickly dispersed the earlier low lying cloud and mist patches, and prominent landmarks were beginning to stand out clearly. Astern of them the other Chinese ship, now easily recognisable as a large cargo carrier, was following in their wake at about nine miles range. As Thomson remarked, she was a faster ship, but with the distance left to go they should get to Toulage well before her. Even further astern another pair of masts had appeared on the horizon, and these, Halton knew, must belong to the third Chinese ship. He knew now that he had taken the correct - the only decision; not to wait for the arrival of the cruiser.

Presently Captain Morrison appeared on the bridge with the reply from the cruiser. Halton gave a sigh of relief, as he read the message, for he had been half anticipating that his plan might be met with a firm refusal. The Ministry of Defence, it seemed, realised the seriousness of the situation, and had given the go ahead - with a totally unnecessary warning about using maximum caution. That, replied Halton, was precisely what he intended to do; and he began to reveal the next part of his plan.

As soon as they got into a good position, with anchors firmly bedded down, he was going to invite Rhaman on board. The chances were that this request would be met with a refusal, and that dire threats would be made to destroy the Chinese ship - but these threats could never be carried out, for they would result in the permanent blocking of the harbour entrance, which would be a disaster for the communist cause.

179

Therefore, Halton continued, another signal would be sent stating that Rhaman *must* come on board immediately, otherwise he, Halton, would scuttle the ship and block the entrance. Rhaman would know from the events of the past few days that the British Navy did not utter idle threats, and he would be forced to come out to them. Once on board he would be arrested. Never mind about the British tradition of fair play, Halton added, with a grim smile. With their leader gone, the harbour blocked, no outside help available and the pending arrival of a superior British force, the revolution would be finished.

In another twenty minutes they would reach the harbour. With the distance down to a bare five miles Halton was able, through his binoculars, to study it in detail. The *Umled* was lying inside, about three hundred yards from the entrance, with a small tanker alongside busily engaged in refuelling operations. As Halton had estimated, her tanks were almost empty after her long voyage across the Atlantic, and there was not much chance that she could leave before they got there. Even if the actual process was completed in the next few minutes it would still take at least a quarter of an hour to cast off from the tanker and make ready for sea again. The appearance of one of the Chinese cargo ships – after all, they were expected – was not going to cause any surprise, and the *Umled* should not speed up her refuelling. So far, so good, said Halton, with satisfaction. It looked as though the first part of the operation was going to work out.

Giving orders for the majority of his crew to gather just in front of the bridge and leaving Drew in command, Halton went down to tell his men exactly what was going to happen. This did not take long; within five minutes he was back on the bridge to give his final instructions.

Captain Morrison was requested to get a message ready, before they anchored, for immediate transmission to the British cruiser, stating that they were in position, and asking the cruiser's Captain, with his more comprehensive radio equipment, to lay on a series of extensive propaganda broadcasts to Zembasia, letting the country know what was happening. This would give fresh heart to the loyalists, and at the same time emphasise the hopeless position that the rebels were now in. Be sure to let the people know, Halton emphasised, that Rhaman intended to bombard innocent women and children, to show

180

them the kind of dictator he was likely to be. Also, request that a stream of helicopters be seen arriving and departing the scene. This would certainly add tangible evidence that the British reinforcements were getting nearer every minute.

Drew's task was equally vital. The First Lieutenant was to go to the fo'castle and supervise the anchoring of the ship, when Halton gave the signal. As he did not know much about a merchant ship's anchors and cables, the Captain added, it might be a good idea for him to go forward now and familiarise himself and his party with the equipment.

Ringing down to the engine room Halton told Smythe what had been planned. In addition the senior engineer was instructed to find the seacocks and find out exactly how to operate them. It was hoped it would not be necessary to use them, but, if Rhaman tried any tricks then he, Halton, would not have the slightest hesitation in sinking the ship.

Finally Halton told the chief yeoman of signals to stand beside him. This senior rating was to be prepared to send and receive some of the most vital signals in which he would be involved in the whole of his career. Thomson was told to organise the rest of the men into armed parties, positioned at strategic points, to stop anyone from boarding the ship. Taking one last look round before bringing the ship up to the entrance, the Captain noted that all his orders had been carried out – all his crew were in position.

'Look, sir – there's a launch coming out to meet us. I think it must be the pilot boat,' said Sub Lieutenant Gordon, who had taken over as officer of the watch when his more senior colleagues had gone about their special duties. Training his binoculars ahead, Halton cursed himself for overlooking such an obvious hazard. Of course, a deeply laden merchant ship would need the assistance of a pilot to go into a strange harbour. He quickly gave orders for his men to keep their heads well down. In five minutes time, at this speed, the merchant ship would reach the harbour entrance. By the time the rebels noticed she had ignored the services of a pilot she should be in position.

Sweeping majestically by the pilot launch, which got out of the way just in time, the merchant ship headed boldly for the entrance. Halton was certain that by the time the launch got a radio message off they would be dropping anchor.

Carefully lining up with the middle of the entrance, now only four hundred yards ahead, Halton rang down for 'full astern'. Slowly the forward speed fell away. The ship came to a stop right in the mdidle of the narrow entrance, and a moment later, on Halton's signal, Drew let go both anchors. Toulage was now sealed off completely.

Within a few seconds a signal lamp began to flash from the *Alched*, Rhaman's flagship and the headquarters of the revolution, telling the merchant ship to raise anchor and get out of the way. Morrison had got his message off and now, remarked Halton, Rhaman was in for the shock of his life as the chief yeoman commenced his signal.

'*Phoenix* to Rhaman. I will sink this ship if you do not come on board in the next fifteen minutes.'

Halton had decided to dispense with any preliminary banter and get down to business at once. Signal lamps began to flash between the Zembasian warships, and the tanker, alongside the *Umled*, was hastily making preparations to get out of the way. These were anxious moments for Halton and his crew, for Rhaman could react to the sheer impertinence of his message in many violent ways. While they were waiting, all eyes fixed on the *Alched* watching for the first flash of her signal lamp, Morrison telephoned the bridge with cheerful news.

Two helicopters were well on their way to them. They had been launched even before Halton had signalled to find out what the situation was, and should arrive within the next twenty minutes. Other helicopters would arrive on a rotation basis, as requested by Halton, and the cruiser itself was racing to them at top speed – the weather in the Atlantic had improved considerably. Powerful transmitters were informing all of Zembasia what was going on. Within a matter of a mere five minutes the whole situation, as far as Rhaman was concerned, had changed completely.

The anxiously awaited signal from the *Alched* came.

'Rhaman to Halton. I shall be coming out to you in ten minutes.'

A few moments later a small motor launch left the *Alched* and began to head towards the merchant ship. This was too good to be true, commented Halton to Morrison, who had come up on the bridge. He just could not see Rhaman giving up the fight so tamely. Morrison agreed, warning the

Captain to be on his guard against treachery. Every available man, most of them armed, stood ready along the side to which Rhaman's launch was heading. The second Chinese ship had come to a stop about a mile away, waiting for the harbour entrance to be cleared, and in the far distance the other two merchant ships were now clearly recognisable. Even further away, just mere specks in the sky, the helicopters were approaching. The chief telegraphist reported that he had managed to establish R/T contact with the latter.

One hundred yards from the merchant ship the launch came to a halt and Rhaman, loudhailer in hand, stood up to speak. He was in an ugly mood and obviously not prepared to waste much time talking.

'I am surprised to see you here, Halton,' he called. 'I suppose you realise that you have committed an act of piracy on the high seas? However, that matter will be dealt with later. I will give you ten minutes to get that ship out of the entrance. If you do not, the *Umled* will blast you out of the water!'

Halton replied, also through a loudhailer:

'Go ahead if you want to, Rhaman – I shall not move. But I warn you – this ship is loaded with enough explosives to blow us all to kingdom come. Why not come on board and see for yourself?'

'Do you think I am fool enough to walk into such a trap? Now listen carefully, Halton; I will give you five minutes, no more, to think over what I am going to say. If you do not agree to move that ship I will order the *Umled* to open fire, not on you, but on the town. Her guns will continue to fire until you move, so – if you want the deaths of thousands of innocent people on your hands, stay where you are. Five minutes, remember. I shall wait here, well out of your reach, while you think it over.'

Rhaman sat down in his launch. Every British sailor has heard the conversation, and realised the terrible position their Captain had been forced into. Halton would have shot his enemy out of hand if he could, but sub machine guns were too inaccurate, and the few rifles available might not hit all three of the boat's crew in the first volley. If Rhaman got away – or for that matter only one of the crew – all hell would break loose. The revolution would have a martyr, and all that it implied.

Just then, with only two minutes left for Halton to make his dreadful decision, the helicopters arrived clattering overhead. The destroyer's Captain had a sudden inspiration. If the helicopters could get armed men on the deck of that launch – they were equipped to lower marine commandos – it could swoop down and pluck Rhaman out of the boat! Hastily telling Morrison to keep Rhaman talking if he was not back in time, Halton dashed into the radio compartment and spoke directly to the helicopter pilot in command.

Yes, the latter replied, they were carrying eight armed Marines, in case Halton needed more men, and could get down to the launch.

Try and capture Rhaman without shooting, if possible. Halton ordered – but whatever happened, none of that boat's crew were to be allowed to escape. In one minute's time Rhaman would demand his answer. After giving the pilot his go ahead Halton rushed back to the bridge, just in time to see what happened.

Swooping down low, almost like monstrous deafening birds of prey, the two helicopters headed towards Rhaman's launch. The senior helicopter pilot Lieutenant Stanley Mills, had already briefed the other helicopter to break away at the last moment, but coming in together they were bound to cause a distraction. Rhaman was certainly distracted but for only a split second; then, his trained reflexes sprang into action and, grabbing a sub-machine gun, he opened fire on the approaching helicopters. Before the second helicopter could break away, as it was just intending to do, it was hit badly – the pilot and crew did not stand a chance, and plunged into the sea. Tragically with the resultant explosion it brought about a huge distraction that neither Halton, nor anybody else for that matter, had ever reckoned on. Seizing this grim moment of opportunity Mills brought his helicopter hovering only ten feet above the launch. Its doors opened and four burly Marines slid quickly down ropes to the deck of the launch covered, in this lightning movement, from above by more Marines pointing sub-machine guns. Before Rhaman and his men could offer any more resistance they were quickly disarmed and hoisted up into the helicopter followed by the Marines. The whole operation had taken less than a minute.

Loud cheers broke out from the *Phoenix*'s crew, as the pilot requested instructions. Where was Rhaman to be taken?

'Back to the cruiser at once!' ordered Halton, adding 'Our deepest sorrow for the tragic loss of the second helicopter is expressed and felt by all.' The further Rhaman was from Toulage, the better. Meanwhile he ordered signals to be made to the Zembasian warships saying that Rhaman had surrendered and was seeking political asylum....

* * *

When the British cruiser arrived later that day, the revolution was virtually over. With their powerful leader removed, and the pro-government forces taking fresh heart at this news, the rebels gradually surrendered. The captured Chinese ship was handed back to its crew, and the four merchant vessels departed for home. Much of what had happened would never appear in the world press, but it would be a very long time before China tried to interfere in Africa again. Rhaman, meanwhile, had evaded the course of justice. As the helicopter neared the cruiser he had broken free and hurled himself through the door into the sea. A thorough search was carried out, but no trace of the man was ever found.

Tanjong, the President elect, came out to the cruiser to thank Halton and his crew personally for all their efforts and sacrifices. Zembasia's highest decoration was bestowed upon Halton, but he reflected bitterly that he would rather have been given back the lives of his men who had died in the *Phoenix*. Gathering his crew together for the last time – he was to be flown back to the U.K. at once – Halton tried to thank them, but knew that mere words could never express just how much he really owed them.

* * *

One year later Captain Halton was invited to attend the launching of the Navy's latest guided missile cruiser. This warship was the most advanced of its kind in the world, and Halton, by no means content with his office routine in the Ministry of Defence, was only too pleased to take a day off to travel north to the Clyde shipyard.

When he arrived he found, to his surprise and pleasure, that Drew, Morrison, Gray, Thomson, Smythe, Gordon and most of the other members of his old crew were present. All were somewhat puzzled by this unexpected reunion, until Vice

Admiral Halton took his nephew on one side, just before the launching ceremony, and told him that he was going to be this ship's first Captain. Before Halton had recovered from this bombshell, the wife of the Prime Minister, who was to perform the launching ceremony, smashed a bottle of champagne against the vessel's bows and announced in a clear voice:

'I name this ship *Phoenix*. May God bless her, and all who sail in her.'

As the great ship slid gracefully down the launching rails, to the accompaniment of loud cheers and a band playing 'Rule Britannia', Halton, his heart full, thought of his gallant little destroyer, and all the earlier ships bearing this proud name, right back into the mists of time. The legend, 'From the ashes of the old arises a new *Phoenix*' had come true once more.